# Designs for a Happy Home

**MATTHEW REYNOLDS** is known as a critic and scholar, author of *The Realms of Verse* and of many essays in the *LRB* and *TLS*, editor of *Dante in English* and of Manzoni's *The Betrothed*. He spent time in London, Cambridge, Pisa and Paris before settling in Oxford where he lectures at the University and is a Fellow of St Anne's College. He lives with his unruly family in a thoroughly imperfect interior.

# Designs for a

# Happy Home

*Matthew Reynolds*

**B L O O M S B U R Y**
LONDON · BERLIN · NEW YORK

First published in Great Britain 2009
This paperback edition published 2010

Copyright © 2009 by Matthew Reynolds

The photograph of the 'How High the Moon' Nickel Plated Rib Mesh Armchair by
Shiro Kuramata (1986) is courtesy of Sotheby's Picture Library

Bloomsbury Publishing, London, Berlin and New York

36 Soho Square, London W1D 3QY

A CIP catalogue record for this book is available from the British Library

ISBN 978 1 4088 0105 5

10 9 8 7 6 5 4 3 2 1

Typeset by Hewer Text UK Ltd, Edinburgh
Printed and bound in Great Britain by Clays Ltd, St Ives plc

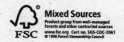

**Mixed Sources**
Product group from well-managed
forests and other controlled sources
www.fsc.org Cert no. SGS-COC-2061
© 1996 Forest Stewardship Council
FSC

*For Kate*

Thank you Kate.

Thank you Ali, Caroline, Finn, Joanna and Sarah.

Thank you Peter, and thank you Helen, Erica, David, Audrey, Penelope and everyone at Bloomsbury.

# 1. The Threshold

You have opened the door. Take a deep breath. Now step . . .

. . . into the world of Good Design. Have a look around you. Isn't it lovely? So calming, but also so alive. Here, colours always *go* – or, if they don't, they clash in interesting ways. Here shapes are in harmony (or else meaningful *dis*-harmony) like a beautiful musical chord. Look, over here, at this Utzon chair and footstool next to the simplest possible standard lamp from IKEA (design doesn't always have to be expensive). Isn't it magic? Or gaze down there at that re-creation of the classic WilliWear showroom in New York: so functional – and also so *funny*.

Don't worry: I know you probably can't actually see these things in your mind's eye yet. And maybe you have no sense of colour, or are psychotically messy, or rubbish at DIY, or simply feel design is not for you. All of us are on our separate journeys; all of us have different hurdles to hop over. But trust me. I have taken this path ahead of you, and look at me now: Alizia Tamé, lead designer with IntArchitec Home-is-Harmony. Whether you want to merely go on a day trip, or else a wholesale design pilgrimage, this book that I am writing will be your guide.

It is a How-To Book; and also it is my Life Story. Why both together? Because the roots of my Designs go deep into my life and their branches (i.e., their effects) stretch out in all directions. You will see my ideas spring up, and watch me bringing them across the threshold of reality. Testimonials from friends and colleagues will show you the influence that I and my Designs have had on them. Finally, I am going to reveal to you my own personal trade secrets – my Magic Mottoes – to help you activate the Design potential in your own lives. A beautiful Interior can make you calmer, more generous – and, in a really startling way, more *you*.

How come? The reason is that your Interior – your thoughts and feelings and fears – and the Interiors that surround you, with their wallpapers and stripped-pine flooring and leather chairs (or whatever), all somehow go together. If a lick of paint can lift your mood, make life seem brighter, and the world a better place – imagine what a full-scale re-design can do. Imagine light-filled rooms. Imagine shining, adorable colours: Naples yellow, cadmium, Manila, cobalt, verditer, burnt vine-wood blue. Imagine spaces harmoniously interlinked. Imagine a bathroom where the shower really works, is really wonderful. Imagine chairs chosen and arranged so that conversation zings like a jazz band or murmurs like a melodious string quartet. Imagine a kitchen where everything you need is miraculously within reach, where your everyday dull chores become a happy dance.

Wouldn't it be wonderful?

When I step into my Home Office (see ch. 4) at the start of each Designing day I take a few minutes to remember when I have been most happy. Of couse good Interiors can make my spirits soar but at this sensitive beginning stage I don't think of them so much as of private things, moments with Poppy or Jem, oh, and other people, other times. I let the smiles rise again inside me, the sunsets fill me with their joy. What's funny is that these moments didn't always happen in beautiful places. It wasn't always sunset! But I remember them as if they did. Don't you? If it was drizzling I remember brightness shining through the wet; if I was in some terrible stodgy blunt Interior it comes back to me miraculously transformed. This is the golden key. This is what I am trying to get through to: these angel Interiors that somehow were there in the air around me even though they actually, physically were not.

Now: relax. Reach back (will you do this for me?) to the happiest moments in your life. What Design ideas do they summon up for you? What colours? Textures? Forms? Or any particular *objets*? Stillness or movement? Brightness or velvet gloom? Visualise these memories: make them real, let them gleam again, let the feeling of them grow. It may help if you jot down some pointers – anything at all: words, doodles, names, shapes. If you like, you can jot them down here:

Did you manage? I don't mind if you haven't actually scribbled anything. Jem wouldn't have done, for instance (he's my husband) – he's a very private person, he likes to keep his feelings nested safe inside. All I need is for you to have accessed that Emotion. The sparkle in your heart. That is what we want to grow and then encapsulate in our Interiors. Through Design, your Happiness can flower and spread.

We have arrived at Magic Motto no. 1:

1. Interior Design Is The Makeover Of Minds.

I know this is a big claim. But little by little you will see it happening. Room by room.

# 2. The Hallway

## a. First Steps

Ready for some actual designing? Where shall we start?
   In the Hallway – of course!
   But how do we start?
   With a question. Actually *the* question:

• What is it for?

Take any hallway you can think of: the narrow corridor of a pinched Victorian terrace, the efficient capsule of a modern Barratt-type home, or the spacious entrance of a country house. Ask: What is it for? And let the answer come to you. Can you hear it?

• For getting people into an Interior – and out of it!

Obvious, perhaps. But it would surprise you how many Designers have ignored this basic fact. Some of them think the Hallway is all about creating 'that vital first impression'. So they try to 'add interest' with incongruous decoration: an 'industrial' theme, or jungle-pattern wallpaper. Or else they try to 'signal comfort' by sticking a sofa in there, or a pair of puffy boudoir chairs. Wrong! Wrong! Wrong! A home is not a stage set. Interiors are to be used: a Hallway is to be walked through. As I put it in the second Magic Motto:

✓ *Design – For Life!*

This brings me to a rather delicate point. Delicate, but essential. Many hallways I have seen have been ruined – not by any Design error – but by a personal failing on the part of the inhabitants: Mess. There is a clutter of shoes and boots and brollies on the floor. It is summer, but the clothes pegs are still piled with winter coats. Maybe there is a picnic blanket hanging there too, and shopping bags. You try to get through – but it feels like clambering over an obstacle course *and* shouldering past a herd of pack animals both at the same time. What I want to say to people with Hallways in this state is: just think about it. It doesn't take much. Think of the effort you (or someone) put into decorating the space and screwing those coat-hooks into the wall. Think of how neat your hallway used to be. You can turn this situation around. All it takes is: a bit of tidying up. Then your Interior will be itself again. And you will have more freedom to be *you*.

What this all comes down to, is that Magic Motto no. 2 is meaningless without no. 3:

✓ *And Live – For Design!*

## b. The Work of Memory

We have grasped the basic *function* of the Hallway. Now we must think about its *character*. In this new stage of the pre-design process we must again draw on our personal experience – but now in a more focused way. The 'Work of Memory' (as I call it) is vital.

As an example, I am going to call up a memory of my own – of when Jem lifted me over the threshold and into the Hallway of the first space we inhabited together. We were not married then, but that did not in any way reduce the significance of the moment. Nowadays marriage is obviously less important than it used to be, and I often feel that the new milestone in people's lives is the purchase of a property – especially joint purchase. That is when you make plans and put down roots. That is when you really have to *commit*.

Well, that is what Jem and I had done. We had shared the excitement of the hunt, and the suspense of offer and survey. We had suffered the agony of the chain. At last the keys had become ours. It was the day of our moving-in; it was morning, we had arrived. There we were, standing in front of the door to the house, which was also the door to our future. But I couldn't go forward. I was stuck.

Above, the sky was a pale, wan blue with high-up streaks of cloud. On either side stretched the empty street and all the rest of the long terrace. In front of me was the door, black (*that* was going to have to change) with nine little panes of glass at eye level, frosted to prevent you seeing through. And in front of that was a cushion of air, invisible but impossible to get past.

It can happen to anyone. I am sure it can! You are in love. Your life begins to alter. Just little things: maybe you dress a little differently, you bother to wear earrings, give extra attention to your hair. People say: You look so well! You wake up with a different feeling, you walk more bouncily, you are quicker to smile. It is all so energising, all such fun! But also, underneath, something much more serious is happening. You don't notice it at first, but there is a sort of deep movement going on down there, like sand sifting through an hour glass, like the shifting of tectonic plates. Little by little, in some secret cave of your personality, a whole new you is being created. In the end, this new you is going to burst out. There is an earthquake! But, just at that moment, the old you, who hasn't quite gone away, who is still there hovering beside you, she touches you on the elbow and says, like the good old friend she is: Alizia, are you sure you are doing the right thing? At least, that is what the old me was whispering (rather loudly!) as we stood there, Jem and I, all ready to go into our new house.

Why? He was the right man, I was sure of it: I simply *knew*. It was the right time, and the right location – near enough to Spitalfields so that Jem would not feel cut off from his Studio and his old friends from the Commune there, but far enough away to mark a break. It meant a bigger break for me, of course: but that was totally fine. It was exciting to be moving East; the area was so stimulating with its energy and variety, there were such charming stalls and shops along Brick Lane.

Still, there I stood, stuck; and though my eyes looked forward my thoughts rushed back, along roads and round roundabouts, through traffic lights and junctions, over crossroads, round turnings to left and right, and left, and left again, along one street, then another, and then yet one more, towards my old flat where I had spent my last night the night before. Everything from there had come along with me: it was all safely piled in the van that stood behind me on the kerb. At least, the bed wasn't – it was too big – but everything else was: my precious Additional Living System chaise by Colombo, the two Ernest Race chairs, and the cutlery and pots and pans, and the photos of my parents and two big brothers and my friends and . . . What I hadn't been able to bring with me was not strictly speaking any *thing* at all, but simply: that space. And the reason why that was upsetting was that it was not just any old space but My Interior. The place where I had been for so long, where I had done – oh not anything so very special, but just all the little things that made me me, the getting up, the coming back in the evening, and going to sleep, and having carefully selected friends round for little dinners; the place where I had stood looking out through rainy glass, the light of the grey sky bright on my face; where I had cried and had long baths, and snuggled up with books; where I had been me.

I dragged my thoughts back to where I was physically standing. I focused on our future home. Well, it was perfect. Just an ordinary little house – an 1860s two-up two-down – but that was what we liked about it. All around us in the early '90s the fashion was to find surprising places to live in: warehouses, of course, and pumping stations, and bankrupted local shops: I had even helped one of my friends from art college convert an old water tank on stilts above a deserted railway line. Jem detested this trend: he thought it was false, tacky, a diversion from the real work of living and creating things that mattered, like his own Ceramic Art. I didn't feel quite so negative, obviously; but I did see that, for the two of us, an 'in your face' architectural statement was completely unnecessary. Loving Jem had shown me that it doesn't take very much to make the ordinary remarkable. The right textures, the right tones, plus the odd really sparkling design idea: that was all you needed to make a place where it was possible to live in harmony, to be, in a deep sense, beautiful. Design for Life! Live for Design! That was what we were going to do in Wood Street. It was going to be divine.

The right textures. The right tones. The odd really sparkling Idea. You would have thought that with all my talent, my training and experience, this would have been not very much to ask (even back then at the time I am talking about I had been in professional practice at IntArchitec for a good five years). But I was used to big projects with generous budgets. Wood Street was small and personal. No, doubly personal, that was the thing that was so scary (though also so exciting). Obviously I was designing, not for any old client, and not just for me (*that* wouldn't have been a problem) but for Us – i.e., for what it was going to be like for the two of us to live together – our moods, our rhythms, our habits. Don't get me wrong, I was longing to be together with Jem, hour upon hour, day after day; just simply to have him there beside me. But when I tried to visualise our lives together in enough detail to begin to project a Design – well, I found I couldn't do it. Of course I knew how we were now: we were delightful. Jem gave me such energy and also strength – and I gave him, well, not for me to say really, but I *think* I gave him happiness: I think that when he smiled it went all the way down. But things change, don't they, when you actually move in together. When there's nowhere to walk away to, when you aren't, each moment, making a choice to be together and not apart. And so the slight being-on-your-best-behaviour feeling disappears, that feeling of slightly being the guest, or being the host, and so being a little bit more kind, a little bit more considerate. When you live together, the Us becomes the Usual. There are the bills to be paid together and the housework to be done together, and waking up in the morning together stops being a miracle and becomes the Usual Thing. Or at least it does if you're not careful. And would we manage to be careful – that was the question – would we manage to nurture ourselves, keep ourselves warm and tender and wide-eyed? The right sort of Design – l was sure – could make a crucial difference. Obviously it was down to me to create it: after all, I was the Designer! But where, where was my Idea?

The door; the sky; and Jem. Jem next to me. I leaned into him. He was solid. My cheek was against his bony shoulder and his arm was around me. 'Hey,' he said. I could feel his other arm wriggling. He was groping in his pocket for the key. The door opened and there was a change in the air somehow; a dusty smell. Then suddenly Jem's big hands were under my armpits. My body understood what he was doing before my mind did! My knees bent, and I jumped, and he swung me up and over the threshold – and then held me for a moment dangling before lowering me gently to the floor. I had been literally swept away! As I stood there after my short, tender flight through the air, I had a new feeling. The floor was firm, the walls were on either side of me, the ceiling was above. I felt that I belonged. The front door to our future had become the back door of our separate pasts – and it was about to close. My eyes were in Jem's, his arms were around me. I felt the moment I was in would last for ever . . .

But of course it did not. His eyes moved, mine lowered, I took a step back, turned, and one after the other we processed on in. Into the gloom, with our feet feeling muffled on the carpet and a dank smell gathering around us. Upstairs? No, left into the back room, which was light. Then something rather odd began to happen. As I took these steps into our Interior I realised that something was changing in *my* Interior too: there was a bulging feeling; lines zigzagged here and there, a flash of colour – the moment was giving birth to an Idea! 'Hang on,' I said to Jem, and I strode back out, threw open the doors of the van and started pulling at a box that was full of papers and books. I grabbed a notebook but then had to look for a black Gladstone bag and rootle in it for a pencil. By the time I was ready a little avalanche of boxes had spilled out on to the road. I sat on the kerb with my pad on my knees: the first firm strokes flowed out of me.

The thing is, the idea was not for our house in Wood Street but for an important project I had been working on at IntArchitec – important for me at least: it really felt like crunch-time in my career. I had been unhappy with IntArchitec's high-concept ethos for a while. Deep down inside I longed to find a way of designing that connected more with people's feelings. A big part of the

11

change I went through thanks to Jem was that he had helped me admit this about myself and think of ways of actually moving forward. So really it wasn't at all surprising that a special moment that had to do with him, with our new house, and with Us, also turned out to give me an idea about this important project at work. It certainly was not any kind of betrayal.

Anyway, this project I am talking about – the Dawson House near St Ives – seemed like the perfect opportunity to try out my (and Jem's!) new mode of design. It was a weekend house, but very much loved by the owners – a banker and his orthodontist wife. I sensed that, imaginatively speaking, they kept a lot of their emotions in the Dawson House. All the life that was squeezed and wired up during their working week in London was allowed to burst out at weekends.

And the Dawson House was a great place for this to happen. It was another 'unusual' '90s conversion: originally, it had been a lifeboat station – basically just a huge shed, high-roofed and rectangular. But it had a really wonderful location: perched halfway down a cliff, end-on to the open enormous Atlantic. The architect in charge of the conversion had done the obvious thing of installing a galleried area at the landward end with bedrooms and bathroom on the higher level. But at the other end, where the great doors had been, just next to the waves, he had created a glass-walled, glass-roofed space which stuck out from the body of the building. The effect was simply magical. When you stood there you saw nothing but the endless restless sea, no doubt endlessly twinkling on a bright, calm day; but endlessly tortured, grieving, almost, it seemed to me on the day I first stood there, the white breakers like a sort of whimpering. Standing in the glass box, you felt completely exposed, but also completely safe. It was as if the aura of the lifeboat was preserved, fixed in glass. As if it, or you, or *something*, was perpetually on the point of launching itself, but never quite letting go.

Obviously, the way forward for the Feeling Designer was to work with this sensation of nearly being launched – and I had got as far as realising that the sofas were going to be crucial. Has it ever occurred to you that a sofa can be a bit like a boat? – not so much because it looks like one as because it can feel like a boat, put you in mind of one. You can curl up in it and drift away: reading, or talking to someone who is also curled up in it, or simply dozing off to sleep. Do you see what I mean? Anyway, my ideas had gone that far, but then got stuck. *Until* I had the experience of being swept off my feet and landing inside our Wood Street Interior. As I landed, I thought: Movement. As we walked along the rest of the Hallway, I thought: Wheels. Which, if they were to be secure, meant Rails. A picture blocked itself into place in my mind. I would fit rails along the whole length of the boathouse. There would be two sofas – preferably curvy Deco pieces with lots of wood and touches of chrome – placed one on each track, face to face. An automated system would move them back and forth. When the weather was mild they would roll forward to occupy the glass space, just as the lifeboats had done before them. In time of storm they would retreat from the angry waves, travelling all the way back through the house to nestle in warmth and safety under the low ceiling of the galleried area.

This was the concept I just had to get down on paper before I lost the freshness of it (see *Figure 1*). And it *was* a beauty, and it *did* open doors for me: in fact, it is not too much to say that it launched me on the journey I am going to re-travel for you in this book. But, back at the moment I am describing, all this of course was in the future. There was just me, my drawing pad, the chilly kerbstone, and Jem coming up behind me saying: 'Leez, what are you doing?'

'I've got to get this down, it's an idea.'

'What?'

'For work, for the Dawson House.'

'Leez' – he was squatting down beside me – 'this is our day. We're moving in. There are all these boxes to unpack and you're . . .' He stopped. His hand grabbed a hunk of my hair at the back and squeezed it, pulling the skin of my scalp. He was standing up, sighing the loving sigh that already meant: 'It's Leez, that's what she's like, let's leave her be.' He was turning and heaving the boxes up from the road. He was carrying them in.

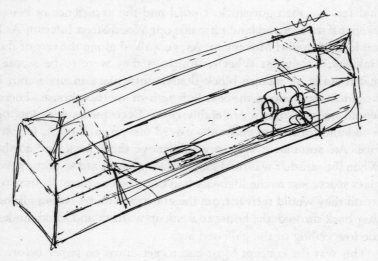

Figure 1. That crucial first sketch for the Dawson House
at St Ives (original now in the Design Museum, London)

After not so very long (maybe ten minutes?) I got up and set about helping Jem with the boxes and chairs. We were humping pretty much everything upstairs to leave the ground floor clear for the knocking-through and the stripping and painting and everything else that needed to be done there. Jem was working fast,

14

sometimes taking two boxes at a time, making the house wobble as he stamped stumblingly up the stairs. He didn't look at me. I was carrying something up and he stood back on the landing, making sure not to touch me, his eyes turned away. Next it was me waiting at the bottom: he came careering down and the side of him bashed into me.

'Jem!'

'Sorry,' he said – but dully, resentfully.

'Jem . . .'

'We're moving in. I'm getting the job done.'

'Jem,' I said, 'I'm sorry.'

'What?'

'About going out and doing those sketches.'

'Oh,' – his shoulders seemed to soften; his face turned and his eyes looked into me.

'I just had to.'

There was the twitch of the beginning of a smile: 'It's all right.'

'It doesn't mean . . .'

'I know' – and then his arms were around me, wrapping me to him, and my face was against the top of his chest, snug in its special den.

That afternoon, when Jem had gone out to get something, I took a rest from unpacking and went downstairs. I stood in one room, then the other, then the first again, both really a little bit grim with their dirty white walls and putrid flower-pattern carpet, but both quietly humming with potential. I imagined the central wall cleared away, light from both windows flooding in so that the polished floorboards shone (this *was* the early '90s). I visualised a distinctive but harmonious colourway of violet, orange and moss green. Mentally, I blocked in my elegant Race chairs, a beautiful new table that we were going to have to find from somewhere and – very importantly – some sort of keystone sofa. I hadn't quite decided what the sofa should be like: gentle and enveloping and snuggly? Or more formal and architectural like the simple yet dramatic Sofa Noguchi? But it didn't matter. I didn't have the answers but I knew I was on the path towards finding them. Life was moving again.

## c. Design Consequences

OK then: what sense can we make of this Work of Memory? What principles can we discover to guide us in our Designs? Well, for me, the Hallway is always a place of

- Transformation.

This is the key *Feel* I want people to get from a Tamé Hallway, whether it is the rotating 'Dinner Plate' Entrance Space I have created for a kitchenware manufacturer in Worcester or the Air-lock Hallway designed for the London house of a billionaire recluse (to protect the privacy of my clients the names and addresses will have to remain confidential). Obviously I am not saying that every time you go into or out of your Hallway it is as much of a revolution as it was for me, that day, about a decade ago. But, if you stop to think about it, you do change a little, don't you, every time? You might put on a coat – or take it off. You might pick up an umbrella or wrap your neck in a scarf. But what interests me are the Feelings you button up around yourself, or shrug off and hang up on a peg. It might be relief: at reaching the harbour of home after a hard day – or else at going out into the fresh air. It might be nervousness or excitement or happiness or resolve. These feelings Transform you. They make you grimmer or

16

smilier, they make you walk faster or slower, they make you more open to the world, or less. Have you ever wondered why a Mirror is such a common element in a Hallway? You may think it is simply a practical thing to help you check your mascara or adjust the angle of your hat. But the real reason is more profound. It allows you to examine yourself at the crucial moment of Transformation. Assess what you are going to look like (if you are on your way out) or what you have looked like (if you are on your way in). Make your 'public face' fit more securely over the private *you*. Or else measure what damage the world has done to you during a day of being out in it: a little bit more sagginess in that bag under the eye? Another hairline crack?

Back in Wood Street I had taken only the very first steps towards discovering these truths. I had had the experience of being lifted into the Hallway; the idea for the Dawson House had come to me there; Jem and I had had a grump and then made up. All this was giving me a very strong feeling that the Hallway was going to be our signature room, the space that set the tone for the entire Interior. But inside my head there seemed to be some blockage, some wad of something grey. I could not convert this Feeling I had into a fully visualised Design.

Bit by bit we had been settling in. The knocking-through had happened (now *that* was a Transformation!), the floorboards had been sanded and varnished, and at last we had a bathroom. But the kitchen was still weeks off, and there was a lot of sanding and filling to be done to the walls before we could put the lining paper up, let alone get started on the colourway. I was back at work 10–6, concentrating on the Dawson House – which was great, but it did absorb my energies. Jem took the view that since I was going to the office every morning he would go to his studio. If this was really a house for Us – he said – we should work on it Together.

Which was fine, of course; I could totally see his point – but it did mean we now had only evenings and weekends for trying to push the project forward. There was such a contrast between the resources available to me at IntArchitec, and our own small pot of money and limited time! On top of these practical problems was a real conceptual challenge: with no clear vision of the Hallway it was impossible to do anything else properly because anything we did might end up having to be changed. It was like wandering through some dark, dark forest with no torch to light the path. We were living on cold food and takeaway. Our joints were achy, our hands were dry and my hair seemed to stay clotted with dust however much I washed and conditioned and combed. So it seemed very nice indeed of Jem's old friends Stan and Marion to invite us over for an evening off and a proper slap-up supper.

Stan and Marion had lived for a while in the Commune, but they had left to set up house together a couple of years before I met Jem. Marion made 'arty' hand-knits which she sold through a stall in Camden Market. Stan had originally wanted to be a conceptual artist but had given up for lack of money: now he worked as a lecturer in the field of cultural studies. He wrote the catalogue essays for Jem's exhibitions, and had once called him 'the only truly postmodern potter, a potter for our times' – so he was an important work contact as well as an old friend. Jem was grateful to him but also – I sometimes thought – rather took him for granted. I think he felt Stan's essays never quite said the right thing – but then Jem himself hated writing and he needed someone to at least try to explain his work to the world. Anyway, I knew Stan and Marion a little, obviously, but this was the first time Jem and I had been, as a couple, to visit them in their home. As I say, it was nice of them to cook us a meal, but I think they probably also wanted to figure as a bit of a beacon for us: two people, living happily together, in a house that was fully furnished and didn't have plaster flaking off the walls!

But when we arrived a very different feeling started to bubble up inside me. Their hallway was as cluttered as a cupboard and it had a dark colour-scheme which – a very bad idea, this – they had decided to continue throughout. Take the sitting room: hessian on the walls, beaded lampshades, heavy 'Afghan' occasional tables, and a squishy plum-coloured three-piece suite speckled with hairs moulted by Spirit, Marion's pet Labrador. 'Souvenirs' crowded every available surface: a Keralan sewing box next to a Javanese shadow puppet and a set of Russian dolls. An actually very mysterious and lovely burial figure, thin and pale, from (apparently) Mesopotamia slumming it in the company of a painted pottery ibis from Egypt and a plastic model of the Rialto Bridge in Venice. What Marion said about all this stuff was that she thought of it not really as being material items but as psychic gateways to other parts of the world (she had been very keen on 'travelling' when she was younger). It is always important to respect other people's beliefs. But the effect it all had on me, visually, as Design, was of a very heavy Interior. Not at all what I was aiming for in Wood Street!

We were full up with the creamy food that Marion and Stan had cooked for us, and nearly at the bottom of our cups of coffee and peppermint tea. Conversation had sagged. Then Jem slithered round on the sofa and reached for the pottery ibis. After a moment of contemplation he said: 'I like it. I like this squared-off shape. Look.' He held the ibis up, then moved his hands so they were pressing against its sides, then held its feet and stroked its back with his right hand, pushing down on the slope of the tail. He looked round at us, wanting our attention. 'You can see how the form came from the maker's hands.'

'It's the aura of authenticity,' said Stan. 'The crucial thing we've lost, in the West.'

'They're sacred birds,' Marion put in.

'For us, "craft" is always self-conscious. Take your work, Jem . . .'

'Sacred to . . . Thoth, that's right, the god of the moon, and of wisdom. Feminine things. What's really sad is that the actual birds don't live in Egypt any more. But the soul of them lives on in the people . . . and in these figures.'

'The primitive' – said Jem – 'is often the most radical.'

Stan and Marion murmured appreciation. Jem was in his 'Artist' mode: they provoked it in him, Stan especially. And when an Artist speaks you don't really agree or disagree. You listen and digest.

I was glad to leave: glad to get out of that Interior. But at least it had made me realise again in my guts how much Design did matter. Even at the small-budget level it was possible to make a difference. No: *all* the difference. I had to find a solution for our Hallway! Colours shifted in my mind like sunlight between clouds; masses almost took on form but didn't quite. But I knew that sometime soon I would find the key. I would make an Interior for us that would be light and energetic and harmonious – like we were. An Interior for Us!

Happiness surged through me. I tensed my arm and squeezed Jem's hand. I pushed my shoulder in against his upper arm. I said: 'That was funny – you being so polite about that terrible ibis.'

He said: 'I wasn't being polite.'

'Yes you were.'

'I liked it.'

'You can't have liked it. It's tat, it's mass-produced.'

'Leez, you could see the imprint of the maker's hands.'

'OK they're not actually made by machine – but they make thousands of them for the tourist market. They're completely commercial.'

He replied: 'That's not the feeling it gave me.'

20

Somewhere inside me a hole opened and all my happiness disappeared. The shadowy pavement stretched ahead of us: we walked past tree after tree. We crossed, and walked some more, and crossed and walked some more. The lights of cars came towards us and passed; our shadows on the pavement shrank and grew. Then we went into the tube and stood on the platform and when the train came went in and sat down and when we reached our station got up and got out. And then we walked some more. And then we reached our new, empty home and went inside. We lay down on the camping mats that were all we had to sleep on.

After a while we did sleep.

Such a little thing! A disagreement about someone else's *objet*. But it had to do with taste, and taste connects to every aspect of your life, especially when you are someone like Jem or me, and especially when you are in the middle of creating an Interior. Next morning I woke as usual full of brightness – but then the memory of what had happened came over me and everything turned dull. 'Morning', we said to each other; 'kettle's just boiled'; 'could I have the butter'; 'bye'; 'see you later'. I think we both felt it was a little bit ridiculous. But at the same time we couldn't help but turn away from each other – couldn't help not wanting to touch the wound. So after work I didn't feel like going home: I went for a drink with my nice colleague Simon. We ended up having supper and by the time I got back it was late. Jem was not there. Not there.

Strangely, after the first shock of it, I found a sort of comfort in his absence. So he was feeling the same. We were sensitive to the same things in the same way. It was all part of our being in love.

When I woke in the morning and found his sleeping body safely there again beside me I sneaked out and down to our still-uncompleted ground floor. I walked to and fro, my footsteps echoing. I looked out of the front window at the sun-filled street;

and out of the back window at our shadowy courtyard. I was feeling that surely today the little cloud of our misunderstanding would pass, surely Jem would wake up warm again; and also I was thinking about the Hallway. How dark it was, how glum. Obviously ceiling spotlights would brighten it up (inset LEDs were not yet readily available) – but I needed to do more than that to give it movement and life, to get the all-important feel of Transformation.

I thought of waves crashing on the shore; I thought of rivers flowing to the sea. A sunbeam touched me and I thought of flowers blooming. I thought of children running down a hill. I thought of a swing – that couldn't be made to work, could it? I thought of a see-saw – just maybe, maybe the merest hint of a wobble, a re-orientation as you walked along? No. I thought of roller-coasters, and rafts, and again of rivers. Then I thought of a bridge.

A bridge. Or rather the concept of a bridge. A little slope up, then a plateau, then a little slope down. It would divide the long narrowness of our passage in a rather pleasing way. And it would interrupt the rhythm of our going in and out of the house with just the sort of effect I was after. You would get your coat out of the cupboard under the stairs, you would go up the little slope, and you would pause, in the way people pause to gaze around halfway across a bridge. Only, you wouldn't gaze around, you would look at yourself, because on either side of this central section I would put mirrors. They would be practical, so you could see what you looked like from back as well as front; but also symbolic, because the infinity of reflections would suggest the past, the future, the many things that can happen, the many, many possible ways of being you. And after that pause, that hitch, that moment of contemplation, you would go rushing in or rushing out with renewed energy, a new spark. It could work! It was *definitely* a solution.

Moments of Vision like this one I have described are always wonderful. But, obviously, there is a long, long way to go between just having an idea and actually making the idea real. There are the products to be sourced, and the craftsmen to be engaged and managed. Above all, there are (in normal circumstances) the clients who need to be helped to share your Vision. Of course, in Wood Street, there was no client as such – just Us, just me and Jem. Jem loved my sparky concepts – at least, he loved hearing about the ones I created at work. But here at home, and especially in the wake of our Ibis Episode . . . maybe it would be better to wait, to pitch this idea to him later when we were properly happy again and calm. Then as I thought about it more a different feeling filtered through me. This idea could help. Surely he would catch my excitement! And if he did – it could be a way forward for us both.

I went through to our makeshift kitchen, managed to light the calor-gas stove and made him a little strong black coffee. I took it up to the bedroom where he lay heavy on our pile of camping mats and blankets. I kneeled down and stroked the rough hunk of his hair: 'Hello love.' He stirred.

'I've brought you coffee.'

Creakily he raised himself up, plonked his shoulders and the back of his head against the wall. His eyes were narrowed against the light. One of his cheeks was pink and had the creases of a sheet pressed into it. I was nervous! I waited for the coffee to be sipped and the eyes to widen.

'Jem . . . I've had an idea, about the Hallway.' He looked at me without opening his mouth – but it was the look itself that somehow spoke. It was heavy, sort of like a cow's. But there was a sparkle in it also; there was love. So I told him about the Hallway Bridge, and he objected: 'Every morning there's going to be this thing I have to clamber over . . .' but I could see he wasn't in fact seriously opposed to the idea, so I kept on going and explained about how it was all to do with what I had felt like when he had lifted me into the space, and about how it embodied the change that was happening to both of us, how there were going to be difficulties but we were always going to get over them, how – finally – we were in the Hallway of our lives. And he said yes. He said he thought it was a great idea. Inside me, tension unravelled and flowed away.

So: something to remember in the darkest times is that good can come of bad. The Ibis was the grain of sand that made a pearl. Another thing is that, if I honestly delve into my consciousness to ask where the idea for the Hallway Bridge came from, I think that Marion's terrible miniature Rialto might have had a little bit to do with it. But I am not at all ashamed of that. Magic Motto no. 4:

✓ *Ideas Can Come From Anywhere!*

So the Hallway Bridge was built. It was a pearl of a Design! Even Fisher Paul said so when I described it at the IntArchitec Brain Exchange – and Fisher of course is synonymous with a very different take on Interiors: high concept, high budget, and very business-oriented. When, in the wake of the Dawson House, I persuaded him to let me launch our new family-friendly brand of design, Home-is-Harmony, the Hallway Bridge became one of the touchstones for what we were all about. A brand that was Feeling-Focused, a little bit Humorous, comparatively Inexpensive; and that very much put People First.

Even more importantly, the Hallway Bridge worked for Jem and me. When I came in in the evening I stopped at the crest of it and saw myself and the edges of all the other selves stretching out beyond me, a caterpillar of other me-s, and I thought of where I had ended up and who I had turned into; and I was happy. And when, usually a little bit later, Jem arrived, I heard the drum-beat of his step on the slope up and my heart leaped; then there was a pause; then a bang as he came back down and our evening together began. Jem never actually commented on the piece very much; but from his smile as he came in, and the flush on his cheeks, and simply the impetus the slope gave him as he careered into the sitting room, I could tell that it was having a good effect on him.

Often in those early days we crossed our Bridge together to head out to salvage yards, furniture warehouses, the timber merchant, the paint shop. We were like magpies, spotting stuff that no one else had noticed and hauling it back to add sparkle to our nest. When we finally found the keystone sofa for our sitting area – that was a magical moment. We had been trawling the warehouses by Tower Bridge for hours. Every time we pushed open a door my spirits lifted for a bit and then settled like dust as we wandered through the ranks of chairs and tables and stools and dressers and desks, some shiny with polish, some saggy and drab, but all calling out to be bought and loved and used – by someone, but not by us. Jem is more patient with this kind of thing than I am, but by the end even he was getting bored. And then I spotted it: a huge, curvy piece, the frame of it like the shell of an enormous bean in which a long leather cushion lay lolling. It couldn't be. It was! It was the spit of the Marcel Coard Rosewood Sofa from 1929 – which everyone had thought was a unique piece and which I was sure was in a museum in America! What was it? A replica? Could the Coard have been one of a pair? Whatever, here it was, languishing at the back of a showroom cluttered with dull Victoriana. It was beautiful. Stay calm, I thought to myself, don't let on.

So we bought it for a fraction of its value. What a find! Walking back, we were silent as if we had seen a miracle, and when our eyes met we would smile and smile. When it was delivered a week later we found that it did go wonderfully with my trusty Race chairs and our fantastic Bauer plywood table (another find). And when, at the end of each day, we snuggled up on the Coard to read or watch a bit of telly, it seemed that everything had fallen into place. The Coard didn't literally move like the boat-sofas in the Dawson House; but Jem and I were spiritually launched, in our Hallway House, discovering life together, and one another.

Every Hallway must feel like a beginning. I *so* disagree with the Design Cliché that says the Hallway should be the most polite, least personal room because it is the house's public face. No! It is an introduction, an opening, a passage to the future. When you design a Hallway, let your fantasies explode around you. Create an airlock, an egg, a rubbish chute, a runway. Take your inspiration from arrows, waves, or wheels. Think butterflies emerging from their chrysalises, or flowers in bud. The Hallway is a place of Transformation. Give it life!

*Magic Mottoes*

*2. Design — For Life!*

*3. And Live — For Design!*

*4. Ideas Can Come From Anywhere!*

# Living with Alizia: Jem

*This was my first attempt to gather a 'testimonial'. I am printing the whole exchange so as to give you, not only a little extra insight into my personal life, but an understanding of the delicate negotiations that sometimes have to happen between the Designer and other people who – even if they are very close to her indeed – may not have Design as their no 1 focus.*

*Tuesday 12 June 2003. Sweetie I know this isn't your sort of thing but it would really help me if you could just say something about what it's like to live in our Interior – and about what I am like to live with during the process of creation.*

OK. I am sitting here. I have washed my hands. I am holding a pencil. There are sheets of paper in front of me and they are bright white, different from all the other tones around me here, the wood of the workbench, soft and grey with clay dust, the sandy distemper of the walls, the stone flags, the grey-browns and red-browns, earth colours, of the pots. And I am thinking: What can I say about all that? You and me are there, in my mind. Or else we are in the world. And here in front of me is this piece of paper, bright unnatural white (though I am filling it up now, greying it: nearly a whole page gone), and:

. . .

No. Here. I have made something. For you. Here. This is what I feel. This is what you are like, and we are like. This is our harmony.

*I have to say it was actually very sweet, what Jem had done. He brought up to me a pot that was almost a perfect globe, with just a little pair of lips in the top of it at the centre. Rolled up, clasped in their kiss, were these words that I have copied out. Really lovely – but obviously not at all what I needed to help me with this project. So I asked again: Dear I know it's hard for you. I love the pot. I do. I know what you are trying to say. But is it really not possible for you to say any of it at all in words? How about you begin at the beginning – Wood Street, right back at the very start of Us. Just focus on that Interior. Just say what you felt about it. It would be so helpful to me to have that on record.*

All right then, I will try. Since it means so much to you I'll try. I remember: when it was all a catastrophe around us. You and I. The dusty carpet, the wires dangling from the ceiling; and this was going to be our nest. You were so energised, all lit up. There you were, sitting at that card table piled with directories and swatches and mood boards and your sketches, making order, making lists. Then running down to the phone box on the corner to ring; and then running back. And pacing up and down, and grabbing little sample pots of paint and brushing lines of colour on the walls (how delicately you did that; how

28

intently!). Then stepping back to look at them, and asking me what I thought, only it never really mattered what I thought, you had your Project for the two of us, you were skittish like a foal. I thought you were so charming, so *young*: full of the future, full up with it to your lips. At the end of the day we would sit on those precious chairs of yours, with their protective covering of newspaper and tape. The house was cold: the only warmth came from the gas-canister camping stove. We would cook something childish, sausages and baked beans, and drink rough red wine out of plastic cups. No lights, only candles. We wrote messages in the dust of the floor – do you remember? At night we huddled together for warmth: when you were in my arms the whole house trembled with our joy. Afterwards, I lay there, in my socks, on our thin mat, hearing the tick-tock of pedestrians on the pavement, and watching shadows swing by above us.

But of course the design had to progress. We filled and smoothed the walls, the floors were sanded and varnished. In the end the house was finished. It had its 'Signature Space', the Bridge Hallway, which certainly was striking. Fisher Paul liked it, which was clearly very important. The whole Interior was – yes, I can say beautiful. There was a pleasure to being inside it. There was a pleasure to having people over: they looked around them and smiled; they sat down and felt at ease.

Then I started to make great heavy pots, unglazed on the outside, reddish, like rust. Like huge artefacts that had been underground for centuries. Each morning I left our house like anybody going to work, but where I was going was my studio, my burrow, where I could turn around and snuggle, where I could open myself up in the gloom. I breathed the damp, thick air, and my Art happened. Pots that some earth god might make. They had a gravity, they dragged me to them, they wanted to keep me by their side. Some evenings I found it hard to leave. I walked slower back along the streets, over the railway bridge and past the park; and when I got back to Wood Street there was that bridge of yours to cross in the hallway. I stepped over it into the brightness you had made, so bright it pained me. You might be cooking to calm yourself after your busy day, and we would eat together, talk. Sometimes you might be already cosily on your way to bed and I would wrap my arms around you, pull you into the hollow of me, my chin above your head. The pain would go so far away I hardly heard it, a distant siren sounding the all-clear.

But then, what is it about lives? Sometimes I would go back to Spital, and talk with the people there, new people some of them, they were interesting, just sitting at the sticky table or on the grime of the floor with a beer or a smoke or a coffee, passing the time. When the right amount of time had passed, and the rhythm took me, I would go to the studio and work late. Then I would forget about our lovely house, I would put it away like a tin. There was only me, and the whirring of the wheel, and the thick shadow that the walls of the pot on the wheel would wall in.

Until once I finished, late, and came out, sliding the metal door along behind me until it clattered shut; and there you were, waiting, under a streetlamp, in a pale coat cinched around your waist. You took my arm and looked up at me with swollen eyes. You held me tight all the way home. In bed you sobbed and sobbed. Everything was wrong. We had gone wrong. I held you and we were like tree-boles specked with dew. I dried your eyes. You dusted my face with kisses, like the touch of a hundred dandelion clocks, like the sway of a willow weeping.

There. Will that do?

# 3. The Sitting Room

*a. Sample Conversation*

'So here you are,' said Marion. 'Settled.'

'There's still an awful lot to do.'

'Not for a while there isn't,' Jem said. 'We need a rest.'

'This is' – Stan looked around – 'so exciting.'

'Thank you. But more importantly: it's true. It's Us. Isn't it Jem? We've had our false start . . .'

'I still think Wood Street was very charming,' – Stan put in.

'Yes but it didn't work, that's the thing. It wasn't right for us. But here – don't we? – we feel at home.'

'We do.'

'I am so glad,' said Marion.

There was a pause.

'What next?' – she asked, but Stan asked at the same time: 'And Home-is-Harmony?'

'It's growing and growing.'

'Too fast, if you ask Fisher,' said Jem.

'Oh?'

'He says he wants us to stay niche,' I explained.

'He's feeling threatened!' – said Stan.

31

'No, I think there are legitimate issues. IntArchitec is the established brand. It has to be the umbrella.'

'What does Simon think?'

'Oh Simon doesn't enter into it,' Jem answered rather bluntly in my place. 'Leez is the golden girl.'

'Hear hear,' said Marion. 'Here's to you both.' She raised her stone beaker; and Stan did; and they drank.

## b. Analysis: The Language of Chairs

That snippet of talk took place in, oh, must have been 1997, i.e., about four years after the completion of the Hallway in Wood Street. As you will have guessed, Jem and I had moved to our second house – Allsop Road – and we were celebrating the completion of the Sitting Room. Together with the Kitchen, the Bedroom and Jem's new Studio this meant we now had a core Interior we could live in and forget for the moment about the several unfinished other rooms. Obviously the conversation touches on how Jem and I were feeling about this major change – but that is not the only reason I have quoted it for you here. The other reason is that I want to ask you a question:

• Which of us is sitting in which kind of chair?

Puzzled? I'm not surprised. Yet for the Interior Designer the answer is easy. At least, it will be if the room where people are sitting is well designed (not much point trying this game for Stan and Marion's sitting room!). The explanation is that good chairs have different characters, just as different rooms do. When you sit in a good chair, there is a definite connection between It and You. Of course you remain yourself – but yourself as influenced by the piece on which you are Sitting. This influence can be happy, or else it can feel all wrong. In general, a well-designed Sitting Room should offer a variety of different seating experiences so all sorts of different people can feel comfortable – though you should obviously include some chairs specifically tailored to your client or clients. The 'three-piece suite' is therefore obviously a No-No for the serious designer.

A big, red square chair, for example, suits a forceful character. If you are not a forceful character, sitting in it will be a challenge. You may find you become more assertive than you would be normally. Or you may feel awkward, and even end up unable to speak at all. If this happens it does not mean there is anything wrong with you. It just means you are literally *out of place*. The solution is simple: find yourself more appropriate seating. Think of all the unhappiness that is caused by feelings of inadequacy, and all the money spent on therapy, on lifestyle coaching or simply on chocolate. I sometimes wonder how much of this could be saved if people gave just a little bit more thought to their choice of chair.

Curves – on the other hand – encourage subtlety and quiet. Soft or organic materials such as upholstery and wood create a similar vibe. So if you have a friend who is a little on the brash side, try to sit him or her in a small bent-wood chair and see how he or she responds. I guarantee the results will be interesting!

Now: keep these principles in mind, and let us turn to our sample conversation.

First, who is the centre of attention?

- Well, me.

Therefore:

- I am in a big, rectangular armchair.

33

In fact it is a piece designed by Kuramata and made of steel mesh (see *Figure 2*). But what about the curved back, and the curved arms: how do they fit my theory? The answer is that these 'soft touches' are needed to compensate for the rest of the piece: without them it would be simply too tough to fit into a domestic space. Steel mesh is obviously in itself very hard – almost brutal. But here again Kuramata has introduced a genius detail. He has given the mesh a gentle, opalescent sheen so that it looks almost delicate – like congealed and woven air. The Kuramata is my favourite chair. It always feels right. When I am down, it cheers me up. When I am happy, it makes me happier. Somehow, the *rapport* between it and my personality must go very deep.

Next, the trickiest case: Jem. He is perhaps not as chatty as me or Stan or Marion, but he is still quite assertive, don't you agree? When he makes a point, he puts it forcefully. I think this must have something to do with the way he really does his thinking with his hands rather than with words. It is as if what he says has been built up in advance: and then out it comes like something solid being dropped into the world. Now: what kind of seating fits this style of talk? A curved but metal chair? – maybe a light metal such as aluminium? Or angular but upholstered? It is hard to say.

Let me lift the veil:

• A nineteenth-century chaise longue upholstered in pale grey-blue.

The curved back of the chaise reflects his reticence, his softness (he is actually really rather sensitive). But it is offset by straight, exposed legs with clawed feet. Now, I don't want to push the connection between people's characters and their seating too far: I don't want you to think I'm some kind of obsessive! But, the funny thing is, once you have seen someone in their favourite chair, that

34

chair can become a key to their personality. For me, the strength of those straight legs and the menace of the claws will always be associated with the toughness that there is deep down at the bottom of Jem's character. On the surface: warm and supportive. Further down: spikes, which you sometimes have to tread carefully to avoid.

Figure 2. The Kuramata

Finally, Stan and Marion. Again, if you look closely you can see that essentially they are listeners. They do speak quite a lot of words. But, at a deeper level, what those words do is keep the focus of the conversation on me. So, over to you:

- What sort of chair?

That's right: curvy. But curvy in a special way. They are Sitting on a creation of my own which consists of nothing *but* curves.

- ??!

Let me explain. When I first turned my mind to the Sitting Room I realised I needed a signature piece to go in the crucial position in front of the French windows. It had to be low so as not to block the view; it had to be quite big; and (since Jem and I had found our Character Chairs already) its main function was to be guest seating – so it had to have the sort of 'feel' that would be right for a range of friends and visitors. I whited-out my mind and waited for ideas to come. And come they did. A car flowing up and down over the rolling English hills: an old-fashioned car, with a lady and an upright gentleman inside, doing the careful, dignified thing that used to be called 'touring'. A train jiggling – no, better, a train of camels, laden with boxes and rugs and silver bottles, plodding over dust and gravel, sharp mountains in the background, pillowy dunes ahead . . . and there it was. A mirage? No, my Idea! The piece would be an undulating landscape. A nowhere land, over which all sorts of people might travel. A place where anyone might pitch their tent and feel – not at home exactly, but at ease.

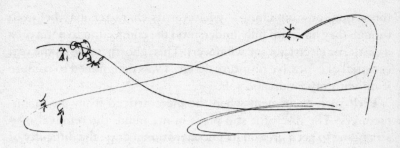

Figure 3. Conceptual Outline of the Spiritual Landscape

I turned to my sketchbook and drew a series of undulations. Good – but not quite right. I tried again – and again. It must have taken me a hundred attempts to achieve the perfect combination of curves (see *Figure 3*). If there was one thing I had learned by this stage in my career it was: time spent in development is never wasted. What is important, is to be faithful to your vision. I have enshrined this truth in Magic Motto no. 5:

✓ *Never Compromise! (Unless You Absolutely Have To!)*

When I had finished the Design it was constructed in compressed foam (a comfortable and durable material, despite its unpromising market image). For the covering, I chose a soft woollen fabric of palest olive green. This was not exactly the colour of the English countryside, nor of the desert. As with the boat-sofas in the Dawson House all those years before, what I wanted was not to *copy* the landscape, but to *suggest* it. The strange, wonderful thing is, that often people's imaginations respond to this sort of hint without the people themselves realising what is happening. You hear clients saying: What a calming piece

37

(or strong, or stimulating – whatever its character may be) even though they have not fully understood the connection to nature, or a castle, or electricity (or whatever). This 'ghostly sense' is the real essential of evocative furniture design. I was determined to conjure it up with my landscape sofa.

I felt such excitement when the piece arrived from the manu-facturers! The disc of it still plays in my mind: the removal men struggling to get a grip on its unconventional lines; the difficulty of squeezing it along the corridor until at last it reached its proper place, low down on our lovely bare old oak boards in front of the high back windows. I took a knife to the rough plastic cover (shocking pink, I remember it was) and tore it off. I dragged the ripped plastic to one side and stepped back to give my attention to the piece.

'Going in for war-games?' I think one of the removal men said – but I never mind that sort of quip, and in any case I barely heard him. I was concentrated on the piece. At first sight it was wide, low, perhaps a little featureless: it didn't grab the eye but allowed it to pass (as I had wanted) out into the light beyond and the shadowy presence of the chestnut tree in our courtyard garden. But if you let your gaze rest on the new seating land-scape, even for a moment, you found yourself drawn towards it, drawn into it by the lines of valleys and hilltops which went on, rising and sinking and twisting, till they reached the horizon (i.e., the edge of the piece). I moved forward, turned, sat in one of the lower seating positions which looked as if it had been carved out by a glacier. Such calm came over me! Of course I had modelled and colour-boarded the room in advance; but there are some things you can't predict, however much you plan. In this case, I hadn't guessed quite how harmoniously the curves of the new piece would echo and yet also contrast with the chaise longue and Kuramata, and how the olive green of its fabric would

38

combine with the dark boards and the paler paintwork like some beautiful musical chord.

I sat happily for a while on the Spiritual Landscape – as I now realised it should be called – and then I got up and went out on to the little balcony and shouted for Jem to come in from his studio. I watched him lumbering across the courtyard, and then darted back in to wait excitedly on the SL. In he stomped, in grubby overalls, his hands all clayey. He stood. He focused on the piece. He took a step back. Gently he stretched his arms out sideways, lifted them, lowered them, turning his hands all the time as if he was feeling something like mist or drizzle in the air. Then he brought his hands together, hunched his shoulders, and stepped forward.

He stopped. 'I can't sit on it. I can't even touch it with these hands,' he said. Then he crouched down. 'Yes I can.' He leaned in towards an especially plump undulation that rose beside me, stretched his head out, his mouth, and touched the fabric with his lips. Then he revolved and sat on the floor, legs bent in front of him, elbows like buttresses behind.

'Leez, it's great,' he said. 'I was worried it'd feel contrived, but it doesn't. It brings the earth into the heart of our house. It's beautiful.' He looked at me; I looked at him. We smiled and smiled.

It was only really in the aftermath of that moment that I realised how nervous I must have been for months before. Such a lot depended on the success of Allsop Road! The story of Wood Street – the wave of it rising from hope to a crest of achievement and then the tumbling, miserable feeling of something being not quite right – well, it had been sad, but it had also made me feel I had a lot to fight for. Jem and I were right together. We were in love. But the fact is there are three corners to any relationship: the two people, and also their environment. By 'environment' I mean not only the home, but the whole way you live your life, your work, what you believe in, the pressures you are under, the patterns that lock into place around you. What I had to do in Allsop Road was learn from Wood Street and somehow bring all the different struggling forces into harmony. Jem's words gave me hope that I was going to achieve that aim. I had been so anxious about him, about us, about the project, about everything. But now those worries were caught up like rubbish in the wind, and blown far, far away.

So: that is the piece our friends were sitting on during the sample conversation. Marion was cross-legged in a dip, Stan was lounging against a rise. And, to get back to our opening question: their supportive, secondary role in the conversation does I think owe something to the welcoming but temporary feel the Spiritual Landscape was designed to produce.

The four of us were often together in the Sitting Room at Allsop Road. And the seating arrangement I have described was natural to us. It simply felt right. Or rather, it simply felt right except during an uneasy period a couple of years after the sample conversation. One evening, I came in with coffee and saw that Marion had claimed the Kuramata. As you can imagine, I was surprised.

'I've got news,' she said. 'I'm pregnant.'

'Woah!' – cried Jem, leaping to his feet and giving her an awkward hug and kiss on the cheek and then taking Stan's hand in both his hands and pumping it. 'Beat us to it. Well done. It'll be wonderful. The two of you. A little one.'

'Yes,' I said. 'Congratulations.'

I *was* happy for Marion. But her announcement also stirred up my feelings in a very muddling way. Let me explain.

## c. Marion, the Kuramata, and Me

Allsop Road was just around the corner from Marion and Stan's house – and over time Marion and I had, I suppose, become good friends. But our relationship wasn't ever totally straightforward. Stan struck me as a very open person – all brainy, quick and alert, with his round eyes looking out through purple rectangular glasses, interested in anything that was going on. But Marion was more mysterious. She was tall and graceful – though not exactly slim. Pale-skinned, with freckles and red hair. She was very keen on Nature – always packing poor Stan into a camper van and taking him off to some bit of Wales by the sea. But she wasn't one of those feisty outward-bound types. She was into yoga and meditation and baths with aromatic powders dissolved in the water. She had a calmness about her which seemed to me just a little bit self-centred – as if nothing from the outside world ever really quite got through to her. And she was very quick to offer advice. Often that advice was right! – at least, it worked. But still, there was something about it . . . Sometimes I'm not sure I really like being helped in quite that way.

Let me give you an example of what I mean. During the delicate period of settling into Allsop Road, Jem had some difficulties adapting to his new studio. We went through days of him arranging and re-arranging his materials. Of him starting out on a new pot and almost at once giving up. Bringing his hand down on the half-shaped mound: squelch! Grabbing and pushing it and then chucking it back into the wet clay bin, and then coming and sitting in the kitchen for a bit, looking at the paper, and then getting up and going up the stairs and out, the door slamming behind him. I tried to smile at it; I tried to be supportive. But I began to worry that it was going to be Wood Street all over again – or maybe worse! In the evenings I would wait for him at our stop-gap

41

kitchen table. In he'd come and I would look up into his face for a sign of change, of happiness. But he would look away, or shrug, and go straight to the pile of boxes where the wine bottles were, and pull one out roughly. Such stifled anger he brought in with him, such thwarted hopes! Sometimes he'd struggle to open a bottle. He looked stupid, his big body bent over, heaving at a little cylinder of glass. He couldn't do it. He let go and straightened up, then bang! – his fist punched into the wall or his hand went slap against his thigh. 'Fucking plastic corks,' he'd say, as the pain passed through him. Then he would reach down again. This time he would pull more effectively, the bottle would be opened, and he would pour us drinks and sit down opposite me, his face hanging sullen. I knew better than to make suggestions. I so much wanted to help, of course I did – but I knew that, for Jem, this was a spiritual logjam that only he could ever clear. So I sat calmly, tried to be discreet and understanding and receptive, nothing more. In the end he raised his head and said: 'I'm going to sleep in there. What's wrong is that it doesn't feel me. But if I sleep there, and wake up there. If it's all around me, all the time . . .'

'Dusty, smelly . . .'

'Yeh – if it smells of me. If I could just feel close to it. Do you see?'

I did see. Of course I did. Most of all, I was glad there seemed to be some glimpse of a way forward.

The thing was, when I happened to mention this episode to Marion, she took a completely different view.

'Oh Alizia, I *am* sorry.'

'Why?'

'It's a rather bad sign. Don't you think?'

'No.'

'If Stan stopped wanting to sleep in my bed, I'd be very worried.'

'Marion . . .'

'Physical closeness is the heart of a relationship. The physical *is* the spiritual! When a man stops needing to dream next to a woman's body, he very soon stops needing her at all. Especially a very physical man like Jem.'

I simply couldn't make her see that things weren't that simple. Jem is an Artist – which means he can be very sensitive. When things change, he needs time to get accustomed to them. He is like some sort of plant that has to be dug in and grow roots. Moss that needs to spread.

Marion sat me down. She made me a cup of lemon verbena and watched me while I sipped. Then she came and stood behind me, put her arms on my shoulders, squeezed.

'You're very tense.'

'Am I?'

'Deep breaths.'

I tried. I *think* when people are being massaged they are meant to make their minds go blank. Or imagine rustling palms. But I am no good at that. I was wondering how long Marion would stay, thinking would I have time to email Simon at IntArchitec before he left at six.

Then she said: 'You know, I feel you're quite a tense person. I mean, you're lovely, obviously, but you are also, aren't you, a little, well . . . tense. If anyone touches you, you jump. I bet you don't have massages very often, do you?

'I don't usually like it . . .'

'You should. You and Jem. Foot massages. You really need to work on that bodily connection. Make it so he needs your touch. Think of monkeys. They touch each other all the time – they have to, for grooming, they pick out ticks and nits. It's so intimate. And even when they just brush against each other, their hair touches. Hair is so sensual, isn't it? . . . I wish I was covered in hair: thick hair like a monkey, so I could feel that frisson of brushing past

43

things. Stan could comb it and pick through it. We've lost all that, us humans. We're wrapped up in our clothes, painted over with make-up. Unless we make an effort we can end up very distant from one another.'

'Hmm.'

'What I'd do, is leave Jem there for a few days so he gets a bit lonely. And then do something really romantic. Wait till the evening. Put candles all round the courtyard. No, a line of candles leading from his study to the back of your house. And incense. Bit of an Eastern feel. Give yourself a nice relaxing bath with ginger and cinnamon salts, so your senses are all opened up and your body is glowing and tingling. Put on something flattering, something see-through. Go out to him, and invite him in.'

By now she had stopped pressing at my shoulders, so I could turn and stand. I was outraged. This was *so* intrusive. I wanted to hit her! But all I said was: 'It's a bit corny.'

She said: 'It's what men like.'

The horrid thing was . . . she was right! Well, not completely right – but more right than I wanted her to be. Jem did stay in his studio for several days. From the food that went missing I knew he must have come into the kitchen to raid, but I never saw him. I went out to him twice, as my usual self, to ask how things were going. He didn't open the door but communicated through an open window. He said he was fine, he was getting there. But he showed no sign of wanting to come back to our bed. So in the end, partly in case it did work, but mainly to prove that it wouldn't, I tried the Marion method, modified version.

Evening. Skip the slow aromatic bath (I'm more of a shower person) and *certainly* no pathway of candles – so naff! But I did make a nice meal, knowing that he could see me through the big back downstairs windows (see ch. 4). And put on something slinky. And foundation and eyeshadow and mascara and lipgloss

44

and just a hint of blush. And lowered the lights in the kitchen-diner, and placed a single candle on the table. And then pressed the switch that connected to the gong in his studio, and walked out to his door. It opened. Fawn-like, I looked up at him. Dove-like, I cooed: 'Sweetheart, I miss you. Will you come in?'

And he did.

And the evening was lovely. I was thrilled to have him back in the house: it was like being on a date again. But there was also a part of me that was uneasy. Wasn't it a bit artificial? We shouldn't have to go on a 'date' now when we had been together for, what, more than four years! Jem was always saying how important it was to just *be*. So why couldn't he do it? Why couldn't he actually just *be*, and stop going on about it?

Another thing I didn't like was: Marion should not have been able to give me advice on how to handle my boyfriend. I suppose actually, to tell the truth, that was what upset me most.

So: that's Marion. Or rather, that's Marion and me. Mixed feelings. Friendship, and . . . something else. What it all added up to was: that when she sat there in my Kuramata and said 'I'm pregnant', I didn't really manage to feel as happy for her as I should have done. It wasn't simple envy. It wasn't that I was desperate for a child of my own (though, as I was in my mid-thirties by then, the issue of WHEN was very much on my agenda). It was more . . . oh, I don't know. Some things she could just do better than me. I suppose I felt she was more confident, more sexy, more fertile. Altogether more of a woman. There.

Anyway, it wasn't just the *fact* that she was pregnant; it was the *fuss* she made about it. Hot flushes, cravings, dizzy spells, indigestion – what happens to you when you fall pregnant is really very peculiar. But you don't need to tell the whole world about it – and

*certainly* not when you are Sitting in a chair designed by Kuramata. Yes, that's right: she took possession of the Kuramata for
the whole nine months. There was always a new excuse: morning
sickness, a sore back, the difficulty of getting up from the Spiritual
Landscape (in fact the Spiritual Landscape had been designed with
ease of use very much in mind). In the end I stopped caring. But I
do firmly believe we owe it to ourselves, as women, to behave with
more dignity. Magic Motto no. 6:

✓ *Proportion In All Things!*

## d. Concealment

We have begun to understand the nature of seating. But now we are
faced with another big challenge. How do we fit into the Sitting Room
all the 'stuff' that is necessary for everything that happens there other
than sitting down – all the 'life tools', as I call them? We can't just leave
them lying around. The mess would be unbearable – and so would
what I like to call the 'noise'. Because the truth is that objects are not
simply objects. They have a kind of life. They call out to you, asking to
be noticed, admired, and used. Imagine a room where stereo system,
TV, computer, bottles of spirits, decanters, books, CDs, jigsaw
puzzles, assorted ornaments and vases – where all these are crowded
around us, begging. Marion and Stan's Sitting Room is a bit like that,
you'll remember; and it makes it very difficult to feel relaxed.

If a Sitting Room is going to be a space where it is actually
pleasant to Sit, then *effective storage* is crucial. One possibility is to
conceal all objects completely. Fisher – and IntArchitec in general –
has always been very pro this line. His three principles for a good
sitting room are clearly laid out in the 1978 IntArchitec pamphlet
'No Buts':

- Line
- Tone
- Calm

Not much room for personal clutter there!

Fisher's own sitting room is in his penthouse, which forms the top floor of the IntArchitec building. He uses it sometimes as a very intimate extension of his office, and it is in that role that I have seen it – though only on a few occasions. It has always made a very strong impression on me. What that impression is of, is: Nothingness. Limestone floor. A wall of pale ash cupboards, so precisely engineered that you can barely see the edges of the doors (they have push catches). A low, grey rectangular divan of Fisher's own design, made to harmonise with the tones and proportions of the rest of the room. And then three of John Makepeace's lovely Millennium Armchairs. With their delicate pale curves, spindly legs and the cobweb tracery of their backs the Makepeaces introduce a just slightly contrasting note. Fisher has always made me sit in one of them, and I think he must do the same to all his visitors – while he reclines on the divan, relaxed and yet immoveable. The dove-grey clothes he always wears (Miyake, Yamamoto) blend with the upholstery and the other muted tones around, making the whole space seem very him. There you sit, in your little cobweb cup, balancing on stick-like legs. You are meant to feel unsupported, disempowered, totally at his command.

The thing is, there is something about the simple beauty of those chairs that also buoys me up. Maybe it's the way they are a tiny bit reminiscent of the Kuramata – like little, well-mannered cousins. Or maybe it's because – as a designer myself – I can see the designs they have on me: I can enjoy feeling their influence, and also fending it off. Whatever the reason, I have somehow managed to find a bit of strength in them every time I have entered that room: whether to be hired by Fisher all those years ago, or when we had the discussion which resulted in my setting up IntArchitec Home-is-Harmony, or much more recently when he was urging me to take on my first solo international project, the Bleunet kitchen and dining rooms in Paris – even though it would mean a major adjustment to my lifestyle and career trajectory. So I don't kowtow, I really don't. I gather my courage and I blurt out things like what I said to this Bleunet proposal:

'Obviously Home-is-Harmony has to come first.'

I do have to be quite assertive like that because, really, he is a very implacable man. You say something and it seems to be swallowed up into the heart of him, silently, without a splash. Then there is a pause. His round face is unreadable: the greyish, tight skin stays motionless but his pale blue eyes behind his little wire specs lose focus for a moment while he considers his reply. Then it comes, and it is like a wall being built, brick by brick. You look at it. It seems immoveable:

'The continuing prosperity of Home-is-Harmony could depend on your decision, Alizia. I think you need to grasp this opportunity. And you need to make it work.'

Years ago, way back at the time of Wood Street, I had been very surprised when I got Fisher to support Home-is-Harmony's original concept. I had gone in there trembling, even though I had the success of the Dawson House as capital and the ingenuity of the Bridge Hallway to lead with. The whole idea seemed to me too small-scale for him, and too individual, not major in the way IntArchitec projects traditionally had to be. I was prepared to have a spat about it. I was prepared, in the end, to leave – at least I think I was. And Fisher did pause. He did ponder. He did look at me appraisingly. But what he said back then was: OK. While now . . . well, now I don't know what he thinks at all. Not what he really

48

thinks, deep down inside, beneath the surface courtesy. That is what is so unnerving about him. You think you see what he is up to, what he stands for. You think you can rely on him, even if only to disagree with you. But he is cannier than that, and more complex.

That's why everything he says has to be weighed up from all angles.

Anyway: Fisher's sitting room obviously suits the kind of person he is and the sort of thing he does there. But I think very few other people would be happy in that room for long. The reason is that – in my view – Fisher's design forgets that objects have a vital second side. They don't only 'beg' at you in an irritating way. They also offer stimulation – which is good. The danger of the completely 'empty' Interior is that it literally does nothing for us. It gives us no ideas – and, just as importantly, it gives us no temptations to resist. In Fisher's room this means that all there is to concentrate on is *him* – and, as I say, for his purposes, and for the sort of person he is, that is a very effective result. But the rest of us, who simply want to Sit in our sitting rooms, to chat, be comfortable, to be together with our families, and welcoming to our friends, we need something more. We need our life tools around us. We need to feel enlivened by them, and wanted by them. We need to feel *at home*.

So the question is:

• How can we make the necessary living-room objects feel *available* – but not *intrusive*?

Take a moment to formulate your own ideas.

. . .

. . .

I will not go through all the answers I have come up with over the last few years. Suffice it to say, that there are all sorts of ways in which the concealment approach can be made less total. You can place photographs of the objects on the cupboard doors. You can employ colour coding. In a high-spec project, it is even possible to situate LCD screens next to each seating position so that, at a mere touch of the finger, the appropriate cupboard springs open. In all of these strategies, I have been guided by Magic Motto no. 7:

✓ *Stimulate, But Not Too Much.*

But the solution I do want to tell you about is the one I found for my own sitting room in Allsop Road. The property is a 1760s town house, with rooms that have high ceilings but are narrow for their size. And they are blessed with really exquisite cornicing, dado rails and fireplaces – period details which should be respected as part of the character of the building. These features put even a modified concealment strategy out of the question. I simply was not prepared to cover one of the original walls with cupboards. But how then could I keep our life tools under control?

The answer came to me as one word:

• Height

The life tools should be raised above our sightline. But if they were so high up, how could they be made readily accessible? Solution:

• Pulleys

I had four blocks fixed to the ceiling, screwed firmly into the joists. Four pulleys were attached so that the steel cables dangled within easy reach of the four main seating positions which the chaise longue, the Kuramata and the Spiritual Landscape provided. Hooked on to the cables were a beautiful Hillé cabinet, a Wirkkala coffee-table, the stereo and of course the television and video ensemble. Very careful counterweighting was necessary to avoid accidents and ensure ease of use. When our life tools first rose hesitantly into the air, my heart lifted with them. What a victory over the problem of Sitting-Room clutter! There would be no need for any of the usual awkward ways of hiding the television – in converted tea-chests or behind paintings or under a specially commissioned TV-cosy (yes, they do exist). One yank on a cable and it would be hoisted away. But, even more than the practical advantages, what really excited me about the Design was the visual effect it presented. At ground level: the chairs. They were made to seem especially solid, especially welcoming, by the life tools which floated above them – like ministering angels. The space seemed full of possibility, but at the same time very rooted. And in a family home, a feeling of rootedness is vital.

## e. Continuity and Community

To Sit is to establish a special relationship with the ground. When we stand, we dominate the earth: we can see into the distance, we can hunt, or run from danger. But when we Sit we give the earth our trust. The earliest hominids had no chairs: a rock or a patch of soft grass were their chaise longue and Kuramata.

Obviously Design has advanced a long way since the Palaeolithic era. Still, in the creation of a Sitting Room, the concept of earthing remains key. When you are securely seated, you can open yourself to your surroundings. You can connect with the past, with the future, and with other people.

This is why (I now see) the move on from Wood Street was always going to have to happen. Life has bad things in it as well as

51

good; the sunshine is streaked with cloud. I think there are several reasons why dark feelings gathered round us in that house, why we came to feel so frustrated. But one of them definitely had to do with seating. Of course we had a room with chairs in it – my lovely Race chairs, and the magnificent Coard – but was it really a place where we could Sit in the full sense of the word? It wasn't only that the space was small: it was the feel of it. The so-called Sitting Room was really just a lobby where we rested for a moment before moving on: back to work, or out, or up to bed. When people came round, they were picking us up or passing through or dropping by. They didn't really linger. And we didn't really flower. We simply were not grounded then in the way we are now. In a deep sense, we were always going somewhere: we were in the Hallway of our Lives.

But now; now the two of us are thoroughly dug in. We are Sitting Down. Not long after the Sitting Room had been finished I was in the Kuramata, waiting for Jem to get changed out of his work clothes as we were going out for supper. I looked through the back windows at our courtyard: Jem's studio, the kiln, and the big, branching chestnut tree that brought nature's magnificence right into the heart of our space. It was a warm dusk (early autumn), the windows were open, and I listened to the leaves swaying and rustling. I did so hope that Jem had really settled here. My eyes came to rest on the grey-blue chaise longue, which looked so distinctive now it was framed by the cables dangling down to the life tools on either side. I imagined Jem sitting there. I imagined myself sitting where I was sitting. We looked so solid. Then I heard feet coming down the stairs: there Jem was.

He was so lovable! All scrubbed up like a little boy, his face pinkish from being washed and shaved, his chunk of peppery blond hair pushed back, a loose white shirt, camel-coloured moleskin trousers and heavy brown Docs, quite clean. I looked up again into his face and he said: 'Leez, let's sit down together. Let's sit on the Spiritual Landscape.' So we did. I had a nice sudden reminder of what a good piece it was, so soft and so supportive. But I also felt a little bit lost. It was a wobbly feeling: everything looked different from over here.

Jem was next to me. He put his arm around me and for a moment we were close, shoulder to shoulder, our heads tilted, higgledy-piggledy lean-tos. Then all of a sudden he had twisted round and was on the floor in front of me, kneeling.

'I've made something.'

'Fantastic' – it would be the first fruit of the new Studio! He brought whatever it was round from behind his back and held it out. It was bulbous, about the size of two tennis balls. It was a shiny brownish colour with streaks of red. There were tubes sticking out of it.

'What is it?'

He held it further out towards me: 'Take it. Hold it.'

I did. 'What is it?'

'My heart.'

A twitch went through me and a sound came out of my mouth. It was grotesque! And yet it turned out Jem didn't mean to be grotesque in the least. He moved back a bit, offended, but then gathered himself and leaned forwards and became warm again.

'It's for you.'

'. . .'

'Keep it . . . Leez, will you marry me?'

'Marry you?' I was stunned. I had a very strong feeling of – feeling nothing at all! I seemed to see us from a distance, in a photo, him kneeling, me sitting there looking flummoxed. And then whole skies of nightingales began to sing, whole seas of dolphins leaped.

He was anxious: 'Don't you want . . .?'

53

'I never thought you would.'

'Neither did I.' He looked up into my eyes so searchingly, with such delight. His face opened into a smile, I caught his smile, and our one huge smile went shining back and forth between us; and then we laughed, and then we were in a hug, and then after a while he was lying on the floor with his head on one of the Landscape's undulations. I had my fingers in his hair and he said: 'It's what it all adds up to. That's what I was working out, in my studio. You've done it. It means we can be Us again, for ever.' His head arched back so I could see his eyes. 'Don't you think?'

'Yes.'

He said: 'I am so grateful to you.'

I said: 'I am so happy.'

A couple of weeks later we were married. Just like that. We didn't want to make a display of it. To us, being married was a private thing, almost a secret between Jem and me. Our party was going to be the rest of our lives, in the Interiors we were going to make together. So we just popped down to the registry office. My parents and my brothers were there for me, and Stan and Marion for Jem. And there were rows and rows of empty chairs.

I rather liked those chairs. Not their Design, which was *terrible*: curved and gilded wooden frames, with the seats and backs incongruously upholstered in 'practical' dark diamond-pattern nylon. It was more what they symbolised. They made me think of all the people who had sat on them, and all the people who were going to. They were full of the future and the past. They made me think of the community that Jem and I were going to create – through Allsop Road. Of how we were going to Sit there. And how there would be room for all our friends to Sit there too.

And that is what has happened! Maybe this is going to sound silly. But sometimes I like to Sit in our Sitting Room, with our life tools dangling above me and the empty chairs all around, and let myself feel surrounded by all the other people who have ever sat there. Stan and Marion, of course, and Fisher, and my delightful colleagues and friends Graham and Stuart from Wallpapers Bespoke, and Carlo and Adriana, and Alexander and Jean-Philippe. The heavenly Naomi Cleaver has contributed her aura to our Sitting Room: she finds the chaise longue suits her best. Once, we even had a visit from Jasper Morrison: I happily let him Sit in the Kuramata! All these friends have left traces of their presence in our house – and especially in the bosom of our house which is our Sitting Room. The echoes of their chat surround me there. I see mirages of their smiles.

## Magic Mottoes

5. Never Compromise! (Unless You Absolutely Have To!)

6. Proportion In All Things!

7. Stimulate, But Not Too Much.

# Working with Alizia: Fisher Paul

Talent is light. It changes whatever it touches, but is itself intangible. I love it. I have talent myself, of course; but also I love to grow it in other people.

I am Fisher Paul, the designer. I am me; and also I am Lead Creative and Managing Director of IntArchitec, the world's most innovative interior design practice. Alizia Tamé, who is my colleague there, has asked me to add my contribution to this book of hers. I am happy so to do.

I first met Alizia, plain Alice Tame as she was back then, at her degree show. Yes, that is where I picked her up. I was looking around as I always do, not expecting to discover anything very exciting necessarily, but just wanting to see what the children each year have done. I had drifted past the usual sort of work, a wall papered with leaves, a table made of interlocking knives and forks, but then: good gracious, here was a really very striking installation. A white space. In the middle of it: a spindly, bendy-looking, brownish little chair. In the corner, sitting bunched up on the floor, a figure dressed in black. Quite still, the face hidden. A person or a sculpture? I was not sure.

I looked closer at the chair. Its finish was strong and polished like furniture of the highest quality. Whatever substance it was made of was a little bit translucent, so that you could see through the curvaceous amber limbs to a shadowy hint of bone within. There were lines around each limb like ridges marking the stages of growth, only . . . yes now I saw what they were, something had been wound around: tape, that was it; some transparent tape. I stepped back to assess the overall effect. The piece was profoundly organic: curvy like a vine, and yet also subtly skeletal. It really was a very good chair.

But it was the *mise-en-scène* that was superlative. The big space. The small chair. The figure on the floor: why? – because the chair was too precious to sit on? – or too fragile? – or just too damn uncomfortable? Or else a gesture of abjection? The designer sacrificing him- or herself for the sake of the Design? I stepped towards the figure in the corner. It had not moved. But it was a living person. I introduced myself. She did not stand; she did not move except to raise her head. But she looked up at me with such excitement, such triumph in her eyes.

So I invited her in to IntArchitec for a chat.

From that beginning she has grown and grown. Funny, isn't it, how just one thing, one installation, can be the unerring proof of talent. But so it always is. And so it was for her. Now, as Alizia Tamé, with IntArchitec, she has established a really very enviable reputation. Of course I have subjected her to careful handling. That is what I do for all our creatives: it is no more than my job. To begin with, she had a minder, Simon Sanders, another designer, very understanding and very reliable, though not in possession of the burning talent that she has. He guided her, but did not stifle her. After that: well, the key to the successful management of young talent is to be not too controlling. You give them space. For this is the thing to remember: they are the future. If IntArchitec is to prosper, it must renew itself – and that means: it must do things I could not do, perhaps even would not want to do myself. So I

57

allow Alizia to create Home-is-Harmony – I even help her. Look how she has grown. Now there is talk of branded products. Now she is writing this book.

This book, which is so very you, Alizia. And obviously in some respects a good thing. To spread the word. To open your life to people; to bring them into your world of lived design. It is a lovely ideal. You know the risks – of cheapening, of losing that respect for Interior Design which I have spent my career building up. You know what it was like when I started out. There were no Interior Designers. There were people who dabbled in decoration. No professional training, no standards, no intellectual base, no conceptualisation, no rigour. Now we have all that. IntArchitec helped to make it happen.

I know times change. I brought you in and promoted you because I knew that times were changing. For me, four, even five decades ago, it was about the wholesale re-imagining of the built environment, the creation of spaces that were healthy, that were light, that were not depressing; interiors you could pass through easily; chairs that were not great heavy lumps, that could be moved or stacked. I am sure you are right that my battle has been won. You are right that we are in a phase where greater individuality is possible, and idiosyncrasy, and surprise. I am behind you. Lead the way!

Only . . . but you know this. You must hold on to the principles that matter. I can see there is an attraction, from your point of view, in producing a range of wallpapers and paints and tiles: but can you control how they are used? Think of it: a space dressed entirely in Tamé branded products – but the ensemble effect? A catastrophe! There is still good design and bad design. There are still people out there who do not know the difference, and who never will. What will they make of the words that you are writing for them? What will they do in your name?

58

This is why I have sought now, just a little, to direct you. This is why I turned your attention towards a proper *grand projet*, the Bleunet kitchen and dining rooms. And I was right: don't you agree? Now you must have confidence. I know you look around you sometimes and ask: Where are the great woman designers? You, Alizia, can be such a one. You do not need to dabble in little people's houses, in nurseries, in paint effects, in writing manuals of DIY. You can achieve great things. A path is opening before you. To create landmark interiors across the globe. Beacons, from IntArchitec's new generation, to light the way through this new millennium that has dawned.

I urge you: think of it.

Fisher Paul.

# 4. The Home Office

## a. Un-Design

Let us go back to the very beginnings of Allsop Road. What was the crucial space there, our *alpha* and *omega*, our *sine qua non*? Answer:

- Jem's Studio (of course).

It was vital for him; and so it was vital for me. If I hadn't managed to make it work, none of the rest of the house could have happened and, frankly, I don't know what would have become of Us. Jem's Art has such an effect on him. When he is creating, it is like his roots are in wet soil, his leaves are spread and the sun is shining. He is happy and strong and – well, just so delightful! But when things are not going well – even for only a little while – it is like he folds up and becomes impermeable. Then the world, and everyone, even me – we all turn into a sort of dark, dark cloud. He ignores us, or else grumbles at us. He wants us all to go away.

The thing was, creation was only possible for him when he was in the right space – both emotionally and physically. In the early days of our relationship, I spent a lot of time in what seemed like the chaos of the studio under the arches in Spitalfields: darkness and damp, the wheel in the middle of everything; a swirl of litter around it; a line of old wardrobes and shelving units where the finished pots were stored; a hat-stand; random tables; and a sunken, lumpy two-seat sofa off to one side – where I usually was – with an old steel two-bar fire in front of it. It seemed to me he didn't care about the Interior he was in at all. But no, he told me; on the contrary. This space we were in was special. And what was special about it was that it had simply come into being. He hadn't given any thought to it – let alone paid someone to design it. All that had happened was: he had worked here, and the necessary things had gathered round him. He had spotted them here and there; in a skip or where someone was having a clear-out. He had put them where they had seemed to want to go. That was all. The result was: the space just felt like more of him, really. It orbited around him.

Once – he told me – he had been invited to do a residency somewhere where there was a state-of-the-art pottery, all wide vistas and clean floors, luminous and practical. But it hadn't worked at all; it was like he was a novice again, the wheel not keeping a constant speed, his hands out of true, the clay slipping and slopping.

Jem is such a challenge to me. I think that's what makes our relationship stay so alive. Everything that inspires me in him, that excites me, that lifts me up, also shakes what I believe in. He is probably the most extreme example I know of the connection between our two Interiors – the places we live in, and our thoughts and feelings. Yet what follows on from this, for him, is a deep unease about Design. I had always thought I would prove him wrong, that I could design in a way that was just as organic and nurturing as his thrown-together studio (and actually more practical as well!). This was the impetus behind Wood Street and

Home-is-Harmony and the whole shift towards Feeling Design. I really think I had had some success, with the Dawson House, with the Bridge Hallway, and with other projects that I haven't yet gone into. But when it came to creating a place where Jem himself could work . . .

It had to be done. I had to take the risk. And not only take it, but chew it up and gulp it down: i.e., succeed. Because I do take some of the blame for the, well, not total happiness of Wood Street. After all, it was my design! But I want to say, in mitigation, that when I made that design I did not know what our lives together would be like. I did not know how we would be pulled in different directions, how difficult it would be for us to create a feeling of real togetherness. I was very focused on setting up Home-is-Harmony: of course I was. But I did always make sure there was room in my schedule for us to have Together Time, for us to Be together in our space, to cook together, watch a video, to snuggle and chat. I suppose the mistake I made to begin with was thinking that, because he was an Artist, Jem would be more flexible; that whenever I was free he would be too, or could be if he really loved me. But he said he had to follow the rhythm of his work; that I had my appointments and my deadlines but he was in the grip of a force that was just as inescapable and a lot less easy to predict. If he felt the pulse of his inspiration rising he simply had to let it flow. When he explained this to me I understood it, I really did. I absolutely did not want him to sacrifice one jot of his creativity for me. So I did not mind that sometimes I spent evenings in the house alone, or that even when he was there physically his mind would sometimes not be, or not completely. I would say something and he would just carry on chewing a mouthful of whatever it was that we were eating. After a while he would look up and say: 'What?'

I suppose what really hurt was that earlier, before Wood Street, I had felt that I was totally part of him, and of his Art – of everything he was involved in. I had sat in the mouldy chair in the gloomy space, the clutter of this and that gathered around us. He had worked with me there: with me in his force field, and him in mine. I had watched the swing of his shoulders, the poise of his arms, the taut lips; and when he paused we had chatted, oh, about trivial things, but also about beauty and life and clay. But that didn't seem to happen any more. Partly there was a very simple reason: that actually I didn't go to his studio; that I went to wait for him at home instead. But the reason I did that was because home was not his place but the place we had made together, the place that was meant to be for Us. What was upsetting was that, in the end, even after all the work we had put into it together, he didn't seem to feel the same, he didn't seem to want to take that step. So I sat there on the Coard with the empty space of the rest of the sofa next to me, and the rainbow colours around me singing here, here is your crock of gold (only it wasn't) and the found objects we had put for artworks on the walls reminding me of the happy days of our discovery of the world and one another, the days when we had been getting to know each other and making Wood Street for the two of us. In the end I couldn't keep on sitting there. I did what I always did when I felt low: went out and walked. Walked the shadowy, abstract streets till the surge of unhappiness in me would turn to tiredness and I could reach a sort of calm. Only this time I didn't reach that calm. Pain and hope kept bubbling inside me. I found myself always gravitating towards his studio, wanting to bump into him, wanting him to be on his way back home. But I never did, he never was. Until one night he came out to find me standing there outside. He took me in his arms; and we walked back home together.

We talked. We decided to have another try. To move to a location where we could create a Whole Life Space where all our energies would at last be gathered, where we would live and I could have an office and he would have his studio. Which he wanted me to design for him: that shows how Together he realised we could be. And I was happy to do it for him; of course I was; we were in harmony again, we had a future; he was my love.

But: how?

I pondered the question as I had my morning cup of lime and echinacea. I worried at it on the tube. I laid it down in the back of my mind as I got on with the day at IntArchitec Home-is-Harmony; but I let it come nosing out again at nights as I tried and failed to go to sleep. Could I just transport everything from Spitalfields? It was tempting but, no – Jem's Interior under the arches was totally site-specific. And anyway, even if I could, the Feel would be all wrong: it wouldn't any longer be a space that had organically come into being but an imitation, a dead pastiche. Somehow I needed to catch the essence of Jem's creativity, its pulse, and use that to shape the new things in the new place. The husk of the new Studio would be different; but (I hoped) its heart would be the same.

The answer came to me one bright morning as I was walking along to the tube, a bit more hurriedly than usual, almost marching, my arms swinging back and forth. I thought of Jem's movements at the wheel: the swing of his torso as he turns from sink to bench, the pulsations of the kneading of the clay, the speed at which the pot on the wheel is thrown. *That* was where the pulse of his work became visible. If I could capture those movements – yes, with a video camera: rig up a camera on the ceiling of the studio directly above Jem's work area. Just leave it there and let him pot.

So I did. And then, one quiet, nervous evening, we sat down together on the Coard to watch the results. Jem was oddly upright next to me, his right hand gripping the sofa's arm, his left trailing behind my back. He was shy just at the prospect of seeing himself, and I think understandably a bit reluctant to have his rhythm tracked: it was so much part of him, so fundamental. I snuggled close and stroked my hand along his thigh. I rested my cheek for a moment against his shoulder. Then I pressed the remote.

There he was, on TV, a bird's-eye view of him, the scramble of his hair, his broad, bowed shoulders, his feet popping out comically in front and behind as he moved. We watched. On the screen, the virtual Jem settled to his wheel. Next to me, the real Jem was fidgety. On the screen, the virtual Jem rose, and took a finished pot over to the drying shelves. All of a sudden something struck me. I reached for the remote and touched fast forward. I was right! I leaned back so I could watch the real Jem's face. To begin with, he was bewildered. But after a few minutes more, I knew he could see what I had seen. He was hunched forward, arms on his knees. His eyes were wobbling as he tracked the fast-moving image on the screen. He watched. And he watched. And then I heard him murmur: 'Beautiful!'

And it was. What we saw, underneath the comic quick jerkiness of the speeded-up movements was that, as he worked, Jem literally went round in circles (see *Figure 4*). What he had always said, was right. A shape came from somewhere deep inside him, or maybe from the ground. It came out through his body and imposed itself on the pot. At once, I realised I had the concept for his new Studio. Clay bins, sinks, workbench, wheel and drying shelves would be arranged in a ring. The Interior would be like an enormous potter's wheel.

I said: 'I'll take that, that's the heart of it, that circle. I'll work with that.'

All Jem said was: 'Yes.' But he said it in such a sighing, solemn way. He leaned back in the Coard, resting his head on the thick leather and rosewood rim. His eyes were closed but his hand was reaching out towards me. I knew he trusted me. We were on the path to a solution.

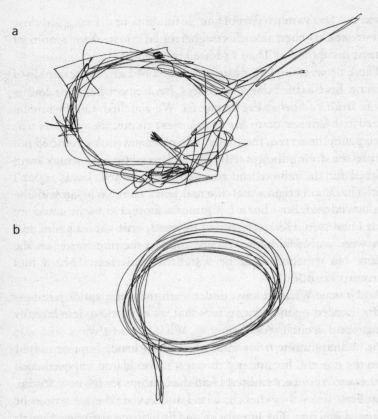

Figure 4. Kinetic diagrams of Jem at work: a. in the old Studio
under the arches; b. in Studio II, Allsop Road (projected)

Over the next few evenings I gave substance to the plan. The
place we had found to move to was a classic Georgian town house
with a decent-sized (well, decent for London) courtyard garden.
Jem's Studio would be a circular building, nestling in the corner at
the back. It would be made of old bricks to match the rest of the

property. The windows would be gothic slits to create a gloomy, cave-like light-scheme; and there would be a low, sloping roof of terracotta tiles. The kiln would be conveniently placed outside. As soon as Allsop Road became ours I channelled all my energies into creating – or rather reincarnating – Jem's special space. And it worked! There was always going to be a time of worry while he settled in. But after that: such happiness! He found his rhythm of work again; there was the proposal, and our wedding. And that's not all. A few months into that special, special time we were sitting in Studio II (as I called it). Jem was showing me the new Works he had been making there: tall, thin creations, some rectangular, like hot-housed jewellery boxes; some circular like narrow chimney pots; some sloping like miniature volcanos. All had lids like tiny roofs. He was looking out through one of the narrow windows.

'You can see right into the back of the house from here. When we have kids . . .'

My heart leaped and I heard him again – 'When we have kids' – and echoingly again and again: 'When we have kids I'll be able to watch them while I work.'

He had put into words something about Allsop Road that I had known since the beginning but hadn't ever dared to speak out loud. It was a house that needed children. It was just too big for the two of us. The only way I could make sense of the half-basement was as a Kitchen and Family-Room thru-space with big French windows opening on to the garden. What did it say about us – I had wondered – that we had chosen to move to that sort of a house at a time when – as far as we knew with our conscious minds – children weren't remotely on either of our agendas? What did it show of the currents that were flowing underneath?

I had taken it for granted that Jem didn't have the same perception. His Art, the life force, his creativity – I had always thought he would see children as threatening all that, as being an obstruction.

So I had tried to shut the whole issue out of my mind, to make myself completely unconcerned by it. That was why I was so shocked when he came out with those simple, totally un-anxious words. I didn't actually say anything about it at the time, though I'm sure I must have looked at him with more than usually sparkling eyes, I must have squeezed his hand. But inside me it was as if piles of rubble had been cleared away, a new stream had sprung up.

The odd thing was, that in the months and years that followed, when I began to wonder if it might not actually be time to paddle along that stream, it turned out to be rather hard to get Jem on board. He never mentioned the subject – and if I ever brought it up myself he always had a good reason for pushing it away into the future. All his creativity was going into the hatted pots at the moment – or else, simply: Do you really think we're ready? The fact is, I wasn't totally sure I did think that. At least, I wasn't sure I *knew*. For the committed, professional woman, motherhood is never going to be an easy issue. Having a child is a tremendous responsibility. You have to give it, well, if not your all, then at least a very large part of you. Could I manage that, while also realising my ambitions for Home-is-Harmony and not disrupting my relationship with Jem? These were big questions – and as I say, Jem never seemed to want to talk them through.

But that's all rather off topic for this chapter – and you probably don't want to hear about it anyway. So: there was Jem in his studio in the courtyard. Here was the Sitting Room and the rest of our Interior-to-be. But what about my Home Office?

## b. The Meaning of Work

At first sight, a potter's studio is very different from the sort of office that many people these days want to create in their home.

But the key principles we discovered in Jem's case are vital to the Design of any workplace. Even the most stationary, un-physical occupation has its rhythms; and of course the Feel of an Interior matters wherever you are and whatever you are doing. So: as with any room, when you are designing a Home Office you need to take account of who You are, and what sort of Interior will suit You. But you also need to ask – crucially – what your Work is, and what sort of Interior will suit It. By this, I don't just mean what kind of computer it needs or whether you have lots of filing cabinets or use an angled drawing board – though these practical details are important. Magic Motto no. 8:

✓ *Look After The Basics! (If You Want Your Vision To Be Workable!)*

The really crucial thing is to recognise that Work has its own demands and impulses – almost a will of its own. This means that when you bring Work into the Home you need to think very carefully about how to create harmony between it and all the other living that is going on in the rest of your Interior. How often have you settled down to what you hope will be a productive day in your home workplace – only to find that hours of it get wasted making cups of tea or watching daytime telly? How often have you meant to have a relaxing lie-in on a weekend morning, only to find that some unfinished task in the office downstairs starts beeping at you like an unstoppable alarm clock? Why is this? Because your Interior is not fully in harmony with the Meaning of Work for You.

In my own case (as you have probably gathered!) Design and Me are very thoroughly wrapped up together. When I look over the misty landscape of my past I find it hard to see when my vocation for Interiors began. Was it with my first fully achieved creations, my barbed-wire-pattern duvet cover and abattoir tablecloth, that date from when I was still at school? Or earlier still, when – as a toddler – I first noticed there was something rather striking, and actually a little bit oppressive, about my parents' 1960s Robin Day suite? Or was it even before that, right back at the very beginning of anything that could be called Me, when I was curled up and snug in my very first Interior, my mother's womb? I simply cannot find the answers to these questions.

What I can say is that right from the beginning I realised Design could be a force for good. I cherished the idea of reaching out to people through the objects and interiors I created. Human beings I had never met would sit on the things that I had made; would eat off them, would lie down on them and go to sleep. By touching them physically, my designs would also touch them emotionally. I would be the guardian angel – or rather, *guiding* angel – they never knew was there. This was the ambition that drove me through A level, art school and then graduate work in London. This was what propelled me into my almost unprecedented straight-out-of-college job at IntArchitec.

So, one aspect of the Meaning of Work for me is: Design is my Vocation. But that doesn't mean it's easy for me. It doesn't mean I'm always certain of the way.

They were so exhilarating, those early years at IntArchitec! To work with Fisher Paul on modern classics-in-the-making such as the Factory Office in the City of London and the Zen shopping centre in Marseille. How I relished taking on my new identity, no longer plain, ambitious Alice Tame, but Alizia Tamé, junior creative with the world's most innovative design company. Fisher had assigned another designer – Simon – to be my associate, basically concentrating on the practical side of things and leaving me free to come up with ideas. Together, we rose fast. Before long, now senior creatives, we were being put in charge of significant commissions. A dream come true. Except – that that was when it all began to pall.

There was something so routine about so much of what we were doing. Stark lines, empty spaces, floors of polished granite (this was the mid-'80s), lots of chrome and leather, with classics by Jacobsen, Le Corbusier and the Eameses always on display. Oh, I know Fisher is famous for some really very innovative designs – and rightly so. But what underlies those moments of magic, at IntArchitec, is such discipline, such rigidity. The principles of impersonality, and of a very literal idea of function, were never up for debate. Once, Simon and I were given the task of remodelling a block of apartments maintained by a private bank as medium-term accommodation for its international employees. Ten interiors, all high-spec, and each one to have its own distinctive character. It should have been such fun! But the IntArchitec ethos was so restrictive! All it seeemed possible to do was change the colour of this or that wall or alter the arrangement of the kitchen or maybe use steel instead of granite for the bath. The reason was, that each Design had first of all to shout out 'IntArchitec!', and only secondarily to express the wishes of the clients or the personality of the individual designer.

We did find a way of giving each Interior a little bit of a distinctive twist. My famous 'Impish Touches' had their genesis at this time: a row of porcelain ducks on one wall of an otherwise minimalist Interior; a corpse-studded flypaper in a kitchen that was in every other way pristine. But it wasn't enough. This wasn't what I had dedicated my whole life to becoming. I was suffocating. I had to find another way.

At weekends I liked to spend time in markets – Camden, Portobello – just to charge myself up with the energy of colour and form that I so badly felt the lack of during my working week. One day, one happy moment, I came upon something that startled me. It was a vase, or a kind of a vase, glazed in an exquisite pale green. The mouth of it was stopped up so you could not put flowers in it. *That* was peculiar enough, but the really interesting thing was that all around the blocked opening were little arms, stretched out or bent at the elbow, full of life with angry gripping fists. At once I understood the concept. Each of these fists would hold the stem of a flower: the same flowers that could not be put in the vase itself. Of course they would quickly wilt, but that – I thought excitedly – would only add to the effect. Whether you thought of the fists as angrily trying to stuff the flowers into the vase, or as angrily chucking them out, it was a perfect symbol of my frustration. It was exactly the thing for my next Impish Touch. Only, I was going to need two.

'Who made it?' – I asked, and the stall-keeper gave me a name – Jem's name – and an address in Spitalfields in East London. There was no phone number. I decided to set off at once.

I got out at Liverpool Street and walked East. Behind me, the over-designed office-blocks of the city. In front of me, increasingly narrow and dirty streets. It was a place I hadn't ever really been to before. Such higgledy-piggledy clutter! And such a whirl of history: Victorian warehouses plus eighteenth-century weavers' houses (the Live–Work spaces of their time!) plus '60s condos plus a fabulous weird church with a high conical spire, totally black – a rather sci-fi effect! But I needed to press on. I consulted my *A–Z*, and walked further, angry vase in hand. Soon the bustle of people dropped away. Here were the railway arches on my right – oh, and a *terrible* smell of sewers. At last I found the place. A wall of corrugated iron closed off the arch from the pavement. There was a door. I banged on the metal wall. It rattled and rumbled. Nobody answered. I tried the door. It opened. I stepped through.

Inside: gloom. I let my eyes adjust . . . and I saw a man kneeling with his hands sunk in what looked like a pile of earth.

'Hello . . .' I said enquiringly.

'Yup,' he grunted as if irritated.

'I bought this.' I lifted it up. 'I love it.'

'Uhuh.' This time he rose and walked towards me. He smeared his hands on the trousers of his overalls and held them out. I realised he wanted the angry vase. He took it in his dirty hands and turned it around and pressed it with his thumbs. They were enormous hands. Hairs like grasses grew from the backs of them where the clay had dried to cracks.

He handed the vase back to me.

'Would you . . .' I said, 'could you possibly make me another?'

'Why?'

I told him again that I loved the angry vase; and I told him what I thought it meant. I explained about the Impish Touches. And then I found myself spouting: about IntArchitec and my dissatisfaction and how the Impish Touches were all I had that felt like life; and if he could only make another . . . And then I stopped.

His shoulders had dropped and his face was open, smiling: it was like he was warming himself at a fire. He said: 'That's good. It does mean that.'

But then his eyes flinched and his face half turned and he said, not looking at me but looking at some distant corner of the floor: 'Can't make another though. Sorry.'

I wanted to cry out: *But it's me! Notice me! Make it for me! Look at me again!* But what I did was say: 'I can pay. A lot.' Which was so obviously the wrong thing to have said.

He scoffed. 'It's not money.'

'I know it's not. Sorry.' And louder: 'Sorry!'

For a moment his eyes were in mine again, searching; and then he was looking at the floor. 'It's – I need to have the feeling. I don't have the feeling for making that kind of work any more.'

'What are you making?'

He led me in to the back of his cave – I mean his studio! – and showed me. I asked him about the work and described what I saw

73

in it; he answered and he listened. After a while I left but soon I had got in the habit of going back there and perching on the mildewy, lumpy sofa in the middle of the whirl of everything; and talking and helping him talk. In turn he helped me understand what I had always somehow felt deep down inside. That Design is about responding to other people, about enabling them to be themselves – only better. That what the Designer does is take people's energy, their feelings – wit or love or rage – and channel them into forms. Design for Life. I realised I needed to work on a smaller scale – in homes that people actually lived in, in the places where they had their messy, textured, energetic lives. So, when the Dawson House commission came up I jumped at it (in fact no one else at IntArchitec was keen). Then there was Wood Street, and then – now – Home-is-Harmony, the solution that allows me to stay with IntArchitec while also doing very much my own thing.

There.

What does it all add up to?

I mean, what pointers does it give us *re* the Design of my own Home Office in Allsop Road? Well, this: I needed a space that would hook into the inspiration Jem kept on giving me, but that was also completely open to the needs of my clients. A space that was welcoming, responsive, generous. I needed a listening space; and a space where I could imagine anything. An Interior where other Interiors could be born.

Sitting in the Kuramata, I focused my mind on the problem. What came to me was: White. Walls: white, and ceiling: white. Actually, white everywhere, for everything: white laminate desk; white drawers and filing cabinet, white cotton blind; white resin floor. Why? Because white is the colour of Vocation (think the cells of monks and nuns). Also, it is the colour of openness, i.e., of generosity. Finally, it is the colour of channelled energy because it includes all colours in itself and can be split to give you any one of

74

them. A variable lighting scheme would show this happening: at the flick of a switch, the walls could turn to mauve or plum, jonquil or apple green. My Home Office would be nothing, and yet everything; empty, and yet full. As for its location, it would be in a small room, just to the right of the front door, which had probably been used as an office by the merchant for whom the building was originally constructed. Magic Motto no. 9:

✓ *Work With The Character Of The Space – Not Against It!*

The practicalities woud be utterly simple. A u-shaped desk, centred beneath the window. To my left, computer and telephone; to my right, a bare surface on which to leave sketches and mood-boards lying about (this 'lying about' is an essential part of the imaginative process, for me at least). Filing cabinets were integrated underneath. And everything was gleaming white.

So there we were. In our new big house, Jem and I. Our house for our future. I loved working in my Home Office – or the Whiteness as I came to call it – knowing that Jem was simultaneously at work down in his Studio. I could almost feel the circling of his wheel sending out little psychic waves of stimulation. And I hoped he could sense beams of concentration shining back from me. In practical terms it took a little while for us to find the rhythm of this new Living-and-Working Together. To begin with, I would go down for my apple and ginseng just as Jem was finishing his coffee and itching to get back to work. He would be ready for lunch at twelve, and me not until half-past two. But bit by bit our cycles got closer. It was just like we had hoped. Our Home-Lives and Work-Lives were integrating – and so were we.

Except, except . . . At the professional level, Jem and I were all about creativity. But in the personal domain . . . what was the meaning of creativity there? Oh, we had good times, and Marion and Stan and lots of other friends were always coming round. But when they left . . . what happened to our Energy then? Familiarity can become routine, and intimacy can start to feel like isolation – especially when you are living in a really rather spacious property. As we have seen, when Marion announced that she was pregnant I was already in a bit of an anxious state about the whole issue of maternity. Then Stan, inspired by our live–work complex at Allsop Road, asked me to create a Home Office for him. Of course, I couldn't not say yes.

*Magic Mottoes*

*8. Look After The Basics! (If You Want Your Vision To Be Workable!)*

*9. Work With The Character Of The Space – Not Against It!*

# Working with Alizia: Stan

Extracts from my manuscript 'Diary of Our Pregnancy – and of the Funnel Office'.

*2 Feb 1999*

Pregnant! Ouch! What's that going to be like?

No. Let me write it with proper dignity.

Today we discovered that Marion is gravid with our child.

Tangle of feelings: Excitement! Growth! Delirium! Helter-skelter!

Man hands on dreariness to man – as Larkin so memorably said. But how would he have felt about it if he had been a father?

A great imponderable unknown.

. . .

*17 Mar*

M makes the announcement to J & A. J very warm and congratulatory at once. A less so. Strained? NB: *must* ask her about the home office idea. It could make such a difference. Query: Cost?!!

. . .

*21 Mar*

She said yes! Seemed very excited. There's this warmth that just erupts out of her sometimes. I'm not sure many people see it. She's usually so driven. At work she must be ferocious. FP probably doesn't have to twist her arm at all to get her to work the hours she does, she's a sucker for it. Or part of her is.

AND – she's going to waive three-quarters of her fee. Which seems to me incredibly generous.

Even so she says we're not going to come out at less than 30K.

*22 Mar*

The schedule for my home office is tight, Alizia says, so we must set to work at once. No overrunning THIS deadline! First step is for me to jot down some pointers about the significance of work for me.

Hmm.

*23 Mar*

Work should not be work.

For the historian of culture everything is grist to the mill, and therefore nothing is. How does my work relate to what my work is about? It is all part of the same thing. The prison-house of language – or rather, the Nike sweatshop. There is no meta-language – or rather, all language is meta-language.

NB: What does this correspond to visually? How can I explain it to A?

*24 Mar*

No problem. A very much up with Theory – was dosed in it at art school. Says she's going to go with the idea of infinitely reflecting mirrors. Given the location [front half-basement, next to Marion's Knitting Place which later turned into Doris's Playroom – A. T.] this will help with light but otherwise I'm not sure I'm convinced. Still, I'll wait to see what she comes up with. M says she's happy to give me a free rein here since it is after all my space.

What will that be like, though, working more at home? Just go in for lectures. Waste less time on email. Might go stir crazy. But if we're going to have a child we need to do it properly. Can't get stuck in the oppressive gender construction of M staying at home with the baby and me going out to work. There *has* to be another way.


*27 Mar*

Have heard nothing from A and I'm still not happy about mirrors. However much you ironise them or complicate them they still return you to a logic of representation. My work is more like picking up rubbish.

Like the church of St Anthony at Padua. All that clutter on the wall, the coats, the handkerchiefs, the umbrellas, the motorbike helmets, the lost babies (joke), the six pairs of false teeth (not a joke), the toys, the books, the hats.

– Q: suggest a lost-property office theme for my home office?


*28 Mar*

Or a dustbin?
Or something to do with recycling?


*30 Mar*

A funnel! That's it! A funnel! All the world flows through it – into an infinity of different bottles. Just as all the world flows through me – and through each one of us. Plus, it's domestic. A plastic epitome of the nature of existence. In every kitchen cupboard.

*31 Mar*

A went for it in a big way. Grasped the concept at once. Said it was *full* of design interest. She's done some excellent sketches [see *Figure 5* – A. T.]. Part of the excitement of it for her, she said, was my courage in seeing that a radically reduced floor area needn't mean less *useable* space. (Hadn't thought of that myself.) Bright yellow would be the best colour – plasticky, but also warm. The floor would need to be porous – a grille – otherwise the feeling of *flow* would be lost. She said it was the opposite of feng shui, that if ever I wanted to disappear a feng shui consultant all I'd need to do would be bring him into the funnel office and he'd collapse on the spot.

There'll be a two-stage build. 1. Heavy work: digging of the conceptual drainage hole in the centre plus creation of a new skylight window plus construction of supports for the funnel structure plus electrics. 2. Installation of the funnel itself, which will be pre-cast in plastic sections. Stage 1 will be noisy and messy and will probably drag on, builders being what they are. Stage 2 should be clean and quick – if the sections manage to squeeze through the door and down the stairs.

*3 Apr*

M very anxious about how the work will affect her knitting. Says she wants to keep working as long as possible. She has orders to fulfil and anyway she'd go *mad* without it. Pregnancy is an unsettling, magical time and she needs something she knows, something routine, to hang on to – otherwise she may well feel

80

all at sea. And she *obviously* can't keep on working with building going on in the next room, builders tramping through her space, the noise and the mess. It'd feel all wrong. Who knows how her body would react? I suggested hiring a studio or something, somewhere for her to work in during the build but she says she's not going to be moved out of her home at this crucial time.

4 Apr

Stalemate. M says why do I need something that will cause so much upheaval, why can't a simple room be enough. I say: What do we believe in? In doing things out of the ordinary. In asserting the specialness of life by, at each point, taking a step back to ask: What can I do here in order to be me? OK, anything you do will just be another instance of the circulation of narratives – but you can try to make sure that it really is *an other* instance: that's the main thing.

M: It's Alizia, isn't it – she's having rather an effect on you. You think she's rather fabulous.

Me: I think we're very lucky to know someone like Alizia who can help us live in the way we want to.

M: Help *us*? – it's *your* home office we're talking about here. Yours.

Me: Yes it's my home office to make it possible for me to be here more so I can spend more time with you and our child.

M: You know what I think? – I think you're jealous. Here I am, pregnant. Which means: creating. Making something wonderful and new in *my* interior. And so you want to do the same. Don't you think? Isn't there a little bit of that? The male cuckoo? And then she cooed: Cuck-oo, cuck-oo. 'You're all such boys. Come here.' And she reached out to me, took my hand, guided it to the hard place at the bottom of her tummy. 'Here – this is you too. We don't need all that Alizia-style upheaval. I love her, you know I do. I love her energy. I just don't think it's very *us*.'

Interesting evening at J & A's. I think that in spite of everything we're going to go ahead. J said that M could move her knitting place into the downstairs of their house – the big empty space next to the kitchen. It would be calm and clean. It wouldn't be lonely like a studio. It would be in a home, OK not her own home, but our friends' home. It's really very nice of him, of them. He is supportive of her, despite the way it sometimes seems. Except I suppose she is going out of her way to help people who were originally his friends rather than hers. Anyway, A very keen to press on: we've gone so far ahead with it, she said, and it's so good. She said we would almost certainly get interest from a magazine and that it would add considerably to the value of our house to have a Tamé space that had featured in the pages of *Wallpaper* or *Elle Deco*. M *seemed* to be persuaded . . .

The builders are in: digging the 'drainage' hole and concreting the rest of the floor. M goes over to J & A's house every morning and I go off to uni. Except I find it hard to stay there. So I come back, make tea for the builders, get involved. I have heard the incredible racket of the drills, smelled the damp warm smell of the earth giving way to the damp bitter smell of the concrete. An interior space is not just a space: it is the result of a process. I want to follow that narrative.

The builders are all right. Two blokes. A uses them a lot, apparently, for her smaller projects. One of them: 'You're a friend of hers, are you, she's something else. Her ideas . . . What are we making for you here then? Water feature?'

I tell them to wait and see.

To be honest, I like it better when they're gone. Then I can walk through the space, hear the echoes of my steps, imagine the future. A drops by sometimes then as well. She's mainly working on some big project over in Primrose Hill but she seems very committed to this one. 'It matters to me,' and for a moment her restless eyes look into mine.

Then she walks through into the space itself, peers into the cavity, bangs on the wooden supports that have already taken, on the funnel shape. I drift in after her.

'Why?' I ask.

'What?' Then she remembers what we were talking about. 'Oh . . . it's nice to do things for friends. That way you can really make the design grow out of their lives. You can be sure it's really right for them.'

I wonder if that's the whole story.

*16 June*

M is perfectly happy at J & A's. Or rather – J's, since A is almost always out. Says being there, with J across the courtyard in his studio, helps her to imagine what it will be like to be back here with me when the works have been completed. Odd, our being so much apart at this very sensitive time. But it does build anticipation. M is very warm always when she gets back. Hard heavy ball in the middle of her like an enormous cannon shot. The rest of her softer as though in compensation, a gentler look and way of moving, sort of hazy. She says there's some discomfort (how could there not be?) but that she is basically very happy.

J has opened up to her a lot, apparently. He's started making these half-filled-up pots in celebration of the idea of pregnancy. He says he very much wants a child of his own but it's difficult with A's career. Actually I can see that. J is so creative, surely he would want to make this miracle-work, a child. And there's a macho thing in him too, cock of the walk, destined to be father of many boys. Whereas A is so fixated on structure, so tidy, so – unbodily. It is hard to imagine, her letting herself swell up, her giving herself over to a messy natural process. And what would a baby do to her beloved Interior? Anyway, so A's career turns out to be the cuckoo in *their* lives. And that's the reason for her commitment to this project, obviously. Classic displacement activity. Not literally pregnant but metaphorically with my Office.

I think that's rather sad.

15 Aug

The plastic sections are here! Somewhat delayed but still OK: my baby will be here before M's, as we jokingly say. They arrived yesterday afternoon and were piled in the front garden. I could hardly sleep. Worrying they might be nicked. Worrying what they would look like. And today, now, literally as I write, they are being carried downstairs and slotted into place. It is astonishing, like some ginormous kids' construction kit. Hadn't thought of that association before but now it's here I like it. Appropriate.

A is flitting around, up and downstairs, in and out. She is illuminated. M of course is over at J's. Not that she's not interested, she says. She just really wants it to be finished. Then she'll be able to appreciate it.

Just been down to have a look. It's half in place. There are the inset shelves where my books will go, and the inset steps so I can reach the higher ones. There

. . .

What happened then was the phone rang. It was M – waters broken. She had thought she might be having contractions earlier on, she said, but she hadn't wanted to tell me in case it spoiled my special day (!). So obviously I had to dash.

And I'll always be grateful for what Alizia must have done when we were at the hospital. I got back to find my Office completely finished. My books in place. Everything clean. And so when Marion and darling little Doris came home the next day we just slotted into our new life. And that is where we still are now. I am sitting here at the centre of my yellow funnel. There is this astonishing yellowness all around me. And Marion and Doris are next door. Perhaps it is a *little* dark in here – the inset halogens almost always have to be on. But then the light they cast is so warm. It makes the plastic glow like something wonderful and alien. Like the life of the mind. The Funnel Office is like a radar dish: it collects thought-waves and focuses them on to me. And it is like the funnel of an old gramophone, projecting my ideas out into the world. I feel that I am levitating, for beneath me is a grille, and beneath that is empty space. But I also feel I am on the stage of an amphitheatre, and the rising circles of books around me are my audience. And yet also – whenever little Doris is distressed I can hear her and go to help.

To be honest, I was rather nervous about the prospect of paternity. I couldn't see how it could not just stifle such a lot of things – going out, thinking . . . being awake. Obviously, there are challenges ahead. But now, here, in my Tamé space, my Funnel Office, the way forward looks very clear.

Alizia: Thank You!

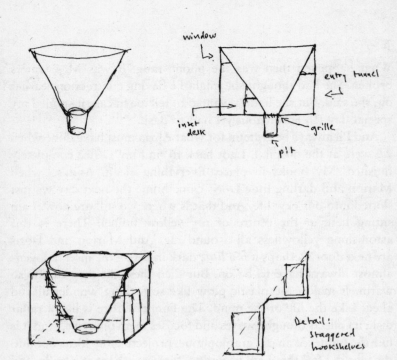

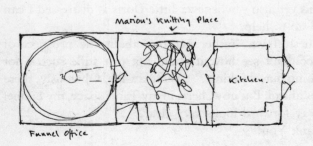

Figure 5. Visual notes towards an understanding of the Funnel Office

# 5. Kids' Rooms

## a. Making a Baby

I expect you'll have guessed this from Stan's 'Working with Alizia' contribution but let me say it anyway: the Funnel Office was not an easy project for me to be involved with. I was pleased to be able to help my friends – and, Design-wise, the result was excellent. But the more I imagined myself into Stan and Marion's Interior, the more I realised that I was helping to create for them, what deep down I wanted to create for Us. It was really very troubling. Especially when Marion came to spend her days at Allsop Road.

I did try to throw myself into the project. I told myself that I was pregnant too – pregnant with invention. But, by bottling up my feelings, I simply made them bubble all the more fiercely. I could see that Stan, like Jem, had his anxieties about paternity. But the difference was, that he was able to face up to them – with the help of the Funnel Office – and go forward. Why didn't Jem want to do the same? Or else, why couldn't I make him want to? I got more and more puzzled, and more and more unhappy. Sooner or later something was going to pop.

I had had a hard day. The builders had started to make the skylight in the wrong position. I told them to move it, they said the plans hadn't been clear: I said of course the plans had been clear. Just a routine building-site disagreement, but I'm afraid I rather lost my temper. When I got home, Marion was on her way out of the front door. Very chubby around the tummy now and walking with a bit of a waddle. I asked her how she was. She said: 'Wonderful.' I said: 'Oh good.'

Downstairs, Jem was in the kitchen. He came towards me, wrapped me in a warm hug. He seemed so strong, so happy, so affectionate. He put the kettle on. I tried not to notice Marion's bloody knitting machine stood in the middle of the emptiness that was going – one day – to be our Family Room and Play-Space.

And then he started talking about her. How relaxed she was, how she loved the aches and the queasiness because they were a sign of Growth, how there was a slow grace in her movements even though she was so bulky which you would have thought would make her clumsy, how at home she seemed to be in her body.

'Jem,' I said. 'I want a child.'

'I know.' He reached out across the table, took my hand. 'We're going to have one. Of course we are. We're going to have lots of them.'

I looked at our hands linked together. And then I looked across towards his face. 'When?'

'Well . . . not right now. Not when Marion's here.'

'Why does that matter? What does it matter if Marion's here for a few hours during the day?'

'You need to have your ideas for the Nursery and the Play-Space.'

'I'm not doing that till I'm pregnant. You know that. We've talked about it.'

Our hands had come apart. My palms were pressing at the edge of the table, and he said: 'It's . . . I don't think we should force it. When it feels right, it'll feel right.'

'To me it feels right now. Right now. You know my age. We've got the house. My career's in a good place. Your work's going well. We've been together for, what, five, six years. What doesn't feel right?' My voice was breaking and my face was twisting up; my eyes were hot suddenly: 'If it doesn't feel right now when is it ever going to? When?'

He just sat there. His eyes were distant as if he was looking at something that made him sad. Then he looked at the rough fingers of his big hands; and then he looked out of the window. And in me, it was like I was sand, draining out of myself between my toes. I saw my face as if it had been painted in a fresco, great black hollow eyes and a black wailing mouth from which no sound came out. 'Oh god,' I said. I went out, and climbed the stairs, and went into our bedroom and lay on the bed. Then I curled up in the centre of the mattress and pulled the dark duvet over my head.

But after a while I got up and – we carried on with our lives. Routine is a very powerful thing. I think it is especially important for me, despite all my creativity, and despite the fact that I am always working in different places. Actually I think it is *because* of those factors. Allsop Road – like any well-designed Interior – is arranged so that it guides people's movements. It leads the eye in one direction rather than another. It makes you feel happier moving *this* way rather than *that*. These invisible pathways create a sense of harmony: when you follow them, things simply feel right. So, when I woke up the day after that scene with Jem, I found myself making the usual movements from bed to ensuite to walk-in wardrobe to dressing room, and down to the kitchen, and then back up into my office, without really meaning to. And this rhythm gave me a little bit of comfort.

Still, all through this time there was a real sense of emptiness inside me. Stan's theory is that, for me, the Funnel Office was displacement activity. And he is right – except that the displacement wasn't actually terribly effective. When I was physically there, it was OK. I could give myself up to the work, I could feel part of something creative, something happy. And Stan was such a good person to work with – so nervy, and sharp and – Alive. It was when I was back at Allsop Road that things were really hard. The Whiteness was bearable as long as I was busy. But if for a moment there was no email to respond to, or if my mind wandered from whatever project was on the drawing board, then suddenly I would be rushing forward through time, as if each second was a year and I was ageing at a terrifying pace. Wrinkles ate into my face, and the whiteness all around, which had meant to be so energising, so full of hope and generosity, meant just one thing: sterility.

So I would go downstairs, and maybe Jem would be there and we would have a cup of tea or cook. But that was terrible too, because of the great lump of unspokenness between us. I could see he was trying to make up for it by being extra warm and sympathetic. He said about how hard I was working. He almost always did the washing up. But no amount of sympathy was enough. Only one thing would be enough.

The day after Marion went into labour was the most difficult of all. I had stayed late at Stan and Marion's sorting things out for them. How could I not? The phone had rung and Stan had rushed off, so scared and yet so happy. Only a few minutes later the builders emerged from the Funnel Office to say that they were done. I went in, switched on the halogens. I came out to get a chair and went back in and sat where Stan would sit, in the centre, with the crescent-shape of desktop in front of me. I checked for practicality. Desk at the right height, plugs correctly situated, bookshelves conveniently placed (apart from the very high-up ones that were reached via inset steps), integral filing cabinets smoothly operational. I sat back and let myself absorb the 'vibe'. Light. Warmth. Yellowness. It was like being in a flower. It was like being the stamen in the centre of a flower with sunlight pouring in and bouncing into me, soaking me, warming me, filling me with growth. And yet of course . . . Well. There was a haziness in the air like pollen, only it was not pollen. It was settling all around me, settling on me, on my hands, my jacket: dust.

I got up and went and found the vacuum cleaner and hoovered and wiped. Then I opened the boxes stacked in Marion's knitting place, and lifted out Stan's papers and his books and carried them through and filed them and put them on the shelves. I went up to their bedroom and got his laptop and carried it down and put it on the desk. Then I stamped and stamped on the boxes and kicked at them and tore them and took them out and put them with the rubbish. And then I mopped the floor.

And then I left. I walked along the pavement back to our house. And went in. Jem was not there. I went upstairs and showered and lay down in our bed, my bed. My thighs and my upper arms and my wrists were so tired that they were sore. They pulled me into sleep.

I woke up. Still no Jem. I lay for a bit and then I started to think about the fact that there was still no Jem. He could have got up earlier than me. But he didn't usually. Usually he was rather a slugabed. Oh yes of course he hadn't been there last night. Uneasiness began to spread through me. But then I remembered about Marion, which changed things. The uneasiness receded and I felt a pulse of anxiety about her, of concern. But what did her giving birth have to do with Jem's not being here? Did it have to do with it? I needed him here. Despite our problems I wanted him near me. Today above all other days!

I pulled on my dressing gown and went downstairs. No Jem. Maybe in his Studio. I hurried out. The odd thing is, that even though I was flustered, the brightness and the chill still struck me. I can see the scene now, the chestnut branches overhead, the autumn sunlight bouncing off the dewy cobbles, the wall all around, the brick kiln, a wheelbarrow and coiled hose in a shadowy corner, and ahead of me the Studio. I rushed across and looked in through one of the narrow gothic windows. It was dark inside so I kept on looking until my eyes adapted. There he was. He was in the corner curled up on a pile of mats, a rug pulled over him, his face nuzzled into a fold of it.

I was so glad! I had an impulse to creep in and snuggle in beside him, and he would stir and draw me to him . . . but then I changed my mind. What was he doing there? *Why* hadn't he come into my bed with me in the night? Was this going to be like that other time all over again? I wasn't going to go in and just get a hug from him and force him to say some kind words. I may have been fragile – but I still had my pride.

So I made my way back to the kitchen and began my usual breakfast-time routine. I put the purified water on to heat for my tea. I opened a cupboard door for the cereal, went to the fruit bowl for a pear, got milk and yoghurt out of the fridge. But today the invisible pathways didn't have their usual calming effect. I found that when I had chopped the pear and poured the yoghurt and eaten them and was sipping my lime and echinacea I still had an angry edgy feeling. Jem's being in the studio must be something to do with Marion's labour. But I was the one who needed comforting. I was the one who was not pregnant. I was the one who should be in hospital now with a little bundle of life in my arms.

I felt sick and stood to get a glass of water. Then I went to the sideboard, to the month's pile of Design glossies. I picked them up, *Wallpaper, Elle Deco, Homes and Gardens* and the others, took them to the table and started flicking through. (I don't ever get

92

*ideas* from these publications, let me hasten to add: but it is important for me to be aware of what the current trends are.) I don't know how long I sat there, the shots of taupe and beige *Interiors* passing in front of me, advertisements for furniture by Cassina, colour ideas from Missoni. What I mainly remember is the feel of my face: heavy, as if the skin were grey; as if there were a clamp around my forehead. Then at last the French windows were open and Jem had come in.

'Hey,' he said. 'I need a coffee.'

I didn't answer. I wanted him to be quiet. I wanted him to want to come close to me, but instead he moved away towards the worktop. He stepped gingerly, as if there were something in the room he had to be careful about, something that needed not to be disturbed.

'You OK?' he now asked. But there was an edge in his voice and again I couldn't see how to reply. I felt pushed back. There wasn't the right atmosphere for speaking in. I had so much inside me waiting to pour out. But I needed him to want to listen.

In the end he had made his coffee and came and sat down heavily opposite me, his arms on the table, his face towards me. His eyes were tired, the lids were narrowed and the skin was puffy around them.

He said: 'Marion's had her baby.'

'Oh that's wonderful news,' I said at once. But as the words left me I flinched inside. I felt like I was shrinking: 'Were you there?'

'I was at the hospital. You know it started when she was . . . when she was here? So of course when the taxi came I went with her. Weren't you still at Stan's when she called him? Anyway' – he shifted his gaze – 'when we got there I found I had to stay. It would have been wrong not to, when a new life was being born. I felt they kind of wanted me there. I mean I wasn't in the room with them, but I felt they wanted me near by. Just in case.'

He lifted his head to look at me again. I held his gaze for a moment: I don't know what I saw. Then he turned his head to the window and after a moment carried on. 'It all happened as Nature intended, apparently. I just sat on a plastic seat in the waiting room, waiting. For hours – I must have gone to sleep. There were screams coming from down the corridor, the screams of different women. Echoing. Nurses went past, hurrying – they didn't seem to mind I was there. Then another couple came in – in tracksuits. They looked too young to be nearly parents. She was big – twice as big as him. She was the one who was in pain. But she was confident. She was the centre. Marion had been the same, going in, but that didn't surprise me. She's got such . . . naturalness about her. She's got wisdom . . .'

'Well . . .' – but he was intent on his story.

'Looking at these *children*, you could imagine them chewing gum. But it was the same for them too. They were in something sacred. It was like a kind of beautiful sacrifice. The woman's pain was *good* pain. Later, Stan came out – I could tell he had been crying. He seemed surprised to see me – but I think he was pleased. He smuggled me in so I could see it, see her. Doris. It was a little baby, Leez. They said did I want to hold her but I said no. I just wanted to look at her. She was all soft. Folded up. Pink; wrinkly. It was strange because I'd seen her grow, you see, when Marion was here. There was that great bump. Enormous. And heavy – you could see the weight of it pushing down inside Marion from the way she walked and sat. You could feel it, just watching her you could almost feel it. And now there's this tiny creature.'

He reached his hand across the table and held my fist, pushing the tips of his fingers into the grip of it. He looked up, and again I looked into those watery eyes.

94

I felt very bitter. Jem was my husband. He does not want to have a child with me but when another woman has a child he is so moved! I sobbed and sobbed.

At last he came round to my side of the table, and crouched in front of me. He took my face between his hands, wiping the tears with his thumbs as if he was moulding my cheeks. 'It's all right, Leez. I understand now. I don't know what was wrong with me. I've been a fool. Seeing them . . . well, whatever the reason is. I've changed now. Let's – well . . . I mean let's – go for it.'

'What?' My hot, heavy head was resting on his forehead and my body ached. 'Really?' The pounding in my head began to quieten. 'Really?' Bit after bit my unhappiness cracked, and broke up, and began to drift away.

It took a while. More than a year. There were some false alarms (never think that a pregnancy test is the be-all and end-all). But in the end, one day, I was three months along, we'd been for a scan – and it had been OK. At last the magic time was here. At last I let myself be happy through and through.

Jem put his arms around me and held me and held me and said such a funny thing: 'I wish I could drive.'

'Why?'

'To be able to help, to be able to take you around.'

'It would be convenient.' And then: 'You'll never drive.'

'I know. I think actually I don't want to really. Probably couldn't. But what I mean is I really want to take care of you, now you're having my baby.'

'Our baby.'

He stroked my hair with his rough fingers and kissed my forehead. Then he sat away from me a bit and said: 'It's been a difficult time.'

'We've stuck together.'

'I know but it's funny what it does to you, when Nature gets blocked like that. Where can your life force go? I was like a river with a dam across it. You know those filled-up pots I started making? They were substitution, no what is it . . .'

'Sublimation.'

'But after that . . I was floundering, didn't know where to go. I'm sorry, Leez. I really am.'

I held him closer and said: 'Now we both know where we're going.'

As my pregnancy advanced, I found I wanted to reduce my usual busy schedule. Partly this was due to practical considerations. Morning sickness may sound like a little thing: let me tell you – it is not! But also, I discovered that I could not really get interested in other people's projects – or not in my usual way. I wanted to concentrate on me. Which meant: I wanted to concentrate on Us. On the surface, Magic Motto no. 10 may not seem to have much to do with Interior Design. But in a deep sense, it is crucial:

✓ *Know When To Put Yourself – And Your Family! – First.*

## b. The Nest

Of course I had designed Nurseries before. And what had increasingly worried me, was how the parents assumed the Nursery should reflect their ideas and not the child's. Why are so many Nurseries painted pastel blue or pink? Not because those are every Baby's favourite colours! As for the cot: what Baby would choose to go to sleep behind bars like an animal or a criminal? When it came to designing the Nursery in Allsop Road I felt I needed to break completely new ground. The challenge was:

- to create a space that was essentially Baby's, not mine.

That meant, making the choices that the Baby him-or-herself would make, if they were able.

I sat in the Kuramata and pressed my hands to my swelling tummy. I cleared my mind. I channelled all my energy into communicating with my Baby-to-Be. 'What Sort Of Thing Do You Like?' I asked. 'What Is Your Ideal Interior Space?' The words that came back out of the depths of inside me, were these:

- Dark
- Wet
- Snug
- Very *me*

Of course: The Womb. Any new Baby must be full of excitement at coming out into the wonderful bright interesting outside World – and probably rather proud of what they have achieved. But they must also be a little bit overwhelmed. What a Baby must want from their Nursery is, above all: reassurance.

'Wet' was obviously a no-no. But the other features? I dashed back into the Whiteness and went busily to work. Corners, edges and angles: all should be filled in and softened for a curved, feminine look. Dominant colour: dark red, painted straight on to the plaster for softness and depth of tone. And in the centre of the room: an enormous egg.

Can you grasp the Concept?

That's right: the Cot. Of course, one of the top quarters of the egg would have to be cut away: not so much as to destroy the vital feeling of enclosure, but just enough for the child to be easily lifted and laid down. There would be no legs – so that, when necessary, the cot could be rocked in a lulling movement (the lower curve of the egg would be flattened just slightly for safety and stability). For the material, I wanted something magic: translucent red perspex gave the right mixture of smoothness and warmth.

This was a wonderful time. The Nursery was growing; I was growing; Poppy was growing inside me. Jem and I had never been closer. It is hard to describe what it is about a couple that shows they are perfectly together. Oh, there were the obvious things: the hugs, the smiles, the kisses. Don't let anyone tell you that pregnancy kills desire. During that nine months we had some of our most passionate experiences! But there is more to it than that. Don't you think so? The way, every time I raised my eyes – or it seemed like every time – Jem had raised his eyes to meet them. Whenever we walked or sat or stood up or turned it seemed to be in harmony, even if we were just, say, making supper, moving around the kitchen from cooker to fridge to sink. Every touch was a caress. Not that I would have called myself graceful, especially towards the end. But as I grew and slowed he seemed to slow down too. I was a planet and he was my moon. He orbited around me.

## c. The Kids – Life Balance

When a couple is in a special space together, any sort of intrusion can be irritating – however nicely it is meant. So, just as I gradually cut back my work commitments, Jem and I gradually reduced our social life. We had Life enough between us!

Pretty much the only people we did still see were Stan and Marion – though I have to admit there had been a bit of a distance between us for a while after Doris was born. I had found it hard to get over my upsetness at Jem's reaction to the birth, even if it had ended up reconciling him to the idea of paternity – and the upsetness spread into my relationship with Marion and Doris, even though it obviously wasn't their fault. But Stan and Marion were so focused on the baby in those early months that they probably didn't notice. Jem didn't do any more odd things and bit by bit I came to understand that his behaviour during Marion's labour had been more to do with Us and our future than with her. When I finally became pregnant myself, the last traces of awkwardness drifted away. I could really throw myself into my role of being Doris's 'friendship mother', knowing that we were soon going to be joined by a real child of my own.

Babies do bring women closer together. Marion, as you might have guessed, gave me lots of advice and reassurance in a way that, in normal circumstances, I *might* have found a little stifling. But now I was simply grateful for the help that she could offer. It is lovely to have a friend to share your intimate anxieties and hopes with at this special time, even if you know you are not going to follow exactly the same path as her. I remember one particular day we had gone over to their house to be shown the mysteries of washable eco-nappies (for me, though I didn't say so, these were definitely a step too far). I sat there feeling cosy as she talked through the importance of establishing breastfeeding from the beginning, and of letting the baby find its own routine (she was right about the first of those, and *so* wrong about the second!). Cosy; and also dazed, and a bit feeble and – since I was eating for two – very, very hungry.

At last we went through to the kitchen. Marion and Stan were moving around purposefully, Marion at the stove, Stan pulling up Doris's high chair and slotting her into it. Jem and I sat there not seeing a way to help. Marion put whatever it was on the table – some sort of marinated lamb, I think, and a purée of something, and boiled something else, plus a salad and home-made bread. She sat down with a look of triumph.

'This is great,' I said.

She said: 'I can still cook.'

We set about eating. Marion was feeding not only herself but little Doris, who sat to her left at the head of the table. Marion's right hand would reach across and dip the little spoon in the bowl of orange mush and hold it hovering in front of Doris's lips. Marion's left hand would fork up a bit of lamb and skilfully convey it (Marion concentrating all the while on little Doris) under the other arm and up to her own mouth with no spills. It was quite a performance. And it was Marion – elegant, overbearing Marion – who was doing this precise, awkward, tender thing, her cheeks flushed, and blue pools of tiredness under her eyes.

Halfway through our lunch, Doris was declared to have had enough. She was put to play in the space between the kitchen area and Stan's Funnel Office – the space that had previously been home to Marion's knitting business. Now, of course, the knitting machinery had been pushed into a corner and fenced off with some lengths of deconstructed playpen. 'I'm just not interested any more,' Marion had said: 'All my energy goes into Doris.' The rest of the room was given over to the chaos that a toddler brings: heaps of alphabet blocks and jumbo wooden steamrollers and cement mixers and dolls and a teddy bear and a pink hippopotamus and plastic jumbo Lego and a beanbag and a big red trolley that played snatches of Beethoven's Fifth Symphony shrilly, very shrilly, when pushed in the right way.

'Adult time,' said Marion as I turned back to face her.

I tried to think of what to say. There was a good show at the Design Museum, there had been a lovely party at Conran's a couple of nights before. No. What I ended up saying was: 'Watched any good videos?'

But Marion didn't seem to hear. Her eyes were on something behind me – Doris, of course – and as I spoke I saw them widening in anxiety. Next to her Stan began to move but behind me there was a crash. Marion's mouth opened in the shape of a howl but the scream came from the wrong place, not from her but from behind me. Stan was on his feet – but before he could take a step Marion had hurled herself around the table and was down on the floor next to her child, picking her up and saying: 'Darling, oh my darling, it's OK, don't cry, Mummy's here.'

But still the shrill cries rose like something automatic. For the rest of the meal Doris was on Marion's knee snuggling into her breasts, or having her nose wiped, or banging the table with a spoon.

Later, when Doris had dozed off, Jem was at the sink washing dishes and Marion was drying and putting away.

'How's the Funnel Office?' I asked Stan.

'It's great.'

'Good.'

'I mean, it's a great design . . .' His eyes looked past me towards it, and then met mine, and then went down to the table where his fingers were pushing breadcrumbs to and fro. 'I haven't been able to use it much. I sit down to work there but every moment, it seems like, Doris is banging on the door, or there's some problem that Marion needs me to help with. When it's not that it's the noise. I can't hear Doris scream without having to come out to see what's the matter with her. Toddlers scream a lot.'

'So you haven't been getting much done . . .'

'I've ended up going back to work in my office in the uni. The ironic thing now, is that if you look at what we actually do for Doris I might as well be an accountant and Marion's pretty much a

101

housewife. I go out in the morning and come back in the evening for bathtime and stories. Marion does the rest.'

'I like it!' Marion called out.

'I know you do – that's not the point: I'm *not* criticising. But it is ironic that we've fallen back into absolutely bog standard traditional gender roles.'

'I don't think you should worry about it,' Jem said. 'Do what feels natural.'

'That's right,' said Marion.

'I'm not saying we should change anything,' said Stan, 'I just think we should all feel some irony about it. Get some perspective . . .'

I felt I had got a lot of perspective during that visit. And the perspective I had got, was this. In a way it was lovely, the muddle of Stan and Marion and Doris, the struggle, the carrying on. What is the point of having a baby if you do not let it bring its chaos into your lives? And how giving it was of Stan and Marion to let themselves be so pushed aside, so beaten down. But I knew it would not work for Jem and me. Oh, of course I wanted to do everything possible for the child I was going to have, to be there for him or her as much as I could. But at the same time I didn't want to lose the togetherness that Jem and I had. I didn't want our lives to be upended. I didn't want Jem to be prevented from working at home. I didn't want to have to betray my vocation. How were we going to manage it? How? We had to have the right Interior, obviously; and the right equipment. And also we were going to need help. Which meant people – or at least somebody. And the trouble with that was that if I wasn't careful it could utterly destroy the family intimacy which is so crucial for a baby, especially in its early weeks and months. This was a new sort of Design challenge – possibly trickier than any I had faced before.

## d. After Birth

And then she came!

Poppy – because a poppy grows wild and free; because a poppy waves in the wind like happiness; because I have always liked poppies, and because when I heard I was pregnant I was using some poppy-patterned wallpaper in a Design; and because she started off little like a pip, and was snuggly like a puppy, and her face when she was born was wrinkled like a poppy in bud and unfolded like a poppy in flower; and finally because she just popped into our lives! Now, when anyone says 'poppy', I don't see a poppy flower, I see my own flower, my daughter. If anyone says – for instance – 'There was a wonderful field of poppies' I am left wondering, what do you mean 'poppies'? – there is only the *one*. This is just a tiny example of the wonderful feeling I have tried to express in the happiest of all the Magic Mottoes. No. 11:

✓ Childbirth Changes Everything!

I am not going to tell you about the birth itself. Some things are just too private to talk about – even in a book like this! Suffice it to say a Caesarean section can be a really wonderful, loving experience – every bit as good as the water birth Marion had. I know some women feel alienated by surgical intervention and disempowered that they cannot hold the baby for themselves immediately after it is born. But I think there is something very moving about this marriage of nature and technology. It is literally magic! One minute, you are a pregnant woman. The next, your baby is out there in the world, being passed from hand to hand. Of course some rummaging around does have to happen between those two moments. But it gets completely forgotten in the astonishment that a totally new person has suddenly appeared. Poppy was so small, so noisy, so assertive, so needy! It was like the whole room was being sucked towards her. Of course, when I looked at her, I felt a great rush of motherly love. But I also felt: How peculiar! In one sense, she was completely powerless. But, in another sense, she seemed very self-possessed. Jem took her in those big, strong, sensitive hands of his and cradled her so her face was against my cheek and her urgent, mouse-like cries were in my ear. It was heavenly, but it was also a little bit like being snuggled up to by an alien. This is going to seem strange, but what I felt most strongly for Poppy was: *respect*.

Some mothers think that only they have total connection with their child, that it will only be happy when it is close to them – or, preferably in their arms. Obviously mothers and babies do have a very special bond. But I can't help wondering if there isn't something a little bit egotistical about this way of thinking. I like to take my cue from primitive (or as I prefer to say, 'unspoilt') tribes. For them, the mother plays a vital role. But the burden of childcare is divided among all the members of the community.

To me, this approach simply felt right. From the beginning, it was clear to me that Poppy was a treasure who deserved to be shared. This wasn't only for my good, nor only for hers, but for the joy of everyone around us. I know that I am lucky in having a wonderfully supportive husband. Even in these days of the 'new man', not many men would be as 'hands on' as Jem. And so sensitive, too! When it turned out I couldn't make as much milk as Poppy seemed to need (she was such a hungry baby) he was a very calming presence. He said it didn't matter, he thought it would be good for her to have a bottle every now and then, he'd like to do it. When it was time to go home and we had said goodbye to the marvellous staff, we walked along the wide, battered corridors with Jem carrying Poppy and also holding my hand. I was the happiest woman in the world!

All mothers must feel happiness at this time. But I believe I was specially able to be happy because I knew I had created a good home environment for my new family to settle into. This was partly a Design thing. But it was also – as I have said – a *people* thing. It is important to see that, in 'Designing for Life' (see Magic Motto no. 2), the people you surround yourself with are just as important as the colours, patterns and *objets*; probably more so. But people are obviously a lot more tricky to work with than wallpaper or fabric. What could be more challenging than choosing a person to help look after your child? To come and be with your family in your Interior. To have such a tremendous influence on the little creature who is so fragile and so dear! I know that lots of parents have managed to do this – often quite successfully. But that doesn't stop it being a very difficult decision.

Jem, in particular, was uneasy. He felt that because Poppy was our creation only we should look after her, at least for the first year. It was about nurture, about continuity. He wouldn't let anyone else put the finishing touches to his pots – and Poppy was going to be a whole lot more precious and delicate even than them.

I did respect this point of view. Jem wouldn't be the Jem I loved if he didn't have strong feelings! But I also thought it might be a teensy bit naïve. Jem had this vision of the baby sleeping in the corner of his studio while he worked; and then of the toddler operating the treadle of his wheel while he threw and shaped the clay. But hadn't he seen what had become of Stan and Marion who had had exactly the same idea? Babies don't just sit there! They need feeding and nappy-changing and playing with and taking for walks. It was going to be very time-consuming. There were going to be sleepless nights. He wouldn't be able to work with a baby there beside him. And, if she wasn't there, where was she going to have to be? With me. But I *had* to go back to work. Financially, Jem's trust fund was a helpful cushion; but without my income we simply would not be able to survive.

I outlined the research I had done into the childcare practices of unspoilt tribes. I explained that, in many ways, it was the modern nuclear family that was an unnatural construction. The natural path was to share, just as the tribespeople did. Finally, I promised that if we did not find someone we really liked and felt we could relate to, we would try going it alone.

Luckily, I had already heard of Carla, the daughter of one of my Italian contacts (a creative working for Missoni). She wanted to spend some time in London, first to perfect her English and then to go to art school. She said she was very keen to come and live in the home of a top English Designer.

Of course I asked for references, I stared at her photo, I interviewed her over the phone. But still it was a nervous few minutes when I, very pregnant by this time, was waiting for her to arrive for our first meeting. At last the bell rang and there she was: one big smile. Above it were little white cheeks like powdered ping-pong balls, nice deep hazel eyes, dark hair in a neat crop, and, dangling from her plump lobes, glittery earrings in the shape of crescent moons. She wore a sheepskin gilet, with its woolly collar turned up even though we were in spring. Beneath that, a black top, and then a little skirt and thick black tights oddly spotted with pink sparkly butterflies. On her feet were sheepskin boots. She held out her hand like a continuation of her grin. 'Hello it is Carla,' she said. She hugged herself like a symbol of cold: 'What chill.'

I liked her at once. So vivid! So effusive! The Italian dress sense has always puzzled me. Often, the women wear bright or jokey patterns which, to me, look wholly inappropriate on an adult. But a child would *love* Carla's butterflies and her moons! I ushered her through into the sitting room. There was a lovely bounce to her walk, as if the world was a trampoline, and when she stepped into the room she stretched out her arms and looked around, taking everything in. 'Eet is fantastic!' she said. 'Look!' – she was pointing at the life tools hanging on their pulley storage. 'And look!' – she pointed at the Spiritual Landscape. 'May I?'

'Yes of course.'

Gingerly she sat down, and then let her fingertips wander over the contours of the piece. 'Eet is lika the Eenglish countryside,' she said, beaming.

'Yes, exactly.' By now I knew I was going to take her. She just felt right. But still, I led her downstairs where I had laid out a doll and some nappies and checked that she knew how to use them – and also, vitally, that she possessed the rudiments of First Aid. I was very pleased at what I saw. Finally, it was time for her to meet Jem. He never liked being surprised when he was at work. So we had installed an early warning system – a switch in the kitchen which operated a gong by his wheel. By the time Carla and I were in the courtyard, he was at the door of the studio, watching us.

'This is Jem,' I said.

'Hello,' Carla called out, and waved.

Jem watched as she bounced over the flagstones. When we reached him he looked into her eyes. His eyes narrowed as if he was sighting some animal against a bright horizon. 'Perfect,' he said. 'I won't shake hands,' he said, for his hands were covered in clay; 'Oh' – looking at them, he had noticed one clean little finger – 'here,' and he held it out like royalty or a bishop. She took it (it filled her tiny fist!), shook it, and giggled like a child. Suddenly, oddly, the two of them seemed to belong together. It wasn't that they looked like a couple. It was that they were not pregnant. I was going to split open, erupt, create. I was going to have a child! And they were going to help me.

Despite all this preparation I was very nervous indeed in the taxi on the journey home from hospital. What would it be like? Would we be able to cope? Would the baby ever forgive me for handing her over to another person even for only a little bit of the time? I made the driver go very slowly, partly so Poppy wouldn't be jarred by any bumps in the road but also I think to delay the moment of our arrival, which would be the beginning of: everything. Carla was such a warm, capable person. But even so . . . Well, here we were. We were out of the car, and the three of us (the three of us!) were walking up the steps and through the front door. I was calling for Carla, and here she was. I gave the baby over for her to hold. 'She ees beautiful, she is a darling,' Carla was saying, grinning, and tickling little Poppy under the chin; and Poppy was lying in her arms, quite calmly, observing her with wide dark eyes. I stood there. Part of me wanted them to get on. Part of me wanted them to not get on too well. Poppy's little lips opened and some pale goo dribbled out, following a contour between the bottom of her cheek and the top of her jaw. Carla reached for the corner of a tartan cardie she was wearing and brought it up and wiped. Then she passed the baby back to me.

In fact it all went very smoothly. During the early days – and, more importantly, nights – Carla was a tremendous help. Of course I was determined to do most of the feeding. But on the other hand, I didn't want to get up to Poppy *every* time she cried. It is important for the mother to sleep properly. If she doesn't, there is simply no chance that her milk will keep coming through. In any case, I wanted to be always at my best for my baby. I don't mean looking good, but having the patience to look after her properly, and the mental space in which to love her. How many parents have you seen, perhaps in a super-market queue or in a park, yelling at their toddlers as if they hated them? You can see the psychological damage this causes: damage that will last for much longer than a day! Obviously in a deep sense these parents do still feel love for their children. It is just that their love has not been able to grow and flourish. Why? Simply because they are too tired.

## e. The Play-Space

Of course I was deeply emotionally caught up in this very moving time. But Home-is-Harmony needed me; and a month or so after Poppy's birth I began to try to get a moment in the Whiteness each day so I could keep properly in touch. It was hard! Carla had really bonded with Poppy, and Jem was of course her father. But still, I felt a real pang each time I tore myself away from my baby and whichever of them was looking after her. I would only be in the office for five minutes or so before I started to wonder what was going on downstairs. I had to find a way to concentrate. I had to meet my commitments.

I set myself to think of Marion and Stan, and to remind myself that Marion was letting down not only herself but her baby by her abandonment of serious creative work. I was not going to let that happen to me! Next, I installed little webcams in the Kitchen, the as-yet-undesigned Family Area, the Sitting Room, the Nursery and our Bedroom and connected them all to my computer. This meant I would feel involved with Poppy wherever she might be. Finally, I decided that in the crucial first few weeks of professional 're-entry' I should concentrate as much as possible on the one area of our Home that remained to be designed: the Family Area or Play-Space in the part of the open plan downstairs that was not occupied by the kitchen. It was work, but work that kept me close to Poppy.

Unlike the nursery, I had not been able to imagine the Family Area or Play-Space in advance. But now, after everything we had been through, its theme was clear to me:

• Change

The Space would have to encapsulate Magic Motto no. 11 (Childbirth Changes Everything!) – not only the practical and emotional upheavals, but also the way it can make the big seem small and the small big, the young old and the old young. Jem, for instance, sometimes seemed just as much a of a baby as Poppy was, the way he cooed and gurgled at her. But also, when he was holding her – all of her! – in just one of his big hands it made his hands look like spades and the rest of him seem giant. Carla too seemed suddenly to have grown up, to be as wise as an old nurse who had cared for a hundred children. Poppy herself was so young, but also so wrinkly; she cried as a baby should, but also had moments of such solemnity and calm!

I gave myself up to the 'Work of Memory'. This time, what appeared in my mind was not a personal memory but a book: *Alice in Wonderland*. Now, books can be dangerous for the Designer. One standard option for children's rooms is simply to take a theme from a book and transfer it into the Interior. I have seen walls painted with the trees from *Where the Wild Things Are*, and a *Mrs Tittlemouse* Interior complete with box bed, cuddly toad and bumble bee, and a larder full of artificial cherry stones and thistledown, ten times life size. I can understand how it might seem like a good idea at the time. But, by definition, this approach lacks the element of originality which is the 'spark of life' in any successful Design.

The key is, to take just a few hints, and develop them. From *Alice*, I took the following ideas:

- Changes of size
- Mirrors

And that was all. There was going to be no white rabbit mural in *my* Wonderland!

Next: development. To get the feeling of size-being-changeable, I decided to alter the proportions of the furniture – and also to introduce some disorienting visual cues. The tricky thing here was that, in a Family Room, practicality is at a premium. There needed to be storage; and there needed to be room to sit and space to play. For storage, I decided to think big. Blocks of flats are a kind of storage: they store human beings. So I envisioned chests of drawers modelled on classic high-rise residential buildings: one like the Trellick Tower; the other in the style of the Barbican. For cupboards, I thought of garages. What could be better than a line of 30cm-high garages along one wall: excellent storage which would double as seating. Of course the garages were out of scale with the tower-block drawers; but that only added to the effect of disorientation. There was something magic in the idea of these big, supposedly concrete buildings being used to store a toddler's toys.

The last piece of surprising furniture was a double-height bench. It was big enough for Poppy to be able to use the underneath as a den until the age of three or four; and small enough that adults could just about perch on it – with their feet dangling childlike off the floor. As I blocked these pieces in, I realised the play with size needed to continue into the structure of the space. In the corner of the room away from the windows, and across from the kitchen, I would create two miniature storeys by putting in a floor at a height of four and a half feet. A little staircase would go up to the higher level, which would be walled and have a window. The lower level would be lined with slightly concave mirrors, so that Poppy and her friends and teddy bears would seem to shrink when they went in.

Once I had this plan down on paper I felt a good deal calmer. Of course part of me wanted to rush into building the new Family Room and Play-Space straight away. But another bit of me realised this probably wasn't such a good idea. Our new life was going along very well and it seemed cruel to disrupt it – especially as we were all still feeling a teensy bit emotionally fragile (I certainly was!). Carla helped out during the nights and then looked after Poppy until lunchtime, when she went off to her language course. Jem then took over. He only really liked to work at his pots in the mornings anyway: and he said that nurturing Poppy was a special privilege he wouldn't miss out on for the world. I made sure I had special mummy-and-baby moments to punctuate the day. I called them 'Jewel Times': a lovely cuddle and giggle once she had been got up and dressed in the morning and a lovely hug and singsong before she went down for lunchtime nap. Bathtime was my speciality. I would always lay her down and give her a little massage (Neal's Yard does a gorgeous fragrant oil), smoothing the excitement of the day out of her shoulders and chest, and down her little soft legs and out through her nobbly toes. I loved lowering her soft pudgy body into the foamy water and supporting her downy head while her arms and legs sploshed randomly. It was in the bath that she smiled her first gummy smile and – not long after – started to giggle with a heavenly bubbling sound.

While I was having this last, lovely Jewel Time of the day, Jem would tidy up downstairs and cook something so that we could go straight into properly ring-fenced Adult Time (NB: the difference from Stan and Marion). We would chat about this and that, maybe watch a bit of telly, but often then doze off in each other's arms. Life was tiring; but also lovely, intimate and tender.

Until, on one of what had become my weekly into-IntArchitec days, Fisher called me to his Sitting Room/Inner Sanctum and started pressing me about this Bleunet project which I think I have mentioned to you before. The great chef – he said – was retiring, or not exactly retiring but wanting to make an extremely exclusive restaurant in a penthouse apartment in Paris where he would cook for only four or maybe eight people at a time. Fisher said he realised this wasn't standard Home-is-Harmony territory, but it was the unparalleled imaginativeness of my work that made him think I was the right person to take the project forward. Well, that was very nice. But then there were these comments that I didn't quite know what to make of: about how I needed to rise to a new level, about how the future of Home-is-Harmony might be at stake. I was sitting there on one of the Millenniums, dazed, happy, feeling that I had left half myself with Poppy in Allsop Road (I couldn't mention these emotions to Fisher, of course). It seemed mad to me, the idea of suddenly taking on a major project; it simply seemed impossible. On the other hand maybe Fisher was right that I needed to try to think bigger, inaugurate a new stage in my career. Perhaps motherhood could be a professional spring-board, not necessarily a honeytrap. Fisher made it sound like this might be the one chance I was going to get.

I worried away at my dilemma. I imagined what would happen if I did start having to spend blocks of time in Paris – and it all seemed fine. I imagined it again: disaster! I woke in the night even when Poppy wasn't calling out to me. I thought about the problem over my early morning lime and echinacea, and over my evening lemon verbena. In the end, one afternoon when the three of us were together in the Play-Space-to-be, I shared my anxieties with Jem. We were all on the big sheepskin rug that, along with some beanbags and cushions, constituted the room's total Design Identity as things stood: Jem was reclining on an elbow; Poppy was sitting in front of him, dribbling, her legs like a frog's, her back absurdly straight; I was cross-legged on the other side of her.

113

'What,' Jem said, 'you and Fisher are going to work together, in Paris?'

'No, he's signing the project over to me. That's what's so surprising. He says he thinks I could do it better than him.'

'So it'll just be you going over there. How long for?'

'Dunno yet. It has to be worked out. Little trips. A few days each time.'

He leaned forward and stroked Poppy's ears and touched the tip of her nose. She giggled, and seized his finger: he pulled; she pulled back; and then he reached down further and grasped her under the arms and hoisted her on to his knee where she sat, happy, shining, gorgeous through and through.

'Do it. If you want to; do it.'

'How do you think Poppy will take it?'

'I expect she'll cope. So long as you don't completely disappear. Other women have international careers.' He smiled – really warmly: 'It's exciting!'

'It puts pressure on you though. That's what I'm worried about. And Us – I'll *miss* Poppy if I have to go away. Even for a night. I'll miss you.'

'We can handle it. Really.'

I didn't make my mind up all at once. I went with Fisher to meet Bleunet and get a better sense of the project. I went through it all with Simon: we made a provisional work schedule and it really didn't look too bad. I talked it over with friends. Stan had this nightmarish interpretation whereby Fisher was basically undermining me by forcing me to take on a project I would find it very difficult to fulfil during this special but demanding time. I do love Stan – but I did think he was being a little bit extreme! Luckily Marion saw things much more in the way Jem did. She said I had a really lovely family set-up, and I should trust it. She said motherhood is such a strong bond it can easily cope with the odd few nights away.

As I waited for my feelings to settle, I found that I kept on imagining the Family Room and Play-Space. I had a vision of Jem and little Poppy sitting together on the outsize bench: it seemed so very reassuring! This became the key to my decision. I was going to take on Bleunet. But I was also going to make sure the Family Room and Play-Space was finished before I went – which also meant, in time for Poppy's first ever birthday. Then, even if I was apart from the family at least they would be surrounded, almost hugged, by an Interior I had made for them.

Jem did grumble a little at the idea of the upheaval, but when I pointed out he could spend his afternoons with Poppy at Marion's house his objections fell away. Luckily, the project moved ahead totally as planned. We had kept the space screened off from the kitchen so Poppy would not realise what was happening – and on her birthday morning, we had such a lovely opening ceremony. There had been a special breakfast of Weetabix and strawberry mush. Then we encouraged Poppy to crawl towards the curtains. A cord lay across the floor. Eventually, after much pointing and squeaking, she was persuaded to notice it. Together, she and Carla pulled: the curtain fell. Poppy went tense (babies are *so* like little animals when they suddenly notice something). Her eyes started to water and I thought for an instant that my surprise might go horribly wrong. But then Carla giggled theatrically. Poppy caught the mood, screeched, and crawled stiffly ahead, her legs slithering on the tiles and her arms stomping like short, fat stilts. Oh, that was a happy moment! – as she made her way around the new space, taking possession in turn of the den under the outsize bench and the ground floor of her 'Mini-Maisonette' (the stairs were gated for obvious safety reasons). She banged at the garage cupboards and sat back on her knees with a gasp of pleasure when one was opened for her. Finally, she pulled herself up on the miniature Trellick Tower, for all the world like a human Kitten Kong! As we followed her in, Jem and Carla and I took up our places where we were meant to – on the little garages and the enormous bench. The effect was that we all looked just like we felt in the magical company of little Poppy: very big and very small, very old and very young, adult, irresponsible, funny, happy, and – at play.

Later in the morning Poppy had a little bit of a party with Doris and a couple of children she had made friends with at playgroup (and of course their mothers). In the afternoon, the celebrations morphed into something more like an opening. Simon arrived, then Graham and Stuart and Jean-Philippe. There were other industry people as well as hacks from the magazines. Naomi flitted by, on her way to somewhere as always: she was warm in her admiration. At last, Fisher came – bringing with him his companion of the moment, Antonia Blythe. They were a very elegant couple, Fisher in his usual dove grey, Antonia a little taller than him, slim, and pale, and very well preserved: she could still manage to carry off a delightful pastel green dress which I think must have been a couture piece by Chanel. I brought Fisher his usual vodka and tonic (he cannot abide coloured drinks), and a mineral water for Antonia. There they stood, a little apart from the crowd, not standoffish I think so much as perhaps a little shy. I imagine they felt themselves to be a touch beneath their usual element: but they were very gracious.

Bit by bit people drifted away until it was just Fisher and Antonia, Marion and Stan and Doris, Simon, Poppy, Carla, Jem and myself. Carla held Poppy's hands and walked her over towards Fisher. He knelt and cupped her face in his hands and leaned forwards and kissed her on the forehead.

'She is a beautiful child,' he said.

'Not bad, is she,' said Jem, rather bluntly. Then Carla took Poppy and Doris off to bed (this was one day when I had to miss a 'Jewel Bathtime'!), and the rest of us went upstairs to the Dining Room (see ch. 10) for a little light something to eat.

Once we had taken our places Fisher tapped his glass to make it ring, and rose. 'I hate – speeches, but why do we not all, now, raise our glasses, to – Alizia. And to Jem, of course, and Poppy,' he said, angling his head towards where Jem sat, 'but above all, to Alizia, for this beautiful Interior, and for the beautiful family it houses.' He sat, there was a murmur, people drank, I was embarrassed, I smiled. It was funny, I heard the words not just with my ears but with Jem's as well: they would grate on him, he would find them condescending.

I said: 'Thank you.' And then I said: 'I want to say something, though. It's not about being beautiful. That's the thing. It's *for* something. To help make us' (I looked across at Jem: he was listening, smiling) 'happy. To help us do things. Design is for Life.'

'Hear, hear,' said Stan.

Fisher was nodding: 'Quite true.'

'Do things like take on a massive project in Paris,' said Marion to the table in general. And then, focusing on Fisher: 'You must be very pleased to be working with someone so dedicated.'

'She is indeed wonderful.'

Simon was at the sideboard (a black lacquered piece – rather a bargain – from Ballard Design in the United States) serving out the food. Antonia was next to me and I was saying 'I'm so glad you can be here' but my attention was with Marion, who kept on at Fisher: 'You've had an enormous influence on Alizia, haven't you – she always talks about you.'

'We go back a long way. In fact . . .'

('It's lovely to be here.')

' . . . Alizia is one of the protégés I am most proud of, and most respect.'

('Is this all right for you?' – I was carrying on my small talk with Antonia – 'I know you're a vegetarian and apparently it does have a bit of egg-white.')

Then Jem put in: 'Do you really think of Alizia as your protégée?'

'Well, shall we say I *like* to think of her like that.' He turned to me: 'Alizia – this is delicious.'

Carla came in, winked at me, then spoke to Marion: 'Doris has need of you. I cannot make her settle down.' So Marion rose and Carla sat.

Fisher spoke across the empty chair: 'And you must be Alizia's new helper. She has spoken to me of you.'

'Well, truly in this moment I am just the nanny. But I desire to become a designer.'

'Carla is very talented,' I said. 'I expect great things from her.'

There was a pause.

'Fisher, has Simon told you about his wallpaper project? It's going to be fantastic.'

'I'm not sure this is the right . . .' Simon objected.

'No, go on,' I murmured. 'Tell him.'

'Tell me, Simon.'

'Well it's very much a Home-is-Harmony thing. The idea is' – he went on awkwardly – 'well, it'll be hand-printed with wooden blocks – so it won't be just wallpaper, it'll be like, it'll make the whole room into a work of art.'

'Like the very first wallpapers.'

'Yes. But the thing is that with my wallpaper we're going for a super-modern Design based on images from nanotechnology, so there will be this contrast between the texture of the paper and the Design.'

'We're planning a range of products, Fisher: this'll be the first.'

'Interesting. We must talk about it.' And then, musingly: 'It reminds me, this principle of contrast, of your very early work, Alizia, from before you knew me. In your dossier.'

'Fisher . . .'

'The barbed-wire-pattern duvet.'

'I don't think I know about that,' said Simon, looking brightly from Fisher to me and back.

'What is this *Barbed Wire Duvet*?' – Carla was asking.

'It's from decades ago,' put in Jem.

'I think it was a charming idea,' – Fisher continued. 'Why not dig it out? You should add it to your range of products, Alizia. Make paradox your theme.'

'Well, I'm not . . .'

But then Marion came back in. 'Kids,' she said, sighingly, 'can't live with them, can't live without them. I'm afraid' – whispering loudly to me across Fisher as she sat back down beside him – 'she's done some drawing on the *wall*.'

'Where?'

'Carla's room.'

'Oh that's not so bad then.'

Jem was leaning forward: 'You *can* live without them. Fisher does.'

'Yes, that's right, I do.'

'No regrets?' – asked Marion.

Then Jem started in again: 'What's not to like? The chaos. The randomness. They wake up in the night, they puke all over the place, and shit. The way they scatter things. Poppy spent yesterday with a handful of wet leaves. Downstairs in the play-space. Tearing them up into little bits. She wanted to see how many little bits, and how little the bits could be, that she could make with her little fingers. You have to let them. You have to let them totally mess the place up. That's what they like doing. That's

119

what they're for. They're pure, anarchic Nature. Just given to us. What a gift.'

Fisher was listening patiently, Marion was gently nodding, Stan had on one of his bright, interested looks.

'I can't see much mess here,' put in Antonia, kindly.

'I've done a lot of tidying up,' said Jem.

Simon and I were down in the kitchen stashing the plates and getting the things for pudding. 'You all right?' he said as I straightened up from the dishwasher.

'Yes fine. Don't I seem it?'

'Yes. Just . . .'

'What?'

'Nothing.'

'Shall we?' – and up we went. I had set our guests a little task, to do with our centrepiece 'Zettel-Z' chandelier – which is a light-source surrounded by lots of tiny bulldog clips on dangly wires. The piece comes with love-messages in different languages written on scraps of heat-resistant paper that are meant to be inserted into the clips. But I didn't like the idea of all that borrowed feeling hanging in the air: I wanted to make the words mine – or rather, *ours*. My plan was that over months and years all our guests in the dining room should write their own messages and doodles, so that the chandelier would grow into a record of their personalities and thoughts. 'Everyone finished?' – I called as I went in. I collected up the cards.

'Do let us see,' said Marion.

'No. It's a secret. To make sure you all come back. Next time you come, you will be able to see what all of you have written.'

'Oh . . .'

'It is a good idea,' said Fisher. 'Very good.'

When everyone had settled down to their tart and crème fraiche,

Fisher spoke again. 'So: Paris.' He was addressing me across the table. 'I hope it will go well.'

'What if it doesn't?' – put in Stan.

'Of course it will,' I said.

But Fisher answered anyway: 'Alizia would still have Home-is-Harmony. Maybe there would be this "product range" we have been hearing about. And then, I wonder what would come next? Perhaps a book. What would you say to that, Alizia? Reveal all your secrets. Reach out to everyone.'

It was a surprise. I wasn't sure that he was serious. Really I didn't know what to think. So all I said was: 'We'll have to see.' But actually, in that moment, though nobody knew it, not even me: this book was conceived.

Soon after, Fisher and Antonia rose to go. In their careful, poised way they said farewell to Marion and Stan, and Carla, and Simon. Jem and I followed them into the hall where Fisher turned to Jem and held out his hand.

'Good luck,' he said, as they shook. 'You're very fortunate.'

'Aren't we all,' responded Jem. 'Good luck to you.'

Fisher kissed me on the forehead, as he had kissed my child. Side by side, close but not touching, he and Antonia went down the steps. He held open the gate for her. On the pavement they turned, and he raised and waggled his hand by way of farewell. I stood in the doorway for a moment, feeling the chill night air on my cheeks and listening to their steps, which slowly quietened, then died away. And then I went inside.

*Magic Mottoes*

  10. *Know When To Put Yourself – And Your Family! – First.*

  11. *Childbirth Changes Everything!*

# Working with Alizia: Cristophe Bleunet

Allow me to present myself. I am Cristophe Bleunet, Chef. Not an everyday chef: I am known. I am very known. It is because I take a very particular attitude to my cooking. For me, cooking is love. Think about everything that you put into your mouth. There is the food, and the drink, and the medicine; and there is what else? There is the mother's breast and there are the parts of the body of your loved ones. For me, that connection is very significant. I must make my clients love their food. And I must make them feel that they are being loved by it. It is a very sensual experience. To understand me, it is necessary to understand that. In my restaurants, people come so that I can love them, and they can love me.

Also there is the hate. I have cooked in many kitchens, and I have hated them all. I have hated the noise, I have hated the clutter, I have hated the crowdedness, I have hated the industrialisation. How can I be sensual in such an environment? And so I had developed a very particular practice of conscience. Each morning, on arriving in the restaurant, I would go to the bathroom, I would take a shower, and I would wash myself with very great attention. I would shave myself, and I would perfume myself: I would make myself beautiful. And then I would dress as if to spend a warm evening sitting in a beautiful garden with a person whom I loved. I did not wear a white overall. In place of a chef's hat, I wore an English deerstalker. There were difficulties with the hygienic regime, of course. Each night, after the cooking, my clothes would be incinerated. And each morning, one prepared for me a new sterile outfit.

Dressed like that, I imagined I was not in a kitchen at all. I imagined that the terrible noise of fans and clattering was in fact the rustle of the breeze. I imagined that the cries and curses of my assistants were in fact the songs of birds. The aromas of the cooking were the perfumes of the flowers. All around me was air and trees and the sky of evening. Each dish that I finished was my lover that I caressed.

Like that, I have become very successful. I am famous. I have earned a lot of money.

So, after many years, I decide to take my retirement. I decide to make a restaurant, very select, which will be my home. And to make a kitchen which will also be a garden. It will be open to the sky. The birds will come and visit me, and we will have conversations. All around me will be space, and the sizzling of my cooking will disappear into the air. I will have no assistants, or very few. I will be alone; I will be tranquil.

I find a suitable apartment, high up, a penthouse, which overlooks the Jardin du Luxembourg. The view is very green, and the noise – well, it is still a little bit noisy. But when the traffic stops, it is possible to hear also a gentle rustle from the trees which agitate themselves. There is wind which comes against the windows, and drizzle which falls pitter-patter on the roof. Sometimes there is a very beautiful light. So I have the place, but who will be my designer?

Alizia, Alizia, it is you!

Why an English? Because I wanted somebody eccentric. The French designers, they are very grand. They make important projects, impressive statements. But I wanted something different. I had need of someone with a little bit of a sense of humour. So I contact my old friend Fisher Paul and he says he knows just the good designer for me.

Alizia is someone very serious. But also, she is drôle. I am not sure that she knows this, but she is. She has drôle ideas, which are also genial. And so she understands me.

I explain the garden-kitchen: she understands. She explains me that all the machines can be covered with hard wood so that I will not see metal, only wood like trees. It is delicious, is it not? I had not thought it would be possible. She tells me there is a tradition in England of the kitchen-garden that she can utilise. And then she has a big and true idea. For me, what you eat is natural things. All of them – except the oysters – are dead. But in cooking them and eating them, in these acts of love, one takes them into oneself and makes them live again. It is like the circling from the day to the night to the day. It is ritual. It is religious.

Alizia shows me pictures of your ancient English temples of stone, your Avebury and your Stonehenge: they are round. She shows me a picture of a sundial: it is round. So the garden kitchen will be round. It will be at the edge of the apartment, looking out over the Luxembourg like a terrace. And behind it there will be the dining room like a fan. But there will be not just one dining room, there will be rooms. Having eaten each course, the clients will budge themselves into the next room. Alizia has made the colour-scheme like the colours of a day, from dawn to the setting of the sun.

I had an idea in my turn. That is what you want, no, from a designer? This collaboration, this provocation of ideas? So, these rooms represent the passing of time, from morning to evening, from spring to summer, from infancy to the death. What menu should there be in such a place? A menu that takes you on a journey from the life to the death. Cooking this menu, in my retirement, I will resume my life, and prepare myself for my own death. As Marcus Aurelius has said, and Aquinas and Rousseau: in your fourth age you must turn towards eternity. And so, with every meal, I take my guests on a journey through the life. You begin with a salad, but a salad that is in a pot, still living. There is rocket, radish, chervil, cress, growing. You pour on the dressing. You take a pair of scissors: snip. And then, by electrodes, you will hear the cries of the young plants who are dying. After that: lobster. After that: fruit. Then fresh fish, then veal. Do you see? The food gets from more to more dead. We finish with the oldest Jamón Ibérico de Bellota from Espagne, and very aged Cheddar. I will cook marvels in this place. My clientèle will be only the most select. I will invite my most appreciative and loyal friends from my restaurants of the past, from Ypsilon and from Bleu. It will be magnifique.

We did have a disaccord about one thing. I want the kitchen open to the sky. I want the birds to fly around me, to alight and sing. I want the drizzle to keep my vegetables fresh, I want to breathe the air. Alizia she tells me no it is not possible. What if there is a downpour, she says. I say, I do not mind, I will put myself at the mercy of the elements, if there is a downpour, there will be no dinner that day. Her eyes grow, I can see that she appreciates my idea. But she says, with a very apologetic expression: what of the erosion of the materials, the cooker will be damaged, it is not possible, you cannot leave your kitchen out in the rain. What of security? What of the hygiene? I insist: I want to cook in the nature, I need to cook in space. And so we compromise – this is very good in your Alizia – she is resourceful. She creates a retractable roof. I have a kitchen-garden-cabriolet. She thinks the roof will keep me safe and warm. But I know, that if I wish to sleep in the drizzle, I have only to leave the roof open and (sorry, dear Alizia) – I do. I do not mind if the materials decay a little.

Sleep? Yes. For me, this apartment is my home and cooking is my life. What do I cook? Bodies – of animals, and of plants. What is a kitchen, but a place where flesh is kept, where it is loved. So I keep myself there. Each night I take my sleeping bag and lay myself out on the beautiful work-surface Alizia has made for me from ancient teak of Africa. If it suffices for duck, for steak, for lamb, it suffices for me. Under the stars, under the clouds, and same in the drizzle, I compose myself for sleep. I imagine that the time is passing through me, round my sundial rooms. And in sleep, well, who can say with certitude what happens when one sleeps. But for me, my sleep in the drizzle is a softening, a marinating. In the cold of winter, in the snow, it is like a becoming sorbet or ice-cream. When there is dry wind, it is like a toughening, a cure. And in summer, in the heat of July, it is a slow, slow grilling.

Alizia is a beautiful person. She is very efficacious, she is full of energy, she is unfazed. I adore her. She is unique. I can say nothing more.

Alizia: to you!

# 6. The Kitchen

*a. . . .*

This is difficult. I *want* to write about kitchen design. I want to be peacefully at work, here in the Whiteness, calm, focused, moving the project forward. But all there is in my head is this:

'At last we have a child. You pause your career, for a moment, so we can have a child. And then you hand her over to someone else. You sit upstairs and you watch her through a computer.'

(I have to work. I longed to have a child. You were the one who kept on making difficulties. Where does the money come from? I spend a *lot* of time with Poppy. I am her mother. It's not fair. You are *so* not fair.)

And this:

'When she's one, you go away. You take the first opportunity. To Paris. For six months. When she's one year old, Leez.'

(I didn't go *away*. I didn't. I worked there some days a week. Not even every week.)

And this:

'What about me? Do you ever think about that? I can't work. Somebody's got to look out for Poppy. I look out of my window and there she is with Carla. Carla's fine but she is not her mother.

So I have to go and, I don't know, say hello, or give her a big hug, or just be there, just smile. If I don't then I feel I ought to, one of her parents ought to. It means I can't create, Leez. I can't get into the right space.'

(The whole point was for us to have a live–work environment. It is what we both wanted. In this studio you have created: the hatted pots, the half-filled pots, and now these new figurines you've started on since I finished Bleunet that you haven't yet shown me. You have done a lot of work. Many, many children have nannies. Poppy gets a huge amount of parental attention. All that's happening is you're going through a bad patch, just now, just for a little while. I really can't see that that's my fault.)

And this:

'Do you talk to Marion the whole time about Fisher? And Bleunet. Since you got back all you've been doing is writing this book and going on and on and on about Bleunet. Where am I, in you? Where's the space for me?'

(Not that again.)


## b. Now

It is about a year after the day I described at the end of the last chapter, Poppy's first birthday. As Jem has pointed out (and as you can see!) I have been getting on with this book. And I have completed a big project in Paris, The Bleunet Kitchen and Dining Rooms, my first solo international commission. It was very exciting. I am sure Poppy will be proud of it when she is old enough to understand.

I am sitting here, in the Whiteness, wanting to tell you about Bleunet and the project and the impact they made on me. But all that I can write are the words that I have written down.

Funny how a word can be said, a few little words, and everything shifts. It's not like we haven't argued before. But this time – just one little speech and you look back in the light of it – no, under the shock of it – and the smile that was a warm smile is fake, and the eyes that were sincere are devious, and the little jokes, the little ironic comments, like when Jem said – do you remember? – at that dinner with Fisher etc. when he said 'I've done a lot of tidying up': did you wonder about the tone of it? I did, at the time, and I wondered about it again when I wrote it down for you to read. But I am not wondering now. Now I know the truth of it. Now it has flipped over and there is no more beetle irridescent shine but darkness and aggression kicking up at me.

These new few little words of Jem I have written down just now, these open, angry words, he said them to me two days ago. No, shouted them at me. Things haven't been very good between us since. I suppose in his view they were not very good before then either.

To think I did not know. Odd, isn't it? I live with someone for so long, and I do not realise how he is feeling. Of course I knew we had had dark days. The end of Wood Street, the settling into Studio II. But they weren't really about us. They were about coping with things happening to us: work, and change, the things that were stopping us being really Us, ourselves, together. But since then, with Poppy, and the Play-Space, as a family, I had really thought that we were happy. What does that say about me? About *Us*? It was all his idea just as much as mine. Poppy. Marriage. *He* proposed. He said he wanted a child. He said it was meant.

I'm sure he hasn't felt this all the time. He can't have done. He feels it now and so he says he felt it always but he didn't. Now when he looks back everything seems dark. But that doesn't mean everything felt dark at the time. It is like the nap of velvet. Back then, he definitely saw the gleaming side. He must have done. He *liked* his Studio when he moved into it. He said he could imagine it stimulating a whole new phase of creativity – and it did.

I know the half-filled pots didn't really come to anything. Hand of Hampstead really did treat him very badly. But we worked through it together. Even though I was busy, really busy, with Bleunet I was also there for Jem during that disappointing time. But now he's got the figurines to think about. And anyway, he always says he doesn't mind about reviews and sales and all that. He says he judges his own success by a personal measure. Only he could know what he meant, so only he could know how close the finished pot had come to honestly expressing it. But how can he say that and then also get so down? How can he get so down because of some everyday professional setback and yet also be so hoity-toity about my work? Because I am the one who is commercial, I'm the tart, in his exalted view. That is something I did manage to realise that he felt – not that he made it very difficult. That was something I did know, unlike knowing or thinking I knew he loved me and was happy. But he was fascinated by it too, he was fascinated by my world. He kind of despised it but he also kind of loved it. He respected me for being able to operate there. I thought he understood me, I thought he respected me for being me, I thought he loved . . .

. . .

To think that I was proud of what I had done. I was proud of the family I had made for us. I was proud of the Interior I had brought him into.

I *am* proud.

Look at him and little Poppy. He wanted a child, he longed for one, he said – but would he really have been a father if it wasn't for me, for *here*? Oh, he would have had a child, children probably. Someone would have passed through and, sure, maybe there would have been a child. But it wouldn't really have been *his*.

He wouldn't have looked after it. She would have gone off somewhere, and it wouldn't have occurred to him. He would have put it down to 'Nature'. And inside him there would have been a knot of pain. But look at him now, look how happy he is. Or rather look how happy he *was*, I thought he was. No, look how happy he is. What he cannot see, is his own face when he watches her. Poppy is the joy of his life, whatever he says. He'll stay because of her.

If I want him to stay.

Of course I want him to stay. He is my husband. He is in my family. When he says they are my 'project' he is right. And what is wrong with that?

What is wrong with *hope*?

. . .

Now: try to turn away. Deep breath.

In . . . Out.

Imagine this is all a very long way away. Get back to what you are meant to be doing. Think of your readers who are expecting to be told about Interior Design. Get back to work.


## c. Paris: The Bleunet Kitchen and Rainbow Rooms

It really felt OK. It really felt that I was doing no one any harm. I was ready for this project – and the family was ready to support me, yes, why not, to give me a bit of support for once, after two years, after I had set everything up for everyone and it was working. There was the Transformation Play-Space, there was Carla. Poppy loved Carla, we all did, she really fitted in. Jem liked her, they got on well. Jem *liked* 'hanging around' with Poppy in the afternoons after he had done his morning's work.

No: actually it turns out he did not really like it, he only seemed to like it, it was a delusion of liking it.

No: he really did like it, back then, at the time; he really did.

Poppy had grown up a *lot*. She had her Interior, and she was queen of it. She crawled around, wanting this and that, pointing at things and being given them. She could pull herself up, and had even started to totter across from the Barbican to the Trellick Tower. Carla took her to playgroup a couple of times a week where she was beginning to make little friends. Of course she loved her Jewel Times with me – and of course I loved them too. The idea of disrupting those was very hard. But they wouldn't be disrupted completely. I would often be there. She was so secure. She was so much *in* the world.

Carla had got into art college and was very excited at the prospect. I liked her, we talked. She was so interested in things. She was interested in all my old drawings and notes. She said I should create a Tamé Archive: she would love to do the cataloguing. So we went through piles of stuff: plans, photographs, odd jottings. Jem is so wrong to say I am writing this book just because Fisher suggested it. Lots of things went into it: the Archive, the stage I was at in my career, my wanting to, my having the time. I didn't even start it until I was finished with Bleunet! So anyway, before Fisher had even opened his mouth Carla and I had been creating this Archive together. She pointed out some links between my work and Surrealist Art. She was thinking of doing a dissertation about me (!). It was nice.

And Jem was totally supportive. I just don't understand how now he can turn round and hold it against me since at the time he was completely pro it. He said about how there would be times when we both needed space to grow as individuals, about how Poppy was so secure in the Interior I had created for her, it would be like I was still there – because the Interior was so me – and

132

anyway I would be back at weekends, it wouldn't be so different from how we lived already. I was really helped by those discussions. It was like he really understood me, like we were one person. I was giving all the reasons for me *not* to go, and he was giving all the reasons why I *should*.

It should have worked. I thought the two of us were solid. I go back over it and over it and I can't see anything I could have done differently. Apart from just saying no to Bleunet. Apart from just giving up my whole career. But Jem said he didn't want me to. He said he wanted me to be me, just as I want him to be him. I haven't stopped him going on these new trips to the north he's started going on, to look at Staffordshire figures to help him with his new work. I don't want to stand in his way. I *want* him to be successful. Maybe he's just jealous. Which is so crap of him, how can I live with that? It is so mean.

It is so . . . *mean*!

. . .

Come on, Alizia. Pull yourself together.

. . .

Right. I've washed my face. I've had a cup of lemon verbena. I am sitting here in the Whiteness. I have my notes in front of me. I am Alizia Tamé and I am ready to write about Bleunet.

Paris. It was different, designing there, from designing in London – or anywhere in the UK. Here, things tend to be higgledy-piggledy. If ever you find a street of buildings that look like they were meant to go side-by-side it is a surprise. Here, the norm is idiosyncrasy – and design is about creating your own small area of Harmony in the midst of a cacophony of different tunes. Whereas in Paris, everything is much more like one symphony. You can see it in the way people walk. I got to feel it every time I stepped off the Eurostar. People didn't seem to be asserting themselves, to be battling against competing lines and colours as they do in London.

133

It was all much more a matter of being elegant, of fitting in. And what that meant for me, was that my design couldn't stand out as much as Tamé Home-is-Harmony creation might normally be expected to. It had to join in with everything around it, very subtly, and very completely. I had to register the lines of the elegant deco block whose top floor Bleunet had purchased, the calm of the Jardin du Luxembourg that the apartment directly overlooked, and also the busy-ness, the clutter of the major traffic arteries and gyratories on the other side towards Montparnasse. What I had to do then was, not so much transform these signals – as I would have done in London – but play along with them. The tricky thing was how to do this while also doing the Me-thing – which I knew Bleunet very much wanted me to – of expressing his individual vision.

For Cristophe was very much an individual. He dressed conservatively, in a rather English style – all tweed jackets and waistcoats. His hair was thinning, greyish black, and slicked back with Brylcreem, but his face was shiny pink and made him seem much younger than he actually must have been – I think the years spent slaving in hot, steamy kitchens must somehow have preserved him. And he was chubby – so he looked like a jovial bon viveur, except he also had this . . . well, intensity about him. He would take a line of thought and pursue it very quickly, and a very long way, with an air of great seriousness. But then, at the end, he would look up, and there would be a twinkle in his eye, and I would think he was joking. And sometimes he was – but more often he wasn't. Oh, he was a difficult man to be sure about. For instance, when I had the idea of the succession of different dining rooms arranged in an arc: the Rainbow Rooms as I came to call them (they weren't actually arranged like the stripes of a rainbow, obviously – more like the spokes of a wheel). This was a great concept because it expressed a feeling that was very key to

Cristophe – natural cycles, the great are of existence – while also connecting (though I didn't tell him this) to the systems of traffic circulation that were very much part of the local environment. Anyway, at once he leaped from this plan of mine to his idea of the Menu de Vie, starting with living food and ending with the long-dead and even mouldy. A joke, surely? But no – it is now one of his most celebrated creations. It was the same with the idea of the kitchen doubling as his bedroom. I didn't believe that at first; but he meant it.

I suppose I *was* fascinated by him. But why shouldn't I be? Why shouldn't I get involved in my work? Who would want me not to be excited by it? And this vision of Cristophe's really challenged me – much more than the technical difficulty of the retractable roof or the mahogany-covered cooker, or the practical hassle of sourcing products in a strange market and working with craftspeople I did not know. For Cristophe, everything was joined up: loving was linked to killing was linked to eating was linked to growing was linked to dying. When we ate, what we ate wasn't meat or fish or veg but bodies, creatures, which not so very long before had been alive. Not beef but a particular cow; not any old rabbit but this distinctive rabbit called Tam-Tam who had had a chestnut coat and a white patch on one ear. That meant we had to give our food the greatest respect because we were, actually, finally the same sort of thing as what we were eating. Viewed globally, each of us was just one fleeting speck among gazillions of other living creatures. We too were edible. When we were buried – he was very against cremation – we too were going to be eaten: by worms and creepy-crawlies. One day he said that, frankly, he would rather, when it came to it, be gobbled up by human beings than by arthropods: it would feel more friendly – and he was sure he would taste very nice. People donated their bodies for the advancement of medical science – so why not for the advancement of culinary experience?

He would leave instructions that the choicest cuts should be taken, and cured very carefully, and then sent out by courier to his dearest friends and most inspirational colleagues. This obviously was a joke, for once: we had a very good giggle about it indeed.

But still it nagged at me. All of it did. Maybe I was just vulnerable because I was away from home. Or maybe . . . Oh, I don't know. Anyway, I started to feel very differently about myself and my place in the world. I began to have very peculiar ideas about my body. I looked at my fingers and saw bits of asparagus in them and lettuce and beef. My fingernails were like the hooves of little, little lambs. As I stood under the shower the water ran down me like droplets over fishy scales. I had night-mares about being dead and buried; about mould spreading over my tummy which turned into moles who nibbled at my ear. In the evenings I logged on to try to have a Jewel Time with Poppy via the webcam. And that was comforting. I read with her (Carla sent me the words by email so I could read them out while she and Poppy looked at the pictures and lifted the flaps). We pointed and giggled. But at the same time it didn't let me do what I most wanted to each day – which was hug her, make sure she really was alive and safe and also – somehow – that I really was alive and safe too. When she waved her blurry goodbye, and I waved mine, and the pixels went blank on my laptop, and I knew they had also gone blank on the computer she was using at home – then I leaned back and looked up at the ceiling of the perfectly unobjectionable hotel room I was staying in, and felt so hollow and uncertain!

I got so excited every time I was on my way back to London. And when I arrived and opened the front door all the tiredness went out of me. I called hello! – and rushed down to the Kitchen and Transformation Play-Space. There she was, crawling towards me, her head wagging from side to side. I knelt down and took her in my arms; 'Darling!' – I cried. But she pulled away and said:

136

'Daddy,' and wriggled away and went towards him and pushed her head between his knees. I did try not to be upset by this. I told myself it was just her way of showing how much she cared. But I was not really happy until she had come back to me completely. I called out 'Poppy, Poppy' – and then, when I had caught her attention: 'I've got something for you.' I produced whatever it was, a finger puppet, or a little hat or dress (the French make such *lovely* clothes for babies) and she reached out her hands and said: 'Thank you,' so prettily. Again I grabbed her and gave her another hug and a kiss. And again, with that totally understandable reaction that all babies have, she wriggled and escaped and crawled off speedily into the Play-Space, though perhaps looking back over her shoulder this time, and went into her den under the outsize bench or into the ground floor of her Mini-Maisonette. At the beginning of the project it wasn't until, oh, probably two whole days after I got back from each trip that she came round to totally accepting me. As the weeks went by the process got quicker. But I always found it a little bit hard.

Still, when Poppy had been massaged and bathed and cuddled and tucked up, and when Carla had discreetly withdrawn, and when Jem and I were in our Adult Time, towards the end of our meal and a bottle of wine, I always felt a good deal better. I would have told him about some of the challenges of the project (though somehow I didn't ever manage to confide in him fully about the unease Bleunet caused me) and he would have brought me up-to-date with Poppy's development and shared his latest irritations about Hand of Hampstead. Here I was. Here we were. I would sit back in my chair, look at Jem, look around me – and I would get a very strong sense, a very *alive* sense, of all the rooms in the house. I knew they were there, and what was in them. I remembered Poppy's birth, and my pregnancy, and the worry Jem and I had shared before then. The excitement of moving to Allsop Road, the exhilaration of my early career, and the revolution in my thoughts and feelings that had happened, or had been crystallised, when I met Jem. And I thought that all that had ended up here. It had come to this. And this was something solid. It would cope. I could cope with all the new ideas that I was having because of Bleunet. Because there was here, Allsop Road, with Jem and Poppy, and also of course Carla: our place, where we *were*. Obviously it was in a sense not ideal for me to be spending time away working on a project that was emotionally so demanding: it was a strain on the family. But in another sense it was ideal. Strains are part of Life – they are what the Family is for. By living through them you get to feel all the stronger, all the more together.

But no, as it has turned out. All that happiness has ended in the mud. I come back to myself, now, here, in the Whiteness, and I am stunned again. Where has all the whiteness gone? Where is all the hope?

## d. After Bleunet

After Paris I had a bit of a rest. I gave a lot of time to Jem and to Poppy (she was walking now – and so grown-up). I re-connected with Marion who was at last managing to get her knitting business on the rails again: now the Funnel Office was doubling as her storeroom (!). But, before long, news of the Bleunet Kitchen and Rainbow Rooms got around and offers of commissions started to come in from across Europe. Fisher of course was keen for me to take them on. 'Leave Home-is-Harmony to Simon,' he said. 'You have to seize this chance.' But I really didn't feel I could. Home-is-Harmony was mine. I believed in it. And anyway I didn't want to commit myself to more work abroad. Perhaps most importantly of all, my confidence in my design principles was undergoing a significant wobble. Bleunet had made me feel my whole viewpoint was terribly one-sided, just too optimistic. Design for Life! So naïve. Because what about death and emptiness and loss? What about the fact that a step up is always followed by a step down; that growth leads inexorably to decay? What would be the value of all my Interiors, when the people they were designed for were no longer around to live in them? For Cristophe, death was part of the circle of existence. It all made sense. But I was very far from achieving that sort of attitude. For the first time in my life, I had a very real sense of the shadows that lay behind and around and ahead of me – and of us all.

Oddly, helpfully, I found that Carla had done some work which very much connected with my feelings. It all had to do with rubbish – inspired, she said, by conversations with Stan. She had taken the contents of a dustbin. Not just the tin cans that Warhol taught us to see as design items but absolutely everything: polystyrene packaging, plastic bags, rotting salad leaves, potato peelings, chicken carcasses – the lot. She suspended these in rectilinear moulds: a cube to create a simple stool or table; a cube plus square, flat back to create a chair. And then she filled the moulds with clear resin. The result was these beautiful, shiny, clean-lined shapes, with everyday rubbish inside them. The works referenced ideas of redemption, as well as the disposal of nuclear waste in lumps of concrete. But what most moved me, in the wake of the Bleunet experience, was the way the leaves and peelings and carcasses kept on rotting, even when they were encased by the clear, clinical material. After a week or two, the cans and tetra-packs and plastic bags were still there in all their ugly artificial glory. But the things of nature had wasted away, leaving black stains and pools of yellow slime.

These creations of Carla's strengthened my feeling that I needed to dig down to my first principles, have a good look at them, and begin again from there. It occurred to me that starting work on this book might actually be a very good way of doing just that. So, with Carla helping me find material in the Archive, I did. I went back over Wood Street, the Dawson House – of course you know that: you have read all about it. I decided to ask for contributions from friends and colleagues since (as I have said) Design is all about other people. Jem was so sweet: anxious about it, but also keen to be helpful. At first he didn't think he had anything to contribute; but when I explained that his perspective would be vital he went away and; well, again: you have already read it. So loving, his first idea of giving me a bespoke vase instead! Even now, after everything he has said to me, I can appreciate that gesture. And I thought what he said in the rest of his statement was, you know, quite fair. I knew he had had those gloomy feelings, of course I did. It is the sort of thing you can live with – or ought to be. It ought to be all part of the rich tapestry of good things and bad things that real lived-through Love for somebody actually is. The fact that he could write it down, and I could read it and not be upset by it, that only a couple of months ago it was something we could both be adult about and handle – that makes it all the more horrid that now everything has all sort of exploded in the way it has.

But anyway, as I say, Jem's contribution was fine but what actually rather did upset me – was Fisher's. I think he had always felt a bit challenged by Home-is-Harmony; and now, with the success of the Bleunet Project, it was all too much – even though he was the one who passed on the commission to me in the first place. But people do that, don't they? They arrange for something to happen and then, when it does, find they don't completely like it after all. That is why he goes on about how Home-is-Harmony is cheapening Design by spreading the word. It is so not true. I couldn't not include what he had written: if this book isn't open and honest, it is pointless. But I could show that I didn't care for his advice. The way to do that was just to keep on writing *Designs for a Happy Home* in the way that I had started; and to keep on following my Design vocation in my own way too.

So that is what I did.

All day – and some of the night! – images ran through my head. Sand in an egg timer. Wilted flowers. Lighting that altered with the seasons. I was excited by the recent invention of interactive wallpaper which changes shade according to how much noise there is in the room: I wondered if it could be made to react to the age of a space's occupants. Did you know that we flake off grams and grams of skin and dandruff every year? I wondered if it might be possible to harvest it, somehow (some kind of magnetised surface?) and use it for . . . well, I wasn't quite sure! I thought about floors, how solid they seem but how shifting they actually are if you look at them from the point of view of Mortality. Would it be possible to create a floor that rotated imperceptibly, one revolution per day, or per year (perhaps solar-powered?) I spent many happy hours each day at Home-is-Harmony and in the Whiteness, partly working on these speculative ideas, partly revisiting my past in order to write down my *Designs for a Happy Home*. It was a very intense time.

Too intense, as it turned out. Normally I never forget anything! I simply do not mess up my schedule. I suppose something must have made me.

It was the launch of Simon's wallpaper in the IntArchitec display space. It meant missing Jewel Time with Poppy – but obviously I had to show my support for this new Home-is-Harmony initiative. The show went well. Simon had had the excellent idea of framing the samples in antiqued gilt frames just like Old Masters. Some *major* figures were there, and they expressed a lot of interest. Of course, in my profession, people are usually warm to each other – in what they say, at least. To be honest, there is a lot of gush. But somehow you can always tell when someone is being genuine. And these people were. I was very pleased.

So there was a bounce in my step when I got home. I went downstairs for a glass of water. Jem was there. Nothing surprising about that. It wasn't late – about ten. But he wasn't doing anything, not even reading. He was just sitting still with his forearms resting on the table. He seemed to be staring at his fingers.

'You all right?'

'There you are.' He looked at me as if I was a stranger.

'Yes I am.'

'Funny thing, I was working in my Studio at half-past six, trying to finish something off, and the phone rang. It was Sally.'

'Oh?'

'You hadn't picked Poppy up. You were meant to pick Poppy up at six. And you'd forgotten. It's not an optional extra, having a child. She's not a lifestyle accessory.'

'I hadn't forgotten. I was at Simon's launch. At IntArchitec. It's in the calendar. It's been there for a month.'

'Simon's launch is in the calendar for tomorrow.'

'Nonsense.' I went over to check. Jem was right. Tuesday 5th June: Poppy at Dawn's. Wednesday 6th: A out.

'Oh no. Jem. I am so sorry.'

'There were no cabs so I got on the bus. Got there about seven; we weren't back till eight. Poppy was very tired. She wondered what her mummy was doing.'

'I've said I'm sorry. It's work. I've been really absorbed.'

'She was worried you'd gone off to Paris again. Deserted her.'

'Rubbish.'

'It's what she said.' He was staring at his fingers again. And then he raised his head. I remember the look of him there. The bright kitchen lights made his face pale and hid his eyes in shadow. Behind him were the windows. Along the wall to the side of him

142

were the cooker and the work surfaces. A chopping board. There was a knife on it and the remains of an apple. A square of core cut out.

He said: 'At last we have a child. You finally pause your career long enough for us to have a child. And then you hand her over to someone else. You sit upstairs and you watch her through a computer.'

'Jem, I have a job. I have to work.'

'Which means you go away to Paris when she's one. One year old, Leez.'

'Jem, that's not right. We both agreed it. You were in favour of it. I was here – a lot . . .'

'You're *never* really here. You're not here now. You're like behind a wall. A glass wall.'

It seemed so wrong to me, what he was saying. *So* not true. I said: 'I – Have – To – Work. We – Need – The – Money. And anyway, I WANT TO WORK. Even Though I Am A Woman I Am Allowed To Work.'

His chairlegs scraped on the tiles. He pushed himself upright. He put his hands on either side of his head at the top – like he was having to hold it in. He was taking a deep breath. Then one hand was a fist and had turned and the fist came down bang on to the work surface. The knife and the chopping board jumped. I jumped. He was so heavy. So *strong*. I was scared – but he was moving away. He was leaning on the sink in front of the window, looking out. Looking through the reflection of his pale face to the black outside.

He turned again. 'I'm calm now.'

'You frightened me.'

'It's how I feel. I have to break out.'

'Sit down.'

'It's not about you being a woman.'

143

'OK. It's not. Let's talk about it.'

'I can't work. You've put me in that little Studio at the end of the courtyard like your pet artist, shall we see what he's up to today, oh Jem that's delightful, so *now*.'

'We designed the studio together.'

'I can't work in these conditions. With Poppy in here with Carla. She needs me – she needs one of us. I can't get into the right space.'

'OK. Let's sit down and talk it through.'

Still he stayed standing. He said: 'Why did Fisher Paul have to come to Poppy's birthday? What's he got to do with it?'

I felt weary. I felt sad. I said what I had often said before. 'He's my senior colleague. I've known him a long time. He is my friend.'

'Yeh; you talk to Marion about him the whole time. And now Bleunet. Any man who comes along.'

There was nothing I wanted to say to that. There we were. Between us was the great thick central table I had had made from railway sleepers: sanded, bolted together, waxed. They rested on trestle-style legs I had salvaged from a couple of big Victorian mangles.

I was listening so hard for the next word I seemed to hear the room instead. It was like each object was asserting itself. Somehow humming its name. Maybe those violent words made me more sensitive. It was like when you're beaten up – and then someone touches your bruises. Like the wind – the wind can hurt if you are burnt or badly bruised. So I could feel the presence of the objects I had chosen and placed around us. Pushing at me.

In my head there is a picture of us – there, in the Kitchen I had designed. And the odd thing is: we fit in. It looks in keeping, with all the hard surfaces, and the metal, and the knives. What percentage of domestic arguments happen primarily in the kitchen?

• Answer: a lot.

I really want to tell you something about the design of my own kitchen. But I can't. I simply do not have the heart. Spaces take on the feel of what has happened in them and I can't, for the moment, think of my kitchen without seeing us there, physically in the same room, and yet emotionally so far apart.

I think we hated each other then.

Jem . . .


## Magic Mottoes

There are no Magic Mottoes in this chapter.

# Working with Alizia: Simon

Alizia has asked me to write an account of what it is like to work with her.

Delicate!

That's only my little joke. In fact she is a wonderful colleague. Professional, warm, stimulating, supportive, and so very energetic. Sometimes we talk together and we just mention the possibility of something and then, next day, whoosh! she has done it. Just like that. Astonishing. Remarkable. Like the very first time we met, when she was straight out of college and Fisher had asked me to keep an eye on her, help her settle in. I explained the concept for our current project, the Factory Office in the City, and, before I knew it, Bang! a load of plans for desks and chairs and modified computer terminals appeared in front of me. No concern for practicality, that was the problem. Materials? Budget? But that was where I came in, you see. As she said, I took her Vision, and made it Viable.

Which is pretty much what I have been doing ever since. I am her enabler, her connection to the world. Even on our latest triumph, the Bleunet project. The blueprint was very much hers, of course it was, I wouldn't want to take that away from her for a minute. But who advised on the use of mahogany in the kitchen, who fine-tuned the gradation of colours from one dining room to the next? Yes, that's right: someone not a million miles away from yours truly.

I don't begrudge it. I am not frustrated. Because she always gives me credit, you see. And anyway, this is what I have always liked: making things happen, finding the right materials for them, visualising fabrics, textures, tones. I like thinking about how it will feel to walk across a given piece of flooring; what sort of touch-experience a banister or kitchen top will give you. It's the intimacy that attracts me, I suppose. That's why I wasn't really all that happy at IntArchitec before Alizia came along. I hadn't found my niche. Of course it mattered, the sort of thing I was interested in; but I don't think it was felt to be terribly important by comparison with big things like, basically, structure and visual impact. So when Alizia turned up and we hit it off, that was a big improvement. Such fun we have been having ever since! Even our darkest times have a little sparkle in them. That is how the famous Impish Touches came about: they started all the way back then as just a little joke between the two of us.

Then, one day, in she comes, all het up: excited, but also obviously worried and upset. I sit her down and she completely opens up to me. She tells me about this man she's met, what incredible hands he has, how he's made her see everything in a new way, how she doesn't know what to do about it, she thinks she might have to leave IntArchitec but she doesn't want to do that, she feels that, she and I, we have such a strong partnership. And I say: Stop; slow down; see what happens. I can't honestly take any credit for it but I must confess it was lovely, over the next few weeks, watching her become happier and more, well, I suppose the right word is more resolved. Together, we bided our time. And then the Dawson House came up (what beautiful textures there were in that design: the soft, strong tweed of the sofas, the gentle

147

roughness of the wire-brushed bricks, and the hard shine of the polished concrete floor); and not long after we were into the launch of Home-is-Harmony.

That was an exciting time! Our own brand (though of course still very much under the IntArchitec umbrella). Our own big shared office with – in due course – our own dedicated assistants. Ana and Elspeth are such a help to us. I really don't know how we'd cope without them.

So here we all are. Except, just now, as I am writing this (sorry it's a little late, Alizia!) you, Alizia, are not. Not here. And I know you have called in saying you have got a bit of a cold but I'm beginning to wonder if that's really all it is. Because usually you reply to emails, don't you, when you are working at home, or however ill you are. And usually you return my calls. Only that hasn't been happening, has it, these last, what is it now, two weeks? And frankly it's getting to be rather a problem because there are some things I'd really quite like to dicuss with you, such as this odd visit from Fisher I just had yesterday afternoon. Yes, that's right, he just walked in. Ana and Elspeth were very surprised – they tried to hide it but I could tell they were: you know, something just changed in the atmosphere; it got a little more taut. Anyway, so there was Fisher, sitting in front of me. And ostensibly he was just congratulating me on my Wallpaper and this whole plan of ours for the Hints of Home-is-Harmony Range. He said how it had made him realise that with new production techniques and everything it was possible now for top-end Design Vision to become smaller-scale, more individualised and widely spread. So I took that as his blessing. Really it was very nice. But then he went on to say this strange thing which I wanted to discuss with you.

He said: 'It may be that that is where Home-is-Harmony's future lies.'

And I said: 'Well, we've had a lot of international enquiries because of Alizia's big success with the Bleunet project. So I think our future probably lies in that direction too.'

And he said: 'Sometimes it's the apparently more modest thing that's actually the most revolutionary.'

I didn't know what to reply to that.

And then he said: 'Hints of Home-is-Harmony, it's really your brainchild, isn't it, Simon.'

Well, I wasn't having that for a moment, so I told him: 'Everything we do at Home-is-Harmony is very much a joint endeavour.'

He said: 'I understand you. Let me put it like this. Hints of Home-is-Harmony is a very big idea. It could build impressively. If it does, it may be, just possibly, that it would function more effectively outside the IntArchitec stable.'

I suddenly felt even more nervous than I had been feeling before.

He carried on: 'A brand is a very precious thing. IntArchitec is obviously a diamond among brands. Let's say Hints of Home-is-Harmony grows. No longer the little pebble it is at the moment, but a sapphire, maybe eventually a ruby. Synergy between brands is a good thing. Interference is not.'

I said: 'Of course.'

And then what he said was: 'I have the greatest confidence in you, Simon. That's really what I came here to say.'

And then he got up and said farewell to me and graciously also to Ana and Elspeth: and then he just walked out.

Well, what do you think of that? To start off with I was rather pleased. No, actually, I was thrilled. It is very nice to be taken notice of by anyone really, and especially when that anyone is Fisher Paul. But the more I thought it over, the more it came to seem peculiar, especially what with you not being here. So that is why I want to talk to you. Quite urgently, if that's all right.

You are OK, aren't you, Alizia? I can see that Bleunet must have taken it out of you. After a big project like that – and such a big success! – anyone is likely to feel a little bit let down, even someone as full of go as you. So don't be worried by it, if that is what has happened. Be gentle with yourself, and it will pass.

But if there's something more than that, well, I am here for you. You know that, don't you? We go back really quite a long way. And I think it's true to say that we are fond of each other. I can say that, can't I? It's not untrue. Anyway, all I'm meaning to say really is: if you need to open up to someone over a cup of tea (I know your favourite: lemon verbena!) just give me a call. Or drop in. We'd all be thrilled to see you. You know we would.

With love from me, and everyone at IntArchitec,
Simon.

# 7. The Downstairs Convenience

*a. . . .*

So here I am, still. Still here. I didn't tell you much about kitchens. Sorry about that. Everything that has happened got written down instead. I suppose at least some of it happened *in* a kitchen. Anyway. No progress. Still in a tangle of feelings. Still in a mess.

Why?

We have had harsh words before, of course we have, like everyone. But this was a total attack on our whole way of life and on me as a person. Where did it come from? *Where?* In the end he said he would leave, and I said go on, leave then, and he hasn't but I can't see any other way out. Days have passed and he is like a rock. I have been on the point of speaking to him. I have gone into a room where he is, with my feelings melting and my mouth about to speak. But then I have seen him and his body is so hard, it is braced against me. All the warmth I am projecting at him somehow bounces off and turns to ice. And then my body is the same as his. It is so strange, how there can be a voice in you, how the you that you like to think of as you can be there inside you saying: Now be sensible, you really need to make up. Think about Poppy, think about Family, think about Life. And in your body there can be this great electric stifling mass of feeling which makes it all impossible.

Why?

So I am back up here in the Whiteness nearly all the time. And what is so irritating here is that people try to contact me or rather I *know* they are trying to contact me. Emails trill on arrival, the phone rings. I do not want to chat to my friends, I do not want to discuss things with Marion. I cannot deal with work. Look and listen to all these messages from Simon. Obviously I can't reply. I have no voice. I have no place to stand on to speak from. Do you see what I mean?

But there is somewhere else I go for quiet. I check the webcams to be sure the coast is clear but still I have a little feeling of adventure as I leave the Whiteness behind. I snoop through my own house, I am like a burglar, I am in a cartoon animation, my eyes are out on stalks. I am heading for the downstairs loo, or as I prefer to say, the Downstairs Convenience. My arm stretches round a corner, my fingers walk along the wall and find the doorknob and then, whoosh! – I am inside, the door is shut behind me and the bolt is slid across. The gentle light is switched on, there is the purr of the extractor, I am surrounded by pale ultramarine blue (pale colours are always best for a Downstairs Convenience) and my heart starts to slow. I look at myself in the mirror: what I see is that my eyes are saggy and my cheeks are the texture of sand.

And then it is like all of me is heavy, sagging, sinking. I sit down on the loo. After a bit the pee flows. And then so do the tears. And then the knot of wire which is my mind loosens a little and the pain clears. Inside me, a door is unlocked and I can start to think.

# b. Privacy

This happens because of the sort of space the Downstairs Convenience is. It is small, it is functional and, above all: it is private. Much more private than a Home Office – and also more private than a bathroom, even an ensuite. Bathrooms are shared, and baths and showers can be – so even when you are alone in the bathroom with the door locked that feeling of possible sharing is there in the room around you. Not so in the Downstairs Convenience which, I won't say 'never', but quite rarely has two people in it at once and doesn't have that 'feel' of sharing at all. When you are in there, people leave you alone. They are unlikely to even knock on the door.

And so: you can allow yourself to be vulnerable. In primitive times, at moments of excretion, a sabre-toothed tiger might have got you if you didn't go somewhere hidden and safe. I think we still have the same feeling now. Nobody can see you. Your knickers are down. All of you is showing. So all your feelings can show as well.

Breathing slowly, being calm. Thinking ugly thoughts but staying calm. What would Marion say? She would put it down to not enough massage. She would say it was all my fault. And obviously I must be in some way to blame. But I do not think I am the root of it. Where does it come from, this great pile-up of resentment? How dare he say those things?

I lift my shoulders up, sit back. I breathe. I look ahead and a little bit up at the mirror above the basin. In the centre of the mirror there is a reflection, not of me, but of a black-and-white photograph of the Highlands which in fact is placed on the wall behind me above my head.

I look into the distant tumbling glens and bens. A black crag curves across the right like an enormous rib. In the foreground there are scattered great knuckles of rocks. I am launched into the technique of 'Seeing As' which always has a calmative effect on me. I see the crag as a great wave. I see the few stunted bare trees halfway up the rise of it as the masts of boats in trouble. Now the wave is a cave, a shadow drawing me in. Under it there is a road which leads me on into a valley where the hills are gentler. I roll my mind along the road and suddenly I am where I was ten years before, Jem is beside me, we are in my car, on the motorway. We are heading towards Cornwall. Wind hassles us and rain spits but it is cosy inside, even though the car keeps being buffeted to left and right. I am nervous. I am excited. I have known Jem for perhaps two or three months. We are new. We have no child, we are not married, we have no house, no history, we are not yet lovers.

I am watching the glow-worm lights of the cars in front as if we are in some slow ritual procession. Jem is taking me to see the place where his clay is dug. It feels special. It is a step into intimacy, a rite of passage. The lights . . .

But then I heard Carla's voice outside the door. 'A poo, darling? Mummy's in there. Try to hold on . . . No, we go upstairs.'

Not *totally* private then, of course not. But the Downstairs Convenience is still the most private space there can be in a domestic environment. And if it isn't totally, totally private, that shows you something about family spaces, doesn't it? The way families share. The way they have – or should have – such togetherness.

## c. Memories

. . . where his clay is dug . . . a rite of passage . . . the lights . . . the lights led on into . . . I was driving . . . but I didn't know where. I was in a seat in a metal box on wheels, hurtling forwards and forwards but also sitting still.

Years later, in the Downstairs Convenience, I remember what I had been remembering then. One seat stacks on another, loo seat morphs into car seat morphs into the damp sofa I always sat on in Jem's old studio under the arches, my sofa with its familiar animal smell. The fabric must be rotting, I suppose. It is different from the main smell in the studio which is the sour, metallic smell of clay.

Jem has finished his work for the day. He is sitting with me and we are drinking out of little handleless pots that he has made, glazed only on the inside and around the lip. A lovely glaze, iridescent blue and green like a butterfly. The clay itself, which is what your fingers touch, is rough, pitted, red.

'Why do you only glaze the inside?'

'The glaze makes the clay waterproof. Only the inside and the lip need glazing.'

'But it's beautiful . . .'

'Yes.'

His intonation is like a teacher's to a child. It irritates me – and it goads me. I want him to take me seriously. Actually what I want is just for him to notice me, notice me properly, become aware of the real, deep-down me. So I keep on quizzing him.

'Why don't you make it all beautiful?'

'It would be a waste.'

'It wouldn't. It'd make more beauty. That's not waste.' I look at him with my best sparkling eyes, I smile, begin to laugh. But he looks straight ahead, along his legs, which are stretched out, looking past his feet, to the old two-barred electric fire.

He speaks in a blunt, assertive way, very sure of himself: 'It wouldn't make more beauty because you'd feel the waste.'

'I don't see why.'

'Because beauty comes from use. Beauty connects with the body. Look at the cup you are holding. Let yourself feel what your fingers are feeling.' He watches my fingers. I press them into the

155

rough clay, then soften my grip, move my fingertips slightly, rub them against the clay. 'Now put the cup to your lips, and drink. What do you feel?'

'It feels smooth, and cool.'

'The glaze is a tribute to your lips,' he says, looking at my lips. 'What do fingers want? They want something they can hold. Something that is not going to slip. They want good honest grip. In a cup, fingers like roughness. But the liquid and your lips need a smooth surface. The liquid needs to flow. And I wouldn't want to roughen your lips.' Again there is that condescending tone. 'See? The glaze goes where it is needed.'

It is later. Jem has pushed open the metal door. He has switched off the lights and we have picked our way out through the dim luminescence that comes in from the street. I am looking in at the space where we have been, and are now no longer: the door slams echoingly shut across it.

We walk to the end of the cobbled street. We pause. I think of something to say, and say it, to keep him there. I linger close. My shoulder touches his upper arm. I look up . . .

He says: 'Bye then.'

'See you tomorrow?'

'Sure.'

I am watching him. He takes a kneaded lump of clay from the table behind him. Holds it before him in both hands as if it were already a cup, a chalice. Suddenly he slams it down in the centre of the wheel and raises his hands up and away. There is a pause as the memory of the sound fades to nothing, the ripples in the air calm. Now he brings his hands close again and starts to touch around the clay. The wheel budges a little, one way then the other. At last he settles himself on the stool. There is a kick of his leg and the wheel rotates. Another:

faster. His shoulders tense as his thumbs push into the clay. And very fast a shape appears between his fingers: a cup or bowl or vase. It rises into existence so fast! With a wire he slices it off the wheel and places it gently on a shelf to his right where it will sit for days, sometimes weeks before firing. And if at any time it feels to Jem *not honest*, it will be smashed. Many of his creations are short-lived!

Now he rinses his hands in the reservoir of mucky clayey water round the wheel. He begins again. A sigh. Quiet as he gathers his concentration on to the lump. Then a crescendo of clanking, a whirring noise higher and higher then quieter and lower and down to nothing as the next pot appears. At the end his head twitches. He dries his hands, wraps and stores the unused clay, and comes to sit with me.

We have left the storm behind us. Our car has crossed the open endless Bodmin Moor and is in among little hills and narrow, winding, up-and-down roads. Trees meet above us making hoops of dark. Then we go down, across a small stone bridge over white water, into a village. Grey cottages press in: small windows, thick walls, slate roofs. We get out, the air is cold and moist. Low traces of cloud drift across beneath the high, pale sky. I hug myself, stretch, shake the dullness out of my legs. He is already moving, shoulders down in an old stained moss-coloured Barbour with his pale hair heavy above it. I skip to catch up with him, and we stride on, up the road for a while, then over a stile on to a path. Above us a grassy height rises steeply, but we are walking round. Rock breaks through the surface of the earth. There is shale and pebbles underfoot. Now we turn a corner and there is space ahead of us. On the ground an uneven small plain. Pools of murky water edged with grey slime which gleam in the pale sun. Thick rough grass, and odd dark plants made up of narrow spiky leaves. In the distance over a ridge I glimpse the sea.

'Here,' he says. I see that an area of the plain or marsh has been marked out into squares with ropes and pegs. Some of these squares have been dug to varying depths, two feet, or at most five or six. 'Here,' he says, squatting down. He reaches out towards the smooth clay and takes a handful of it, rubbing it between his palms. 'May I?' He takes my fingers in his clayey hands and pulls my arm outstretched. Now he is pushing my hand into the cold wet clay. He pulls it out and holds it in his hand. My hand is cold and it is drying stickily together with his. What is he up to? Overhead a gull swoops, screeches. I wobble, our hands come apart, I sit with a bump on the grass. And then he sits beside me. The wet is seeping through to my bum but I do not mind because he has put his arm around my shoulders and laid his head with its damp hair against my ear, my neck. I lean into him. I am looking ahead at the wet clayey ground, the tufty plants, patches of light and shadow fleeting across it.

We stayed the night with a friend of his who lived there in the village, the man who dug the clay. In the morning Jem went out into the yard at the back of the house to spade the batches of clay that were laid out to weather there. He chopped at them, levered them over: he was helping them to breathe. Then we visited the pottery where he had been an apprentice. I sat on a bench with a cup of hot, sweet tea feeling small and young while he talked with the big, slow-moving potters with their holed jerseys and grubby dungarees, their weathered faces, their thick-fingered, puffy hands.

Once, Jem showed me all the different sorts of pot he had made. Grey, unpolished lumps from his time at Camberwell. A set of black bowls with vertical sides that bulged in and out like they were made of rubber – his 'dark period', as we called it, when he was rebelling against the nature of his medium. Finally, greenish pots, like the piece of his I had seen first of all, with the clay that seemed to come to life.

158

'That was my first inkling of you,' I say.

And what he says as his reply is this: 'They feel like the end of something. I feel I'm moving on.' He is looking at me. My heart is ringing like a bell. He says: 'You can't invent a new style. It just has to come. And when it comes, it changes everything.'

Now I know what is going to happen. I decide what to do. I know that I will take Jem and make a life around him. A life for him, a life for him and me. I don't think it will be easy. But it is what he needs, I need; what I can give. It is all there is to do.

If I had known?

If I had known it would all come to this?

The same. I think that I would still have done the same. Because – because I wouldn't really have known. Because I wouldn't have accepted that I knew. I would have thought, I would have been sure that I could change things. I would have been sure that I could make things better.

And . . .

I can!

There. What I have written down for you is a sort of collage of the remembering that happened during a series of visits to the Downstairs Convenience over several days. The past came in and seemed to flush away all the grief, the puzzlement I was stuck in. It left me feeling strong and clear and calm.

That's what the past is for. Well, one of the things it is for. That's why the images of those early days are so strongly lit inside us. I have so many other happy memories that I could stack on top of these memories I have described. Yes, I really do: Jem walking back together with me from his studio at the beginning of the end of our dark time in Wood Street; Jem helping me walk out of hospital, carrying the baby Poppy; Jem stooped, helping Poppy to learn to walk for herself. But all of them are only echoes of the first bright times. Those are the bones of us.

One morning, in fact it was the day before yesterday, I woke full of brightness, almost happiness. I lay in bed, feeling as if there was no ceiling and second floor and attic and roof between myself and the sky; as if the sun were shining in on me. I got up, threw on my dressing gown, and went straight down to the Downstairs Convenience for one last visit.

Well, not really for the last visit ever, of course: but what I mean is, as a sort of conclusion to the mental journey I had been going through.

Once inside, I turned the lights up to full. I shut the lid of the toilet. I remained standing, fully clothed. Facing myself, with the bright halogens lighting up the pores, flaws and freckles of my un-made-up skin, I decided:

To give way.

Simply: to stop arguing with what he said to me, about me.

To see things from his point of view. Well, try to, anyway: try harder.

To spend less time at work and in the Whiteness. As a mother I had the right to negotiate a part-time commitment to IntArchitec; and that was what I was going to do. I was going to make less use of the webcams and be actually physically present more. I was going to be more mentally open to Jem and the sort of 'hanging out' he liked to do with Poppy.

To listen more. Perhaps I had been going on a bit about Bleunet. I had thought Jem liked to share in my excitements but maybe I did come across as a little bit bragging. Anyway, I would be quieter; leave more space for him to flower.

To have as little as possible to do with Fisher. In the wake of Fisher's Working with Alizia contribution I didn't feel this was much of a sacrifice!

And: to stop (at least for the time being) writing this book.

160

Yes, I am afraid so. Jem obviously isn't happy with it, for whatever wrong-headed reason – sometimes because he can't bear that Fisher gave me the idea for it, sometimes just because he doesn't think we should be written about at all. I can see that. I don't think he is right, but I can see that it is possible for somebody to have that feeling. Especially when that somebody is somebody like Jem.

Anyway, to tell the truth, I'm not entirely sure what I would say next if I did carry on. I know what I am going to do. But I cannot be sure what the results of it are going to be for us, for my Family, or for our Interior. Maybe it will all work. Maybe Jem will change enough, in response to my changes, so that he stops being quite so possessive and I will be able to write again. But maybe he won't. Maybe these words will be discovered in my filing cabinet or on my hard disc only after my death. Perhaps Jem or Poppy will burn them (please don't, my darlings, if it *is* you reading this, and I am no more!). But perhaps they will still be worthy of publication. They might still interest someone.

My last Magic Motto is as vital as any of the others. Maybe more so. Magic Motto no. 12:

✔ *Know When To Stop!*

# 8. The Master Bedroom and Ensuite

## a. Change of Plan

Surprise!

Me again!

I did stop writing. For more than a year. A lot has happened during that time. A *lot*. I have been on a long, dark journey. I have been torn up and the bits of me have been scattered to the wind. Crows have pecked me and cows have trampled me with their hooves in the mud. The result of all this is:

• Things Have Changed.

Now, I am writing from a different place. It is not a happier one. But maybe it is better. There has been a lot of pain. I don't want to look back at it. But on the other hand, looking at me now, looking around me now, things seem sort of stronger than they did before. They are heavier, in the sense of sadder, but also more solid, in the sense of less likely to collapse. And there has got to be good in that – even if what has happened to make this happen is not in itself very good, in fact is not good at all.

Do you understand what I mean?

This book is turning out very different from how I meant it to be. But so is my Life! And the point of a book is to show you how things really are. By doing that, you can make the world a better place. That is what I set out to do. To tell the truth. And that is what I will keep on doing. It's not a reason to stop, just because you discover the truth is different from what you thought it was.

Happiness is so strange, isn't it? You think you are happy. No – you *are* happy. And then in a moment it is gone. In a moment the world changes and everything turns black. You try to remember the happiness you used to have. And you can't reach it. You can see it there. You can see a picture of it, a bit blurred maybe, and in bright colours, Dresden yellow and makka vermilion red. You can see yourself having the happy feeling. But you can't get through to the feeling itself. It is on the other side of a pane of soundproof double glazing. Mouthing at you. Waving. Jumping up and down. Unreachable.

I *can* be happy again. Everyone can.

But I must tell you what has happened.

## b. Peace

After I had taken my vow in the Downstairs Convenience, I went out to Jem's studio and looked through the window. There he was, asleep in his usual doggy place. I decided to let him sleep on. He had always hated being woken. I used to think it was to do with his connection to the unconscious forces of nature and the earth. It simply took him longer than most people to come back to life. But now, from where I am now, I must say it looks more like simple sluggishness. A straightforward selfish inability to bloody well get on with things.

Anyway: I went back upstairs and got dressed in the right sort of clothes for how I was feeling. I.e., just grey cotton trousers and a

163

white blouse. I wanted Jem to see the everyday plain me. Not me as 'career woman' or me as 'threat' – or whatever idea of me I had let him get into his head. The Me who, OK, had a job, but was also a mother. The Me who loved him. The Me who could *help*.

When Poppy and Carla had got up and gone off together as usual, I sat down at the kitchen table with my coffee. In front of me was a piece of paper: I was going to write down my resolutions. I wanted to put them outside myself, to get them really clear and make them permanent. And also – I wanted to have something, some sort of offering, to give to Jem.

I knew him so well. I had known him a long time, and I had watched him with the specially sharp eyes that love gives you. Which meant: I knew what I had to do. My task was, not to 'sort everything out', but to make Jem feel he had 'room to grow into a happier place'. And the aim was:

• For us to be Us, with Poppy, again.

After a while, I noticed movement in the studio. I waited, then made a cup of coffee to take over. I activated the early warning system and went out of the French windows. My throat and tummy felt all tight, and I practised smiling 'spontaneously' as I walked across. The door opened. Jem was there. I kept on walking, stopped, and looked up at him. He looked down.

'Here,' I said.

'Thanks.' He did not move.

'Can I come in?'

'What for?'

'Jem, please. I'm trying to be nice.' I looked up at him appealingly. Around his eyes I saw the wrinkly skin shift a little and the eyebrows rise. His chest was moving backwards. He was letting me in.

I hadn't been inside Jem's studio for ages. I had forgotten how dark it was. Shadowy. Lines of light came in from the windows but between them, and up under the slanting roof, there was darkness. There were sketches stuck higgledy-piggledy on the walls and cupboard doors. There were shelves of pots and what I realised must be the new creations: the Figurines. I smelled the sour smell and felt the dampness of the air on my face; when I spoke, my voice was hollow, echoey:

'I'm sorry. I know I get carried away sometimes. I know I sometimes seem too busy and I'm not here. But I'm always thinking about you. And Poppy. All I want is for you and her to be happy. That's what the house is all about. That's what it's all for!'

'Is it?'

'Yes! – listen, I *know* I can seem too controlling. But that's because I so much want everything to be all right. I so want you both to be happy. It's terrible to know that the thing you want, you're spoiling it by wanting it so much. And that's what's happened here. That's what I've done here. I've wanted to make this life for us, this happy life. And I've mucked it all up. By wanting it too much.' I was beginning to cry. The tightness in my throat had come up into my face, somehow, and now it was turning into tears. And the tears brought that 'relax' feeling which I think tears always bring. As if all of you was going soft and fluid.

Jem said: 'Instead of just letting things happen.'

And I blurted out: 'Yes.'

And he said: 'Instead of just letting things grow.'

And again I blurted: 'Yes.'

The fact is, I didn't really agree with him, even at that exact moment when I said those words. I didn't think things just 'happen', or just 'grow', and I still don't – all the more so *now*.

165

But pretending to agree with him was the first step in my self-sacrifice that I was making for the sake of Us. So I stood there weeping and saying yes. I don't mean that I was lying, exactly. It was just – I was so all given over to the idea of telling him what he wanted to hear.

Bit by bit I pulled myself together. Jem had not moved towards me, not even when I was crying: he had never known how to deal with tears. He was sitting on the stool in front of his wheel, leaning back, his legs stretched out, the coffee cup wrapped in his hands. He didn't look especially upset – more just patient, with maybe a bit of worry in his eyes.

Words splurged out of me: 'I'm going to be here more. I'm going to plan less. I'm going to let things happen. I'm going to go part time at IntArchitec. I'm going to stop writing *Designs for a Happy Home*.'

'You don't need to do that.'

'Yes I do, I know you . . . no, let me just do it for me, it's what I need to do. Here, I've written it all down.' I handed him the bit of paper.

'You don't need to give me a certificate.'

'It's not a certificate. Listen Jem. You know I'm different from you. We work differently. But that doesn't mean we have to be unhappy. We used to love each other for it' – I saw his face twitch, a smile flicker – 'and I think we still do. You may not feel like you love me now, but I think you still do. I still love you. I love you Jem.'

'OK,' he said. 'I'll stick this up.' He turned, took a speck of clay from the edge of the wheel, wetted it with his tongue, pinched it to the back of the paper and pressed the paper to the wall.

'So you won't leave?'

'No,' he said. The word fell through the air like a stone into water and ripples of happiness, of calm, spread all around. I held

166

out my hand to touch his cheek. I moved my fingers across to his rough lips. He clenched them in a kiss.

After that things went along OK. Fisher and the IntArchitec board approved my request to go part-time (the company's structure was so fluid that this was virtually a formality). It turned out to be rather harder for me to stop working on *Designs for a Happy Home*, to stop reading over and over, adjusting, trying to better understand. What I did was give all the papers to Carla to hide away somewhere safe in her room, and emailed the computer files to Simon. So *Designs* just wasn't there in the Whiteness to tempt me. Together, these changes meant I had a lot more time to give to Jem – and to Poppy. Sometimes it was me, instead of Jem or Carla, who collected Poppy from nursery. And sometimes Jem and I 'hung out' together in the afternoons, either just the two of us or with Poppy's little friends Jasper or Dawn and their mums. Occasionally there were strains, of course. Of course I got the lunchtime routine wrong and took her out without her boots and forgot to record her favourite programme on the telly: of course I did. But mainly it was nice. I was sticking to my resolutions – and Jem seemed to appreciate it. I thought I could see that he was making an effort on his side too. The result was that the little things were bit by bit covering over the great wound, healing it.

Still, I didn't want to see Marion, even though Poppy so adored Doris. It would have just felt awkward, it would have felt like we were on show. So I hadn't returned her calls, I had just texted that we were spending time together as a family. I knew Jem usually, when he was looking after Poppy, saw a lot of Doris and Marion. But now he didn't seem to want to either. And what I thought about that was: that it was nice of him to be sensitive to my feelings, that it was all part of the two of us building bridges.

A few weeks after the Peace-Treaty, on a Saturday afternoon, we all set off together to the park. Poppy now had a little trike which she used to race ahead on along the pavement, zigzagging between people's front walls and the parked cars. It made me nervous: what if she smashed her head on something? But I knew Jem thought it was perfectly all right, that she was only ever going to get a little knock and that little knocks were part of growing up: he thought I should give the child more space. So I managed not to shout out 'Stop!' when she was heading at high speed towards the kerb. And he was right: she did in fact stop of her own accord each time. But then she had disappeared round a corner and now I couldn't help myself, I was running after her shouting 'Poppy! Poppy!', and then I could see her again, she had stopped, she was looking round, smiling. After a bit Jem came huffing and puffing up behind us.

I said: 'Sorry.'

'What?'

'Panicked.'

'Oh that's all right, it doesn't matter.' And we walked on again.

After a bit I asked him how his work was going but he didn't seem to want to say.

I pressed: 'Still the Figurines?'

'Yep. Figs.'

'Could I have a look at them sometime? I'd love to have a proper look.'

'Course you can.'

Poppy was waiting again. We were at the busy road, and on the other side was the park. Jem hoisted the trike in one hand and we all joined hands in a row with Poppy in the middle. Then we were across, and separated again, and Poppy was whizzing down the really quite gentle slope. At the top of a rise to the right a fountain pulsed and sprayed. To the left was plain grass. Scattered around were fat, late-summer trees and ahead of us – Poppy had almost reached it – the fenced-off little playground. I drifted closer to Jem, nudged his upper arm with my shoulder. And then he took my hand. My heart lifted and I raised my face and pecked him on the chin – and at once we were going along in the same rhythm together, and I was taking the bouncy, moonwalk steps I had to take to match his stride.

'There's Doris,' Jem said and I saw her, a little figure in a red coat going tick-tock on a swing. I felt my cheeks warming, tightening in a blush. Poppy was shouldering her way through the gate and a languid woman – it was Marion – left the swings and went towards her. Poppy was hoisted into her arms, Poppy was being swung round and round her. Then Marion looked up towards us, I waved, and Marion put Poppy down.

'Hello.' The two of us were facing her.

'How are things?' Her head turned, looking from his face to mine to his.

'Oh . . .'

'Poppy!' – Jem shouted. 'Hang on!' And he went off – 'I'll just . . .' towards the climbing-frame where she didn't in fact seem to me to be that dangerously high. I felt glad Jem had his moments of anxiety as well!

Marion followed him with her eyes and smiled: 'He's such a good dad.'

'Yes,' I said. 'Is Stan around? Not stayed behind in the Funnel Office?'

'No.' There was a sort of not very serious solemnity in her tone and we shared a moment of something, I suppose just a moment of thinking about the same thing from our different points of view. 'He's gone to get a drink for Doris.'

Doris was on the ground underneath the cockpit of the aeroplane climbing-frame and had her arms up towards Poppy – who was trying to manoeuvre herself into position for the jump.

'Doris's so good with Poppy,' I said. 'She needs a little brother or sister.'

'Feeling broody?' She had stepped sort of back and around so she could see my face.

'Well not right now . . .'

'But longer term?'

'Well yes. Don't you?'

'Things are all right with you and Jem then?'

'Yes.'

'Oh good, I'm so glad. Because we had begun to wonder.'

'We just needed some time to ourselves.'

Then we heard Stan's voice calling: 'Hello, you two.' He was coming towards us but he stopped and crouched to give Doris a bottle of something; and then he came towards us again. His arms were open in a long-range embrace. 'How are you doing?'

'What did you get her?'

'Coke.'

'We can't give her Coke.'

'It was all they had.'

'She doesn't like it.'

'In that case she won't drink it.'

'Stan . . .'

'Look, she said she was thirsty, I went to get her a drink. It's a drink.'

'. . .'

Stan turned to me: 'Hello, stranger! Missing gay Paree yet?'

'Actually I like it here.'

'Good,' he said. 'I'm glad about that.'

He too looked searchingly into my face – and suddenly I didn't like how that felt, so I called out: 'Poppy, shall we go on the roundabout?'

She came stumbling across and, next thing, she and me and Doris were perched on the curved metal poles of the roundabout,

170

and Jem was pushing us round and round, round and round, till the sky and the earth were swooping and everything around us blurred. Then we slowed and I moved to get off but I was dizzy so I staggered and bumped into Jem who held me until the world had stopped and cleared. There were Marion and Stan, picking up the children, holding their hands. It felt like time to leave and so we went out of the little gated compound and Marion unleashed Spirit and threw a tennis ball for him to go lolloping after. Doris was a bit ahead on her scooter, I was pushing the handle of Poppy's trike, and we adults walked: together again, up the path and back towards our homes.

Since I was now working part time it wouldn't really have been possible for me to take up any of those big international offers that had come my way after Bleunet, even if I had wanted to. But I still didn't. My feelings were telling me: Stay at home – look after your own Interior. So what I did, was collaborate with Simon on the sort of project I would usually have left to him. Actually, it was a bit bigger than that – a domestic space in Hampstead that the clients wanted made over with absolutely the most sumptuous materials: mahogany, rosewood, cashmere, silk. Their house was to be a lulling, but also luxurious, sensory cocoon.

But my main concern was of course to focus on properly reconnecting with Jem. The keynote, I thought, was 'gently gently'. No Marion-style alluring outfits and candlelit dinners. Just lots and lots of quality time together. Cooking, going for walks, watching telly, holding hands. And when it came to going to bed, lots of tenderness and cuddles. Our bed, I should say, has a bit of the look of a yacht about it. It is made of fibreglass with reclaimed masts where you would expect the posts of a four-poster to be. They are connected by nautical wire and the curtains are of pale gauze – not sails, exactly, but still billowy and light. Instead of being docked against the wall, where beds are usually placed, the 'Wind-Bed' is situated in the centre of the room, at a slight angle. So, that is where we lay, and as we drifted off to sleep, I came to feel more and more sure that now, again, we were travelling on the voyage of life together.

## c. Progress

I did get to see Jem's Figurines – or 'Figs', as he called them: and what they were like, is this. Blobs. Humanoid, with grooved legs and the neck of the pot broadening into something like a head. Some were naked, with a yellowish sheen. Others were covered in a brightly coloured, patterned glaze with a nobbly surface like something knitted. They were bulbous! There were hugely pregnant tummies and balloon breasts and great inflated hips. Some had more than hunchback shoulders, some were all-over bulges and sags of flesh. All of them were women – or rather, I mean, not women exactly, but all of them were feminine. Each Blob had a little hole in it – in the top of the head, or the mouth, or a shoulder or a breast or a hip or a knee. I saw that this hole was designed to take a single flower. The idea – or at least, the interpretation I came up with, and I put to Jem, and he agreed with – was that the flower stood for Beauty, and the different positions it could be in showed that beauty can appear through literally any bit of you, from the top of your hair to the tip of your toes.

This was a completely new style of work for him – and what was new about it was that previously, in his pottery, he hadn't been at all interested in portraying people. It had all been about the Clay, about the shapes that emerged through it. If ever there *were* people, they were always being swamped – like in the green pot with the flailing legs and arms that drew me to him in the first place.

'They're rather wonderful,' I said. 'They're all, they're very womanly.' A lamp was angled to shine on the Figurines which were lined up in front of us, gleaming in a way that was kind of beautiful but also somehow a bit off-putting.

'Yes.'

'Why this nobbly surface?' I reached out and took one of the brightly patterned ones and ran my thumb over the bumps.

'Just feels good. Don't you think? Resistant . . .'

'Is it like the Staffordshire things you've seen in these trips you've been going on? Have they got these bright colours?'

'Maybe sort of. It's more just instinct. I'm not trying to copy anything.'

Standing there in the shadows, looking at these lit-up, shining lumps of clay, I began to have the bubbling beginnings of a seriously happy feeling. As you know I have always greatly admired Jem's work. But it always felt a bit separate from Us – a bit distant from the life of the family. It was all so abstract – all about Nature and Growth and Impersonal Forces. But now, quite spontaneously, without me suggesting it at all, Jem had started making these lovely, interesting pieces which had to do with People. Or really, actually, what I thought was that they must in some way have to do with Me. Because, as I saw it, they were obviously – though I didn't say this to him – Variations on a Theme of Pregnancy. I could see that the feelings coming through in the pots were not uncomplicated. They were not at all straightforwardly flattering. But still, basically, the important point was, that in his silent way – perhaps even without realising that that was what he was doing – Jem had finally taken me as his Muse.

Not long after I finished in Paris, Carla had suggested it might be fun for me or perhaps all of us to accompany Jem on one of these trips he had started taking – maybe even find out where he was going and surprise him. But I hadn't wanted to. They were very much his thing; and anyway, I was preoccupied with working through the new ideas Bleunet had given me. But now I had seen what the Figurines were all about I began to feel differently. When, a few days later, Jem told me he was going to Oxford, to see the Chinese figures in the museum there, and also their collection of English ceramics, I said: 'Why don't Poppy and me come too?'

'I was going to stay the night at Jacob's. You know, in the Cotswolds. He can't cope with all of us.' Jacob was a potter – and apparently rather a recluse.

'Do you have to?'

'It's been arranged. I want to look at some work he's been doing.'

'That doesn't matter: Poppy and I will just come along for the day and come back here, and you can go on to Jacob's.'

'It's work, Leez. I've got to study these ceramics.'

'We'll find things to do.'

'I'm just not sure it's such a good idea.'

'Why not?'

'It's a lot of travelling . . .'

'Rubbish. Let's do it. It'll be nice. A spontaneous family outing.'

When we got to Oxford it turned out that Poppy didn't really want us to stay very long with Jem in the museum. Partly it was the 'Museum' aura – the echoey high ceilings, the still exhibits, people's slow walks: none of that is very enticing for a child! But also, I think, she sensed that Jem didn't really want us to be there either. And the fact is, I sensed it too. When we found the English pottery room – dusty display cases filled with plates, cups and saucers, teapots and the statuettes which Jem had specially come to see – he took on that 'alert' look which went along with his new excitement about the Figurines. It was like Poppy and I had disappeared. He roamed the room, totally focused on the exhibits. He knelt for a while in front of one of them, then sat down cross-legged on the floor and pulled out his sketchbook from his bag. Poppy and I looked around for things to interest us. One surprising exhibit was a sort of box made of heavy-looking pottery, glazed in milk-chocolate brown and dotted with spots of cream. It seemed to be a little cradle for a doll. Three hundred years old! The bed bit was like a lidless coffin, but with a hood like a pram, and poised on rockers. Gargoyle faces poked out from the sides, and the hood was being ridden by a little manic figure fiddling at a violin. It seemed calm on the inside, but hectic on the outside, wild and full of vim. What it made me think of, was Life going very fast, the baby growing, the toddler toddling headlong . . .

But that wasn't enough to keep us there. We said we'd better go.

'Yeh, I'll be here for hours.'

'Hours? What about lunch?'

'Leez, I think I'm going to have to skip lunch.'

'But it's our family day out.'

'I've got work to do. It's a work trip.'

'Jem . . .' But I bit off what I had been going to say. Suddenly I was full of anger but I didn't want to snap with Poppy there. Actually, I didn't want to snap full stop. I didn't want to break the new happy spell that it seeemed to me we were mainly under. So I just said something like: 'OK, we'll go.'

We whisked off through the other rooms. I was baffled at Jem: what did he think the point of the whole day was? But then I told myself he was focused on his work, as dedicated to it as I was – or had been – to mine. I knew what it was to be hooked by an idea and have the bit between your teeth. Maybe I had rather piled into his work time without properly thinking it through. With a sort of great settling-down of feeling I became aware of Poppy's little hand in mine, and I realised that what this day was turning out to be, was a special day with just her. She went ahead through the spin doors while I struggled with the folded-up pushchair – and then we were both outside; a gust of wind slapped us in the face and pulled our hair. Poppy was skipping, and soon she was pointing: 'Look! Look!'

There was a really quite extraordinary number of buses. Left, up to some traffic lights, and right as far as I could see, the road was full of them. It was as if they were on parade, or were trying to be a train or a terrace of houses. It was surreal. Around us there were ancient tranquil honey-coloured buildings. In front of us we could see the upper floors of some big hotel, Victorian Gothic like a fairy castle. And in front of *it* barring the way, these bright red blocks of public transport rumbling and vibrating, darkening the air and putting a sour, powdery feeling in our mouths.

Eventually we managed to get through. Then we were pushing along, through oddly empty streets, past churches and colleges and shops in little Georgian houses. Soon we were by the river, on a gravelly path, a damp, shimmering bank of grass to the side of us, and arching, multicoloured trees above. I put my coat down as a blanket for us and we sat side by side, munching.

'Look at the ducks,' I said, 'look at that funny one that's partly white.' I threw them some bread from my sandwich.

Poppy said: 'Why was he lying on the ground?'

'Why was who lying on the ground?'

'The boy. The sailor boy.' I realised Poppy was asking about one of the paintings we had rushed past in the museum.

'The boy lying on the grass, with a stone there – the one who was dressed in blue?'

'Yes.'

'Well . . . His mummy and daddy had gone away. He was missing them.'

'Where had they gone?'

'Oh. They were having a rest. They had just left him by himself for a bit – and he got sad.'

'At Doris's Daddy has a rest.'

'Does he?'

'We watch a video and Daddy has a rest.'

But she had become intent on the leaves that were falling from high up, slanting and swivelling down. Since the picnic was pretty much finished I let her run to try to catch them. As she ran she turned into a leaf herself, in her yellow raincoat, tumbling and dashing with sudden bursts of speed. I joined her, and we both jumped here and there, screeching, as the leaves came slowly, alluringly down, only to twitch and zoom away at the last minute, out of our grasp.

Jem must have rung to say that he was done, because the next thing I remember is him lolloping towards us with his serious walk. 'Daddy! Daddy!' – Poppy called and trotted to him. He caught her up and swung her round in the classic way, and set her down. We walked along a great avenue of trees. Sunlight glittered on the damp grass. The sky was pale. High above, clouds sped across. He was silent.

'Get everything done?'

'Yes, interesting. Very. Sorry I got so absorbed.'

''S OK. Poppy and me had a nice picnic. Didn't we Poppy?' I took Jem's hand and smiled up at him. It occurred to me he didn't often say sorry. For a moment, resentment flowered inside me. Then! I remembered: Us. Family. Repair. I 'got with the programme' again and swung my hand, swinging his hand along with it.

'You know,' said Jem, 'I think I'll come home with you.'

'You don't need to do that.'

'Jacob rang and – he's got a bit of a cold. Seems like today's not the day.'

'Well' – I squeezed his hand – 'good. It's nice. You can always go another time.'

177

## d. In the Master Bedroom and Ensuite

In Allsop Road, we are lucky enough to have been able to give over a whole floor to our Bedroom, Bathroom and Dressing-Room area. If you have the space for it, I do recommend this solution. It helps you to feel that, during the physical and mental rituals of preparing for sleep (or waking up) and, crucially, during the special transformative time of sleep, you are literally on a different level from your daytime life – and from any other people in the house. This situation is very relaxing.

For me, the Ensuite is a specially spiritual location. Whereas the Downstairs Convenience creates an opportunity for meditation in the midst of your everyday commitments, the Ensuite is all about moving you to a different state of consciousness. Did you know that the word 'ensuite' itself comes from the French for 'next' or 'following'? Well, there you go. I share the Roman Emperor Augustus's view that, each evening, you should take a 'time out' to look back on the day, learn from its experiences, and prepare yourself to fall under the regenerative spell of sleep. For me, the Ensuite is the location *par excellence* where this should happen.

The space's basic 'Function' is, of course, washing. But, when you wash your face or your body, don't you sense that the cleansing process also affects your mind? A properly designed Ensuite can help you to clear the irritants of the day, not only out of your pores, but your brain cells. It prepares your body for the touch of clean sheets (and, perhaps, of your partner!) – and it prepares your mind for sleep's magical embrace.

The floor of my Ensuite is paved with flat, wide pebbles – which are suitable because they have achieved their smooth, calmative form by being *washed* by the sea. The toilet, basin and bath are all in the shape of rocks that look as if the sea has hollowed them. At the time I had to have them specially created out of concrete but I now see that similar, though less distinctive pieces, are being manufactured by Alessi. I have chosen not to install a bath, and the shower has a very basic look – the sort of thing you might find at a beach – except that this primitive exterior conceals a cutting-edge power-shower system. The walls are tiled, but only to the height that is at risk of splashing, i.e., ceiling height around the shower, shoulder height around the basin, waist height elsewhere. The tiles are grey, to match the pebbles. Above them, the paintwork is the soft whitish-grey of the clouds which typify the English summer by the sea. The paint brightens as it rises towards the ceiling, which is tinged with blue. This effect leads the mind upwards, into calm.

But the *tour de force* of my Ensuite is the 'Peace Place'. In physical terms, it is really very simple. A slab of rock, about knee height, with a smooth, undulating surface, just wide enough to sit on cross-legged. But the value of the Peace Place is all to do with how it is used. Each day, both evening and morning, before and after sleep, I spend at least a moment on the Peace Place, breathing deeply. I feel the effect of mask or toner or moisturiser on my face, and I transfer the influence of those beneficial products to my mind.

So there I was on the Peace Place after our 'family day out', cleansed, exfoliated and moisturised, thinking. Or rather, not so much thinking, as bringing thoughts and feelings into my mind, distancing myself from them, looking at them carefully from this new perspective, and – sending them away! I began with my irritation that Jem had gone off to work in his Studio – again – rather than coming up to bed with me. I reflected that we were not much past the beginning of our 'Healing Process', and that I shouldn't expect our problems to disappear all at once. There were always going to be glitches. I reminded myself that he was after all a creative, and that creatives had to be obsessive. I was, after all!

I pressed my fingers on to the pressure points on either side of my head. I moved them around the orbits of my eyes. I flattened my hands and fluttered them over the rest of my face. I dragged my fingertips down to the tip of my chin and imagined them drawing my anxiety with them, away from my brain and forehead and out into the air.

I saw the hunch of Jem's shoulders as he got down to work in the English pottery room in the museum. I saw his odd slow step as he came towards us, as if he was walking into a wind. I remembered, or rather sensed again, his tone of embarrassment when he said he was not going on to Jacob's. Perhaps there was more to that than he had let on? Perhaps they had had a quarrel or something? I breathed deeply, in and out, in and out, and stretched my back like a flower unfolding in the dawn. How odd that he needed to have a rest at Doris's. He wasn't that old. Forty-eight. I didn't like the sound of poor Poppy being dumped in front of a video. And it was odd – it was so different from what Jem seemed to stand for in terms of childcare – hands on, interactive, natural . . . But then the children can just get too much sometimes. Maybe Jem and Marion needed a 'time out', a quiet cup of coffee. Maybe Poppy hadn't properly understood. I stretched my arms out on either side of me and imagined myself floating – in the sea and then like a dove on a current of air. I imagined myself swooping and soaring in the high, cold atmosphere, the far horizon all around. With nothing in my head but lightness and calm, I descended from the Peace Place – and went through to the Bedroom.

In a bedroom, you sleep. You may also read there, get dressed or undressed and (*very* importantly) make love. Even so, sleep is the primary function.

- But what is sleep?

180

When you sleep, you are still. But you are also in motion. Your body is quiet. But your mind is very busy. All your hopes and fears, your anxieties, your longings, all these jump up and run around inside your head. Doors open to the future and the past, and time flows through you, back and forth like a tide, only faster. Going to sleep is, in a profound sense, a liquid experience. In Design terms, this means that strong linkage between the Ensuite and the Bedroom is crucial.

A simple way of creating this continuity is with harmonising paint tones. But in Allsop Road I have found a different solution. Just next to the Peace Place there is a tiny, silver-plated tap, and a small, rock-like basin. From the basin a little canal, lined in polished aluminium, runs along the side of the bathroom at waist height. This is the 'Conduit of Calm'. It penetrates through the wall that separates the bathroom from the bedroom, and continues on. In the bedroom, the Conduit is sunk into a thick shelf. Between it and the wall are displayed a selection of Jem's pots. This is the only decorative element in the room. It works wonderfully. The visual effect is simple, yet striking. The reflection of the pots in the water hints at the 'mirror world' of dreams. And, most importantly, it brings *just enough* liquid into the bedroom, establishing the connection between Bedroom and Ensuite in an unmissable yet subtle way. Of course the 'Breeze Bed' couldn't actually set off along it: the Conduit is much, much too small. But the suggestion is there – and suggestion is what matters. Especially when it comes to dreams.

I got into my pyjamas and wriggled my way under the duvet. I stretched out on the firm but yielding mattress. I felt the pillow gather round my ears. This is always a dangerous moment. However Calm I have become in the Peace Place, it is at this stage of actually getting into bed that worrying thoughts can come to life. The embrace of the sheets made me think of the big hugs

181

Jem had always used to give me, and which he hadn't done so much lately, even after our decision to 'try harder'. I stretched an arm across to where he should have been in the bed beside me – but wasn't, again, despite all the efforts I had made. I turned in the bed, turned again. The tension in me would not let me sleep. I got up, went over to one of the high, twin windows and pulled the curtain a little so I could see out. The houses opposite stared back at me. The road and pavement shone with their orange alien glow. Above, clouds moved across the moon, making the sky around them change from black to blue. I breathed in, felt my chest rise, and out. I walked back through to the Ensuite. Put the lighting on low. Settled on to the Peace Place once more. After a while my pulse and my mind grew calm. Tiredness came, and I returned to bed.

Now images from the day came through my mind. The brown pottery cradle rocking wildly. The leaves falling and flitting away . . .

I have given so much space to describing my Bedroom and Ensuite, and Me in them, because I do strongly feel that I have got them *right*. (The Dressing-Room area, by the way, has a very simple design: wardrobes along each wall, a floor-length mirror, a central banquette, neutral tones, nice proportions – it is not worth analysing for readers who are as familiar with good design principles as you all now should be!) And also, because I now think of them – not for entirely happy reasons – as being a specially *me* Interior.

This book began with a vision of Life-as-Hallway. Well, now, I am sorry to say, it seems to me that for four or five years of my life, until just recently, I was living, mentally, in the Bedroom and Ensuite. I was a woman asleep. Everything seemed quiet and stable. There were changes, of course. The arrival of Poppy, and Carla. The Bleunet project, and other developments in my career. These were like happy dreams. And there were Jem's grouches and our big, big row. They were like nightmares only, really, in retrospect *not too bad* – because they passed. There is a poem I remember from school, 'The Lady of the Shallots', which has a beautiful lady lying in a boat, just drifting through her life, singing. I suppose the shallots must have been growing by the river bank. That is what I was like. I thought that I could make a happy life with my Designs – for my clients, and above all for my Family. But all the time, Life was flowing away beneath me.

Until, one midnight, I awoke.

I had been out late (for once) at a work thing. When I got home, the house was quiet. I did what I still liked to do occasionally at night, even though of course I wasn't doing it so much during the day: I went into my Home Office and looked through the web-cams' infrared eyes. I did it for security reasons. But I also just found it very relaxing to be looking at the empty rooms and my family sleeping.

There was the Transformation Play-Space. Light came in through the French windows. Toys scattered on the floor cast odd shadows. In the corner, the Mini-Maisonette was dark. There was the Kitchen, the units seeming tall on the grey screen, the table-top shining. There was the hall, the staircase rising. There was our bedroom. No Jem – but that was not so very surprising these days. I felt a familiar flatness in my heart.

I had saved the best to last. Poppy's room. Not the same room that I described to you in ch. 5. Or rather – the same Space, but a totally different Design. Children's rooms have to develop along with their occupants. She had been going through a Beatrix Potter phase lately – so I had done her a pond-style look with blue carpet and a big green lily pad for a bed. How I loved watching her there, in the excitement of her sleep. Children are such energetic sleepers! She would curl like a koala then suddenly throw her arms out wide like an owl taking off, then do a karate kick, then roll like a pebble in a wave. I clicked on her camera. Stilled myself in my chair. Felt the tenderness rise in my chest and my eyes. There she was, a darker patch in the grey contours of the image. All still, so still.

Too still. She hadn't moved. She wasn't moving. I rose, my heart was battering, I ran up one flight, another, through the door to the bed. She wasn't there. There was a pillow there under the covers, not her. She wasn't there. I was swaying, floundering. For some reason I went to the window, ripped at the blind, looked down. I came hurtling back, and up more stairs: I called out 'Carla!', battered at her door, went in and screamed at her that Poppy wasn't there. She stirred, looked up, switched the light on. I remember her pale face, her blinking eyes.

Then I was off again, tumbling down the staircase. I slipped, I kicked off my heels, I set off again, down, down to the kitchen and the playroom, searching for the keys, finding the keys, fumbling for the right one, getting the door open, going out across the courtyard, hacking at Jem's studio door. I yelled his name, 'Jem, Jem'. My voice was wild, like a gull's. I banged again, again. There were keys somewhere inside. I didn't know where the keys would be. There were loose bricks by the kiln. I picked up a brick. I hurled the brick at a window. It bounced off the narrow frame. I picked up the brick again. I remember it rough against my fingers. I brought it close to the window pane and smashed it through. I used it like a tool, clearing the shards of glass. I eased my head through. I could see nothing. I called out. The noise came back into my face, loud. My eyes could see better in the darkness now and I could see that there was nobody there. Nobody there. I pulled my head back. I hit the back of my head against the frame, bounced my cheek into a jag of glass, which cut it. My head was back out in the open air and I was standing there, in my dress, trembling, my mouth wobbling, moaning. There was Carla coming towards me.

'They're gone,' I said. And again, quietly: 'They're gone.' And again, screaming: 'They're gone.' She reached for me, one hand on each of my upper arms. At her touch I began to cry. I looked at her as though she knew the answer. I remember her eyes looking into mine, seriously. She said: 'Stan. We must ask Stan.'

I was running. It didn't occur to me to try to phone. I was up the stairs and out of the door and along the street. The street was quiet. Big. There were parked cars. Little saplings growing behind wire. It was taking a long time to run along it. I could hear Carla's feet behind me. Here was the High Street. I ran out. A car braked, shunted forward. I skipped sideways, waving my hands like someone guiding a plane on a runway. I was running along the High Street. Went right, into their road, with its big trees, burly trunks. Streetlights between the trees making cones of light. I stopped. I bent over, hands on my knees. I breathed in and out. I stood up and strode up their path and banged on the door. No answer. No movement. The hall light was on. I banged again. Again. Carla was there beside me, crouching in the little patch of front garden. She was getting a handful of earth and stones. She threw. Up, the little storm went to the first-floor bay window, where it clattered. She bent and threw again. I hammered again. Then the light went on. The curtain was pulled back. A head looked down. Stan's. It disappeared again. A moment later I could see a figure coming down the stairs. The door opened.

'They're gone,' I said.

Carla said: 'Jem and Poppy have disappeared.'

'Right,' Stan said. 'Come in.'

## Magic Mottoes

*None.*

# Letter to Alizia: Carla

I am sorry.

I am very, very sorry. I knew, and I could have said, and I did not. Well, to tell the truth, I did not know exactly, but I suspected. I had seen smiles, I had heard the words that were said on the phone. I looked, and I heard, and a little I suspected. And I did not say anything. I gave you a little nod maybe, a little nudge. But not enough, no absolutely not enough.

What is the reason?

When you leave for Paris and you do not embrace me, you just say 'See you, Carla' – that makes me upset. But then I think on it and I realise that you are English and the English do not embrace like the Italians, or at least not so often. And also I realise another thing which is that you do not want to think of going to Paris as really going away: you want to think of it as nothing out of the common. And so there is no need for a particular farewell. That is the English manner too, and I can understand it. You see, I made some progresses in my studies!

But, of Jem and you what do I understand? I hear him on the phone and I think he is talking to you and I go in afterwards and ask, 'How is Alizia today?' and he says it was not with you that he was speaking. I ask myself, what was it, exactly, that made me think that he spoke with you? I find that it was a brusqueness. I find that it was a tone of voice that if he was not using it to you, then it possibly was rude. That is funny, no? – that you can speak brusquely to someone to whom you are very close, and it is not rude. But it is true.

Another time, after Bleunet, I see Jem coming into the hall after one of his trips away. He stops and looks in the mirror and I remember that you have explained to me how people do this, how in a hallway there is a movement and also a pause. But this is different. He is examining himself. He opens his mouth for to see his teeth, and he raises his chin and turns it a little to left and right: he is looking at his collar and his neck. I am in the summit of the stairs, and when I see him I smile and say to myself: 'Aha, you have been naughty!' For a moment – is this monstruous? – I think it is funny. But then a wave of sadness envelops me and I feel very cold and tired: I think of you. In Milan my father has a mistress. He is a powerful man and so he has a mistress. My mother knows it. They do not talk about it, but she knows it. It is always there, in front of them. And for my mother it is very bad. She does not show it, but it is. For the woman it is humiliating. I do not want this to happen to you. I think it is better not to know. Or else to find out and for there to be an explosion, and then, after the explosion, for everything to become clear again.

So one day I say, like a joke, maybe you should be suspicious of these trips, maybe you should go along one day for to surprise him but you do not pay attention: you are thinking of something else.

Possibly I am wrong in every way. The English words, the English body language, sometimes I understand them, sometimes not.

And anyway it really is not my affair.

When you and Jem had quarrelled, when there was this big freeze between you, I thought you had found out. You were being

187

a strong woman, you were not putting up with it. That pleased me. I wanted to help you – but also it seemed that you did not want to be helped. You were very much doing your own things. Only in the middle of the night, when you came knocking at the door and rushing into my room, screaming, only then did I understand that it had not happened like that. I see you running down the stairs, I see you running into the courtyard and banging at the Studio that you had built for Jem, and hurting yourself on it. I come out to you and your face is so pale like a ghost and there is blood on it and I say we should ask Stan who is Jem's friend and suddenly you are gone. I come running after you with difficulty. Then my heart is full of sorrow for you, and pain. I am so sorry. I did not know that you would lose your child. There are no things worse than that. I could have done more, I should have told you. Maybe it would have prevented this. If I had been sure I could have told you. Even if I had not been sure I could have told you. I should have told you. I am sorry. Now, with Simon, all we want to do is help. Can you understand? Please try to understand.

I am sorry so much, so much.

With great affection,

Carla.

# 9. The Guest Bedroom

## a. Inside

'What have you done to yourself?'

I was in Stan and Marion's house, downstairs. I was standing in the Playroom/Marion's Workroom which was dark. Ahead of me was the kitchen, lit up. Stan was wetting a cloth at the tap. He was stretching up into a high cupboard. He was coming towards me with the cloth and a tube of something. Antiseptic.

'Sit down.' He reached for a chair in the shadows, pulled it towards me. I sat. He wiped at my neck and chin, and dabbed at my cheek. It stung. Carla was in the kitchen. She was in a pink fluffy dressing gown. Her short black hair was squashed to one side. She filled a glass of water and drank. Rinsed it, filled it again and brought it towards me. I shook my head.

Pain was coming from my feet and I looked down. My tights had torn and ripped away from under them, and had pulled back towards my ankles. The tops of my feet were bright in the light from the kitchen. My soles ached. My eyes were tired and I was about to cry. My head was empty. I was lost. I swayed a little . . .

Carla was beside me and her fingers touched my upper arm. 'Here,' she said again. I took the glass and was grateful for the cold water on my mouth and down my gullet into the middle of me. It helped me come back to myself.

'Do you know where they are?' I asked Stan, rather sharply.

'No . . .'

'He doesn't know,' I said to Carla.

Stan said: 'I don't know *where* they are but I think they must have gone to join Marion.'

I said: 'Marion?'

Carla was perched on the table in the kitchen. She was shining – all lit up. Stan had sunk to the floor here in the playroom next to me in the shadows. He was sitting with his back to the wall, his knees up in front of him, and his arms across them. He was looking straight ahead.

'Marion?! . . .'

'And Doris. Marion left here with Doris the day before yesterday. In the camper. I don't know where they've gone. Maybe Wales. Marion likes Wales, as you know . . .'

'Why Marion?'

'You don't know?'

'What?'

'Jem and Marion,' Stan said.

'Jem and Marion?'

I was on my feet again. I winced because the soles of my feet were so sore. For a moment I remember I wondered what I had stood up to do. Then I was rushing! I rushed through to the bright kitchen and stood in front of the sink, gripping the edge of the work surface, leaning forward into it. I didn't really feel sick: it was more that I felt as if I ought to feel sick. I took deep breaths, I let my head hang. I felt my hair flap forward around my eyes, and my earrings press into my skin. Tears felt as if they were sort of gathering in my cheeks but I swallowed and they went away. Carla was there behind me, touching my shoulder. I flinched from her.

Moved again. Got hold of a chair and dragged it to the edge of the kitchen where I could see Stan. Sat down.

He was grinning. I didn't understand why he was grinning.

I said: 'Marion was my good friend.'

He said: 'Isn't it surprising?'

I saw Marion in the Kuramata and my mouth opened in a sort of screech but without noise, it was like I had lost control of my mouth. It was like someone was twisting my tubes round inside and my mouth, which was the top of them, was sort of twitching and jerking. I remembered Marion swaying gracefully as she walked, I remembered Marion telling me how to get Jem back into my bed, I remembered Marion telling me about the importance of massage and physical contact and how my spirit was in every part of me that could feel, even my fingertips, even the calluses on my toes, even my hair, especially my hair, and reaching out and drawing her fingers through it, I twitched at the memory of that touch. I remembered Marion in the Kuramata.

I asked: 'How long has it been going on?'

'Oh' – his voice was airy, careless – 'on and off, apparently.' Carla had moved near me but I drew my arms in, made my body small. I hugged myself.

'It started' – now his voice was sort of sarcastic – 'apparently, when Marion was pregnant. Remember? When you and me were working together on the Funnel Office. We just threw them together.' I could hear that these were Marion's words. 'When a woman is pregnant, her body is very strange, very powerful. It is hungry, it needs nourishment, it needs pampering, it needs pleasure. In ways that I apparently could not supply.'

Now I was just listening. I wasn't feeling anything new. I was just simply registering the words.

'Then they stopped because they were making an effort for the sake of both families. Though I think even Marion can't have felt

191

much like it just after she had given birth. But then you see, later on, you took the fatal step of working in Paris. And what that showed was that, though you didn't know it in your conscious mind, at a deeper level you were driving Jem away from you, and driving them together. It meant that it was *meant*. When you came back they started going on those trips. Didn't you notice? How Marion's trips to investigate possible new knitwear outlets overlapped with Jem's? Not always, obviously – but enough. That was when I twigged.'

He kept on talking: 'Before that, things had been bad between me and Marion for quite a long time. I had thought she was up to something. But I didn't know what. And I didn't want to press. You know Marion – she's got this mystery about her. She's enigmatic. Part of it is that she's a sexual enigma. As a man, you never feel that you can trust her. It's attractive. And also, from the point of view of gender politics . . .'

Stan kept on talking but I wasn't listening. I was thinking about my Poppy. She was on a mattress in the middle of the camper van, in the dark, asleep. The van was bumping and lurching, it was being driven along small bendy up-and-down Welsh roads in the dark. Around it everything was black, there were looming slopes of hills, there was sleet falling, the ground was icy and muddy and my Poppy's pale little face was there in the middle of the van, bump-bumping up and down, being tipped from side to side. She is in her clothes still and her blonde wavy hair is sticking to her forehead, at least she is warm. In the front seats there are two big shadows, Jem and Marion. Marion of course is driving, they are coming to a corner, the wheel turns and the van swings round. Bump-bump: Poppy's little eyelashes move, and her head rolls and her hand reaches sleepily out in her sleep and touches – Doris who is sleeping there beside her. A nail is pushed into my stomach: she is my child! In my family! You can't make another family! You can't take her away!

I speak out loud: 'Do you know where they're going?'

Stan stopped whatever he was saying. He looked bewildered, he seemed to be having to remember what was happening: 'No. I said I didn't know. I'm guessing Wales but there are so many little places . . .'

'The phone! We can ring them! Where's the phone?'

'They won't pick up. Marion hasn't been picking up.'

'Try my phone,' said Carla.

I rang their numbers one after another: phones switched off, please try again later.

'OK, what we need to do. We need to think about what we need to do. What *sort* of place do you think they'll go to?'

Carla says: 'Maybe a hotel, maybe they rent a house.'

Stan says: 'Not Marion. It's more like they'd be camping.'

'In this weather?'

'It's what she likes . . .'

'Or a yurt, it's a yurt, isn't it, that's what they'll be going to, we get on the internet and find all the places with yurts, and then . . .'

'There are loads of places with yurts.'

'OK so what we need to do is . . .' but I am drifting off. I am trying to keep my mind on what we need to do, I am trying to make something to hold on to but I can't make the right thing, it is futile, I am slowing down. I speed up again: 'Call the police!'

'We can't call the police.'

And Carla said: 'I am not sure they could do very much. Poppy is with her father.'

'They can make sure they don't go out of the country.'

'They won't try to get out of the country.'

'They might. I need to know they can't. What if something happens to them? Missing persons they put a notice on the radio . . .'

Carla was saying: 'Oh Alizia, I don't . . .' but Stan talked over her: 'Alizia, I hear what you're saying but . . . I think it'd make things worse. Think of it from their point of view. They're with their children. I know Marion would be offended if I thought . . .'

I screamed: 'I don't care how Marion would feel! Marion was my best friend and she's been fucking my husband and now she's gone off with my child! I don't want her touching my child! I want my child back. Jem can fucking fuck off, that bastard, that . . . after . . . that hateful . . .' and then I was crying. Hunched over in my little dress. My arms wrapped around me. My arms cold. I remember the feel of me there. I was small. I was cold. With a twist in the middle of me, hurting. It was like there was a hole in the middle of me that went on and on, down and down. And the middle of me was so cold, the kind of cold that is so cold it burns! Carla came near me again. And I let her. I remember the softness of her against the top of my back, her cheek on the top of my head, her arms folding round my arms.

'Do you have a blanket, a shawl?' – I heard her say to Stan. I leaned back into her, lifted my head. I felt supported. Comforted. Stan brought a blanket. I remember feeling glad it was not a shawl of Marion's. Nothing to do with Marion.

Stan was saying: 'I just think it's very likely they'll get in touch. It's not a kidnapping.'

'They've got my Poppy.'

'Yeh, but Jem is her father. Marion and Doris are her friends. They'll get in touch, and then we'll work out what will happen. If it comes to divorce, there will be custody . . .'

'Have you frozen your account? Stopped credit cards?'

'No, I hadn't . . .'

'Do that, and I'll do the same. Jem needs my money.'

'Alizia . . .'

'I'll give them till tomorrow morning, and then I'll call the police. Now I've got to go.' I had come to the end of everything that needed to be said. 'Carla, can you call a taxi?' I had sort of come to the end of *words*. I looked around me. Shadows. Whitish walls and grey lino – such bleak colours for a Play-Space, I wonder why, it was because Marion wanted to think the space was still hers, no it was because she couldn't be bothered, there was her machine pushed into the corner, there's a touch of damp in the other corner, and over there through that door there is the Funnel Office, the Funnel Ex-Office, which is so warmly full of light. The space tipped, it veered away from me. No point to this Interior now. I shifted in my chair and wriggled my hand out from under the cocoon of blankets and found Carla's hand and gripped it. Then I let go of it and stood up and felt the pain from my feet again.

Carla said: 'You need some shoes.'

Stan said: 'I can get you some of . . .'

'I'm not going to put on Marion's shoes.'

'Mine'll be much . . . hang on.' Stan went to a cupboard in the corner and pulled out some wellington boots. 'Hang on, I'll just . . .' and he went out of the room and up the stairs. He came back with some thick socks, which I eased on, rough over my sore feet. I said to him we should be in touch tomorrow. In his boots that were much too big for me I hobbled up the stairs and out into the cold street with Carla. We waited until the taxi came. And then we were driven back home.

## b. In a Strange Place

I woke in a strange place. Above me the ceiling sloped up and then down. It was a soft white. Bright lines of sunlight came and went. I was warm, and I was lying down, and I watched the lines of sunlight come and go. There are the angles and the corners and the frames of the Veluxes which are permanent and there is this pattern of lines of light which is fleeting. There. Oh it has gone. When is the next one coming? There. It was cosy. Everything around me was white. Woozily I wondered: Am I in hospital?

I felt – apart from things. I felt high up. The light must have given me that feeling. No, it was the ceiling, of course – I was obviously in somebody's loft room. I lay there – and then I understood where I was. I was in our own Guest Bedroom which was now Carla's room. I turned my head. I hadn't been up here for ages. There was one of her Rubbish Chairs in the middle of the room. The perspex was greyish in the pale light. I could see that in the cavities pretty much everything that could rot had rotted: there was a squashed Pepsi can and a scrunched-up paper bag, and some cigarette ends, and, apart from that, just little smatterings and heaps of black. She hadn't done much to make the room her own. No rug or anything on the whitewashed floorboards. On the cupboard doors at the end some pencil sketches were blu-tacked up, and on the other vertical wall – I turned my head to see – Oh, sweet! – blown-up photographs of Ron Arad and Zaha Hadid. I must be lying on one of the 'Flex-Form' units from Citterio that I had chosen to furnish the Guest Bedroom. I am not usually hugely keen on 'off-the-peg' furniture but what you want in a Guest Bedroom is not to be too startling. My guests may be 'wowed' by the rest of the house, but what they want in their own temporary room is a bit of conceptual peace from the rather *me* stimulation in all the other rooms. They need to be able to simply be themselves.

But where was the other unit? There, behind me, pushed under one of the slopes of the ceiling. I turned and swung my legs out of the bed: ouch! – that was my feet touching the floor. Yes, Carla was there, snuggled up. I could just see her hair, and her little white nose with a bit of a pink flush on it, and her eyelashes, what long eyelashes she had. She had been so good to me yesterday. She had gone and got a bowl of warm water and some soap and cream and bathed my feet. I remembered the gentle grip of her fingers on my ankles, lifting each foot and placing it carefully in . . .

A wave of feeling hit me – a tidal wave! Or, that's not exactly right, but it was like someone had pressed a switch and the whole world had turned red. I was still thinking the same sort of things I had been thinking before, but louder, and faster, and with pain attached. The pictures that were in my mind were of Carla helping me out of the taxi, me waddling up the steps in Stan's big socks and boots. And then the two of us on the landing outside my bedroom, where I suddenly said no I didn't want to go in there. Carla kindly at once understood and so we processed laboriously up another flight to here. I shouted: 'Phones, we need to have all the phones here,' so down she went to gather them up while I sat miserably on the bed. She came back with the three of them – the home phone, my work phone, my mobile – and, as well, a little brown pot that she had found on Poppy's bedside table. There was a bit of paper rolled up in the neck of it which I took out. Jem's pencil scrawl: 'We had to get free.'

When I read it I had really been too tired to feel. But now? Hate – and terrible anxiety about Poppy. Yes, hate. It's odd, isn't it, how feelings can just flip over like that, and all the energy that went into loving someone can turn to hate. I had tried so hard. Here was a man I had looked up to, and adored, and helped, and nurtured. I had made a life for him, for us together. We had had a child. What a mix of feelings there had been – but all finally good ones, all of them with love underneath. Maybe I had done things wrong, maybe I hadn't been sensitive enough, maybe I had been a bit absent, maybe I had been inept. But all the time I had been trying. I had adapted myself to him. I had loved him – I had brought him

197

into the middle of my heart. And now he had simply got a dagger out and was stabbing and ripping at me from inside. 'Get free' – from what? What? He was just spitting at everything. And Marion was too. The two of them. The . . . they were so *conceited*. I saw them floating high up in a dark sky, and this great sneering cosmic laugh came echoing around me. And the way he was hurting me most was by taking my Poppy.

The stupid little pot was still there so I picked it up and smashed it and the shards went scattering across the floor. Carla stirred. She woke and looked at me for a bit, puzzled, then warm. Then suddenly she moved, lifted herself: 'Look out!' I began to say but her head had knocked against the slope of the ceiling. She slithered to the floor and sat there, wrapped in the duvet, leaning against the Flex-Form's base.

'Ouch.' She smiled a bright smile that was nearly a chuckle and rubbed her head.

'Are you all right?' – I said.

'Yes. Yes.' And then, serious: 'Are you?'

'No.' I got up and – ouch – hobbled over to where she was and lowered myself down beside her. 'Not at all.' We were shoulder to shoulder and I let my head droop to the side so it rested against the side of her head. We sat there for a bit like two sacks propped together.

She said: 'Have you checked the phones?'

I said: 'They're on, I'll check them in a minute.' I felt a sudden warmth towards her, almost a kind of joy. She was so young, and she was so kind to me. And I had been a mother to her, I had helped her. I asked: 'Have you been happy here?'

'Yes, I have been very happy.'

'But you don't want this.'

'What?'

'This – this fuck-up.'

'No.'

'You've been very kind,' I said.

'It is OK. You have been kind to me.'

After a bit more time spent sitting there she said: 'Breakfast. We both need a good breakfast. I will make it. You rest.'

She came back with breakfast and we ate. I checked the phones – all on, no new calls – and then I showered in the Family Bathroom. I made a raid on the Dressing Room for clothes but came back up to the Guest Bedroom – Carla's Room – to put them on. And then I called the police. It was the afternoon before they sent someone round. A woman officer in uniform with things hooked to her heavy belt and a cap which, when she sat (I offered her the Kuramata) she placed on her knees. Carla and I sat side by side on the Spiritual Landscape. I told her what had happened and I listened to her say that really there wasn't very much they could do, they could make a record and alert passport control but that really it didn't sound to her as if the child was at risk.

I found myself blurting out: 'He's just not a very responsible person.'

She said that of course I was worried but that really, in almost all cases like this, contact was re-established and then you're into arbitration, or the legal process. Oddly, it was comforting to listen to her, with her solid official voice, not thinking about me as an individual but just as a case. I don't mean she wasn't sympathetic but it was a sort of generalised sympathy – a ritual, that's right, that made you feel you were in a machine of suffering and there was nothing to do but wait until you got to the end of the mechanism – and popped out of it.

What was funny about those days was that I felt rather little actual grief and panic. The real sharp emotions came in waves, in ambushes, like the one I told you about just now. But the rest of the

199

time it was like bits of my brain were shut down, like something dangerous encased in concrete – like a nuclear reactor! There were bits of me that just were not working. Another odd thing was that these affected very ordinary activities like listening. Sometimes I simply tuned out of conversations and then I would come to and there would be Carla's bright face in front of me looking at me anxiously with wide eyes as if she was expecting an answer. All I would be able to say was: 'What?'

It is very hard to be told you have to 'just wait'. How do you do that? How can you *try* to do it? How can you try to do it well? What I found, was that I felt least completely terrible when I was up in the Guest Bedroom/Carla's Room. What I liked to do, or rather what I least hated doing, was just curling up on the Flex-Form unit, pulling the duvet over me and trying to make myself a blank. I would feel my heart beating, I would concentrate on my breathing, and I would focus my attention on the pain in my head. I would lie there, just doing that, in the shadowy, colourless cocoon: and then after a while I would wonder how much time had been got through. I would want to know how much waiting had been done. So I stuck my head out to see what the time was. Sometimes a lot of time had passed, and sometimes virtually none at all. I never knew which it was going to be.

A nice thing about the Guest Bedroom/Carla's Room was it was high up, and it was quiet up there. You could imagine you were in a listening station, like people in the Second World War. The phones kept on ringing but never with Jem's tone or Marion's or even with 'number unknown' so I just let them trill. Or else Carla answered. But the other thing was, you know how sounds from the street echo and get louder as you go up a house? Well I could hear everything, conversations, feet going along tap tap or shuffle shuffle on the pavement. There would be the growl of a car in the distance coming nearer, nearer, and I would wonder if it was a car with Poppy in it, sometimes I would just wonder flatly but sometimes – I don't know what made the difference – I would hope and hope and hope. The car would get nearer and nearer, and the hope would get stronger and stronger until I was filled to overflowing with hope, really about to burst so that the pressure of the hope was hurting in my ears – and then the car would go past. Simply go past, maybe wait at the top of the road, turn a corner and join the flow of other, uninteresting cars, and go into the distance and be lost. Or sometimes (this was the worst) the car would stop, and a door would open, and someone would get out, and then someone else, and the feet would walk along for a bit, and there I would be in my cocoon with my heart trying to hammer a way out of my chest and my tongue getting ready to yodel with joy, with joy, and my eyes seeing the red of red carpets and red streamers of happiness even though they were tightly squeezed shut, only then I would hear another door open, a front door, the door of another house, and the feet would go into that other door, into that other house, and be the feet of totally different people, nothing to do with me, and not come here at all.

As you know, the rest of the house was very carefully and distinctively designed. What I found very upsetting about that, now, was that all that Design projected a very strong identity. It had been designed, not just for Life (see ch. 2) but for *A* Life. It had been designed for particular people. What that Life was, and who those people were, was *Our* Life, Jem's and Poppy's and mine. Which wasn't going to happen any more. All those rooms were full of hope – and all that special hope had been trampled and crushed. So, on the whole, I found it rather hard to be in those rooms, because of what they said to me. But the Guest Bedroom/Carla's Room was different. It was a blank. Of course it had a bit of Carla added to it – but added in a temporary way. And that was comforting. Because it somehow made the change that was happening to me seem not so catastrophic. Carla had come here and 'put down sticks' and been happy. She could quite easily 'pick up sticks' and be gone. I didn't want anybody to be gone from my house, Poppy was definitely going to come back, I was going to fight and kick and scratch and scream until that happened. But maybe Jem wouldn't come back. And maybe I would be able to manage to get used to that.

So I spent many hours each day in Carla's room, curled up. At night she would wriggle in beside me and put her arms around me. To begin with the hurt and the pain would harden into a sort of cannonball inside me. Then they dissolved out through her body and I slept.

I think it was the second evening when Simon turned up. Carla just said: 'Simon is coming to cook this evening. He has been so anxious. Is it OK?' I suppose I should have been touched and, looking back, I am grateful for his concern. But I was so beaten down then, so smashed, that it really didn't matter to me either way. When I went down to the kitchen in the evening he came towards me with his round face full of warmth and sympathy. He put a hand on either side of my shoulders and looked into me. 'How are you,' he asked, and then: 'That bastard! Have a drink.' I felt surprised: this was more assertive than the Simon I knew. I took the glass of red he held out to me. 'We're having steak. I know you don't usually like to eat much meat but I think, the way things are, steak would be best.' The words gushed out of him then his usual shy look came over him again: 'If that's all right?'

'Lovely.'

'Right. I have to cook.' He turned away and went to the work surface where paper bags of things were scattered. He tipped out garlic and mushrooms and unpacked a pot of cream. He gave his attention to the knives hanging up on their magnetic rack and after a moment chose one. Then he put it down and had a drink from his glass and turned back towards me.

'You really don't deserve it, Alizia, you of all the people.' A hand lifted towards me but then changed direction and held on to the table instead. He was looking into my eyes again, solemnly. 'Poppy *will* come back.'

I didn't know how to respond. How could he say those things? How could he say them out loud? I was so vulnerable and he was trying to be sympathetic but what it came out as was he was just jumping up and down on my bruises. He barely even knew Poppy. I had another drink from my glass.

'Here,' he said and filled it up again.

'Simon is right I am sure, I am so sure,' said Carla.

'Yup,' I said. 'I am sure that's right.' Obviously in fact I didn't feel sure at all. How could I possibly feel sure? How could anyone say that they were sure? All that was true was that nobody knew what was going to happen. I could hope, and that was it. Nobody could say anything that would make any difference. I sat and let the two of them bustle around me: the cutlery, the salad, the bread were all put on the table, the glasses were filled up again, and then the hot food came, and Simon and Carla sat down, and we all cut into it.

'Mmm it is delicious,' said Carla and I said so too, but I seemed not to be able to taste it. All I knew was that warm soft stuff was going in through my mouth and filling up my tummy. That was a nice feeling though. Solid.

Then Simon said: 'Poppy will be so fed up now, she'll be so missing her mummy, it's really terrible.'

'Carla!' – I yelped. I had to stop this. 'Your Rubbish Chairs, let's talk about your Rubbish Chairs.'

'Alizia . . .'

'And your wallpaper, Simon, it's so lovely, how are the orders going, are lots more coming in?'

'Alizia' – Simon was insisiting – 'don't.'

And Carla: 'We think maybe to talk is good.'

'It's good to talk.'

'It's not good to talk, what is there to talk about, shall we talk about Poppy starving in some coal mine? Shall we talk about Jem's cock? Shall we talk about how I'm completely crap? What shall we talk about? What? What's the point?' Then the sobs came. It was like a rubber ball was bouncing up and down inside me, hitting the top of my chest. I hiccupped and I yelped and tears squeezed out of my eyes. I felt an arm coming around my shoulder and I wriggled and shook my head and was still in the grip of this uncontrollable jolting and weeping. I heard Simon's voice say something, it said: 'Scream.' I opened my mouth and choked but then a sound came out, and stopped and then came again. I was like a singer trying out a note. 'Scream, let it all out, scream,' Simon was saying again. I gulped some air and tried to calm down but the scream came vomiting back out of me, scratching and scraping, it was a train, it was a hurricane, and I screamed again, and the heavy kitchen table wobbled for a moment and then – bang! – it was rocketed upwards by the scream and hit the ceiling where the impact made the Kuramata jump on the floor above so that it too was hooked up by the scream and shot out of the window, smash, and the dangling life tools swung to and fro, creaking, and then, bang, they were thrown up against the ceiling and the Spiritual Landscape went spinning out of the window and landed gently like a flying saucer in the garden next door and the grey-blue chaise longue went tumbling after, and I screamed and the coir matting in the sitting room was lifting, bulging upward, ballooning until – plink! – one of the nails came unstuck, then another then another until there was a little hailstorm noise of nails and – whoosh! – that was the matting out of the window where it wrapped around the chestnut tree which was already bending under the force of my scream, until a branch went and the ground was lifting and splinteringly the tree tipped over on to the roof of Jem's Studio which was crushed, and then I screamed and the scream seemed to float through the air, I was rising on the billows of it and the Master Bedroom and Ensuite were filled with the waves of my scream and the Peace Place wobbled and – crack! – the Conduit of Calm was dislodged and set afloat on my scream and the Breeze Bed lifted and bobbed and drifted away on it, and I screamed some more, and then I screamed some more, and then I coughed, and then I stopped screaming and I found that Simon's arm was across the front of my shoulders like a bar and Carla's arms were around my waist like a belt, and her head was on my knees. I jolted some more, and then I was just trembling, and then I was still. Simon's hand was smoothing my forehead which was cold and wet. I heard him say: 'Water,' and Carla rose and got some and I drank it, and then Simon had moved away, and it was Carla holding me, and I heard Simon say: 'You'd better put her to bed.' I seemed to be made of polystyrene but Carla had an arm around my waist and guided me upstairs and laid me down.

That was a peculiar experience! The next day Carla came to me with a very solemn face and gave me a little pink envelope. I opened it to find the letter I have put for you at the start of this chapter, in handwriting on pink paper. I read it and told her that that was all OK of course, there was no reason for her to blame herself. Inside me I felt nothing other than my usual pain. She said Simon was sorry, he hoped I didn't think he had taken a liberty, but they had both thought it might help. I said it was fine. Perhaps it did help a little, I don't know. Nothing actually happened to any of those bits of furniture, of course: after the scream they were all exactly where they had been before, not even a centimetre out of place. All that happened was that I was left completely exhausted – and with rather a sore throat. But on the other hand there did seem to have been all that stuff inside me wanting to get out. Maybe my attitude to all of it was what was shaken up by the hurricane, by the scream. I really don't know. But one thing I do know is that nothing could really have helped me during that truly terrible time. Nothing, that is, except . . .

## c. Happiness

One day everything changed. The bell jangled and I went down. The bell had rung before on other days and obviously there were other people it might be: delivery man, Jehovah's Witness . . . Still, I was tense, as I had been every time. When I reached the hall I paused, breathed deeply. Calm. I stepped forward and opened the door.

Marion, and beside her – oh there was Poppy, little Poppy, hurling herself in and hugging my legs. I hoisted her up, she was splayed across the front of me, her head in the crook of my neck. She was *here*!

It took no time for her to get across the threshold into my arms, but I remember the sight of her and Marion side by side on the step as if they were stood there for ages. Marion tall, her loose reddish curls falling over the collar of a thick coat which was open: jersey, jeans, wellington boots. Her pose was defiant. Her face was pink and there was a scattering of freckles across her nose. And next to her my Poppy with her lovely blonde hair which was all greasy and held back by a rubber band. She was in a blue denim smock which was too big for her: it must be Doris's. Her face is pale. It seems to reach out towards me. It is like liquid morphing towards me. And her eyes . . .

I forgot everything in our hug. The *whole world* was in my arms. She was there, the hardness of her, her bones, her muscles, clinging. Her breath stirred against my neck, there was the tart smell of her hair. Then I became aware of a voice speaking. Marion was saying: 'Can I come in?'

'No. No you can't.' I wanted her to – just vanish!

'Alizia, do try to be adult about this.'

I saw she had a bag of Poppy's in her hand. I said: 'Could you give me that bag.'

She said: 'Jem wanted me to say how sorry he is.'

I moved Poppy round so she was saddled on my hip. She pushed her face into the front of my shoulder. I whispered: 'Poppy darling. Would you go downstairs. To your Play-Space. Carla's there.' But in fact Carla was right behind me and she reached out her hands to Poppy and then caught her up in a hug. All my tenderness went after Poppy – like a hand on her shoulder, like a rope attached to her waist. I didn't want to let her go, even with Carla, even for a moment. But also I was full of anger, I had to speak to Marion. No, I had to shout at her. I turned back towards her and suddenly found that I was weak. My knees were wobbling and my heart trembled. She seemed to have power over me. But I made an effort. I looked into her face. The high, wide cheeks. The skin around the eyes, rather wrinkly and loose. The green speckled eyes themselves looking out at me smugly.

My body came together and I was able to say: 'He didn't have the guts to come himself?'

I was strong again. I was like sprung metal. If I let myself go I would be at her face.

'He's been going through a very difficult time. He's had to leave his home . . .'

'He did *not* have to leave *our home*.'

207

'Well, there are always going to be different points of view about that, aren't there?'

'If you have something essential to tell me, say it. If not, please go.'

'Poppy's a lovely girl. Jem adores her. But we're going to live such a different life from what she's used to. I know he has been the primary carer . . .'

'He has *not*.'

'And he knows you're going to find it difficult. But we both thought it would be best for her, and for you, if Poppy came back to live here, for the time being.'

'She's *my child*' – I hissed – 'of *course* she belongs with me. Who the fuck do you think you are, trying to tell me what's best for me or for my child. You abduct her. And you bring her back because her father can't cope when I'm not there to support him. I knew he wouldn't. Look at the state of her! It's not out of fucking consideration for me, or for her. It's for *you*. You deserve each other. He hasn't got a fucking clue about being a parent. He hasn't got a clue about caring for anyone other than himself. You suit him. Now go. Go.'

'Alizia, I know you're upset . . .'

I stepped back, I slammed the door. I turned. I reached out to touch the walls on either side. Behind me, the door was thick. I was inside. There was air here. In my ears, the echo of my shouting rang, and rang, and died away.

Poppy. Poppy was here. I ran back along the hall and skittered down the stairs and she was in my arms and I was turning, twirling with her in my arms, and then I was rocking from foot to foot, asking if she was all right, how she had been, if she wanted some milk, a biscuit, if she was really OK, how much I had missed her – though I could never really say how much I had missed her – how I would never never let her be taken away from me again. I smoothed my hands over her dirty hair and kissed her forehead and her cheeks and her fingers, and her head was there again in its specially designed resting place on my shoulder and her arms were around me and she was there, she was there, she was *totally* there.

## Magic Mottoes

Still none.

# Letter to Alizia: Marion

Dear Alizia,

Please read this – don't tear it up. Well, you can tear it up if you like, of course you can: only I really do think you should make sure you read it first. I am writing as your friend. I know you must find that hard to believe. But if I wasn't still in some sense your friend I wouldn't be writing this letter at all, and it is rather a difficult letter to write. I wouldn't be trying to help you.

I know you must hate me now. I don't blame you: it is inevitable. But that is the whole point, don't you see? Some things are meant to happen, there is no stopping them. But what I want to say to you is this: I did try to fight against it, even despite everything that I was feeling. I tried to stop the irresistible, all-penetrating tide. When Jem was so unhappy after the move to Allsop Road because you were hitting him with all these changes he simply wasn't ready for: I helped you then. And when you had that big row (of course I heard all about it) and he was saying to me let's just go. Can you imagine the difficulty of saying no when he was calling out to me and my whole being was calling back to him? But I did. Because of you. Because I knew how much you had put into your plan of your lovely house and husband and child, and I didn't want to hurt you. I didn't want to be the one who broke it up.

What is it about you, Alizia? You do try, I know you do. Maybe that's the problem. You try too hard, and so you tense up, and so when you try to sing you hit the wrong note. You need to relax. Look around you. Notice the trees budding and the beauty of the dew. Stop trying to change things. Tune in to other people's vibes.

I seem always to have felt a special connection to Jem. I am surprised you didn't notice it even from the beginning, even from that supper we had – do you remember – where I first properly saw the two of you together. Jem was sitting next to you and silently something in him was crying out to me, it was like there was a rhythm rocking back and forth between us, like we were floating down the Nile in two feluccas, being drawn out into the same salt sea. But I was with Stan, and Jem was Stan's good friend, and anyway in that period he was all caught up in his shiny dream of you. But, looking back, I can see that it was always more about *when*, than *if* – especially as you seemed so determined to throw us together. When you and Stan got obsessed with the Funnel Office Jem and I had so much time to share. I was pregnant and the life force was flowing through me. He was so tender, he was so respectful of the mystery of creation. He asked if he could touch my swelling womb and when he did it was like light was pulsing out of me through his hand and arm and then back into me more strongly through his eyes. It was like we were a parhelic halo, it was like he was shaping the creature that was growing inside me – Doris – and making her beautiful. There was no way we could prevent what happened then. It was raw. It was extraordinary. It made me go into labour. It was like the gates of nature had broken open and the tide of life was flooding through.

After that, everything and everyone conspired together, even you. If it hadn't been for Paris I don't know what would have happened. Because *of course* I was asking myself what I was doing. I felt bad for Stan – but the thing about him was that I knew that, deep down, he understood the nature of desire. I knew that, if it came to a break-up, he would be strong. But with you, I didn't know. It was like you were in a completely different world. With your projects and your enthusiasm and your relentless looking on the bright side. You lived in a world of gloss paint but Jem and I were in a world of lichen, a gloomy slow place where the touch of a finger on an arm, the bending of some soft hairs underneath it, the leaning-in of others to caress, where *that* might be more important than any success, more important than anything at all. I didn't know what would become of you if your shiny world was split apart. So I thought that Jem and I could live our earth lives in the shadows. Above us, everything would carry on. The bright god of Family would be honoured. And we would offer our secret rites to the dark god of Desire.

But you started delving down. You started to spend afternoons with him that previously he would have spent with me. What were you thinking? Didn't you know they were his safety valve, the vent that kept your whole happy life from being blown to pieces? Couldn't you sense it? You put a pressure on us that was very difficult to bear. But we did bear it. Or rather *I* bore it. I bore it for your sake.

When I gave way, it was because I saw that good might come to you as well as me. It was in Oxford. I was in a hotel, looking out of the window, waiting for Jem. I was looking at a splendid neoclassical building, built in honey stone with great pillars supporting a wide triangular pediment. It was giving me

212

a very strong feeling of order, of confinement. It was a museum, the same museum that you and Poppy came tumbling out of through its swing doors at that exact moment. Of course I knew you had insisted on coming with Jem so I recognised you at once: Poppy with her wobbling walk, veering to left and right, and you in your black coat and black bob, struggling to open the pushchair and then off after Poppy with your bouncing stride. I watched the two of you, just the two of you, in this strange place, without Jem. You held hands, Poppy started skipping, and then I saw you, Alizia, do a little skip too. Then you both stopped, startled, and looked up and down the street, as if you were fascinated by a traffic jam. My heart convulsed and I felt terrible but I felt wonderful too. I felt the shipwreck was going to come. But also I saw that you and Poppy would survive. You were so beautiful together, so spontaneous. You could be a proper mother to her. You would manage to become one if Jem wasn't there.

When he came up to me a few minutes later I told him it couldn't go on. I told him I wasn't going to spend that night with him, he had to go back, he had to make a clean breast of everything to you. I'm sorry he didn't, you didn't deserve for him not to. And I'm sorry he tried to bring Poppy with him when he left. It is never right to separate a mother from her child.

What I want to say to you is this. Hold on to what you have – what you can have – with Poppy. Love it. Love her, love every fleeting instant of her. I trust to what I saw out of that window, even despite all your going to Paris and your webcams and your keeping on forgetting to pick her up. Poppy will be just wonderful for you. If you open yourself to her. If you allow her to help you to connect.

213

Don't blame yourself about Jem. I really think you couldn't have held him, whatever you did. Jem simply needed more than you could give.

I don't know what the future will bring. What I have found with Jem is so powerful it sometimes scares me. But I do think what has happened can bring all of us to a higher level, including you, Alizia, if only you will let it, if only you will understand. It can help all of us to grow.

In friendship,
Marion.

# 10. The Dining Room

## a. Embracing Change

And she is still here, Poppy I mean: she is still here. Carla is here. And Simon is here much of the day as well. We have been doing such a lot of work. We are brimming with new ideas. And we have also been having quite a good time.

'Quite' – did you notice? Not a fabulous time, and not even a completely good one. I won't pretend that nothing bad has happened. I have been hurt. Poppy has been hurt. We haven't totally got over it. The interesting thing is, I don't think I ever actually want to totally get over it. I don't want to just cut it out and throw it away. I don't want to just remember the good times.

What happens is, you learn to live with the pain. Oh I agree it is not global catastrophe, it is not the Tsunami. But still it is pain, and it is there. But as the days go past and – importantly – as you *do* things, the pain gets muffled. You get to be able to sort of look at it and think about it. I won't say it is behind glass because you can still feel it. But it *is* like it is wrapped in see-through bandages.

So there it is, in a bit of your brain, wrapped up. Life goes on. And the pain is still there. They sort of talk to each other, the life and the pain. Perhaps that sounds a bit of a peculiar thing to say.

But what I mean is, everything interacts. The pain is there, and it is part of you, and the life that is going on is your life, and all of you contributes to it, including the pain.

Maybe I have matured – maybe that's it: I have matured like an expensive wine. No, actually, that's not it at all. It is simpler, and, at the same time, it is more complicated. I have just aged, aged like leather panels in a Venetian *camera d'oro*. I have been rubbed against and stained with smoke and scuffed. The panels don't get more beautiful because of that. It is just a different beauty. And it's the same with me. It's not that this terrible thunder cloud that has broken over me has turned out to be for the best after all. Just: I am in a different situation now. It has good aspects and bad, just like the situation I was in before did. Only different.

I have been trying to sum all this up in a new Magic Motto. But I can't seem to manage it. So let me tell you where I am and how I got here. And then maybe the Mottoes will start to come again.

## b. My Life: Continued

Jem did not get in touch. He did not write, he did not ring, he did not drop by – even though he was living just round the corner with Marion. Of course to begin with I was completely focused on Poppy. We had a lovely tender time, with lots of drawing and colouring and stories; lots of hugs; lots of walks in the park. We had tea-parties with her cuddly toys in the Family Play-Space. It was so nice to be with her as she settled back into all her usual little activities. And lovely, simply indescribably lovely, to see her snuggle down into her lily-pad bed and drift away to sleep.

But bit by bit the thought of Jem began to nag at me. He ought to – well, he ought to do *something*. Perhaps not apologise or explain, but at least he ought to want to see Poppy, to make some sort of arrangement. Obviously I wasn't feeling over fond of him at that precise moment, but I still knew it was important for Poppy to keep on having regular contact with both parents.

But also I wasn't sure I could cope with seeing him. The least that would happen would be that there would be a scene. And what would that do to me? I was feeling stronger, now that Poppy had come back to me. The nastiness of it all, the plain underhand nature of what Jem and Marion had done – that made a toughness inside me, it somehow helped me to keep going. But how real was that feeling of inner strength? If I saw him would it vanish – would I simply collapse? To begin with I didn't want to discover. But bit by bit a different feeling began to grow inside me. I began to think: Fuck it – we might as well find out.

After a week or so I decided Poppy was re-grounded enough to go back to nursery in the mornings – and that I was recovered enough to let her. Still, my heart shivered as she trotted off, even though the nursery was warm and bright and welcoming and all the people there were very sympathetic. Somehow that shiver brought with it the feeling that now was the time for a face-to-face. So when I walked out of the nursery gate I turned towards Marion's house, not mine.

A short walk. Slow steps. Deep breaths – but still my feelings were a storm! As I walked I tried to imagine what I would say. The door would open and which of them would it be? Whether it was Marion or . . . or Jem, I would just say the usual thing: 'Hello!' But after that – I simply did not know.

Here was their road. The long straight pavement and the tree-trunks, passing. Here was their house. I glanced up at the window and suddenly I was back in that night, with Carla throwing gravel and the glimpse of Stan's head, and everything I had discovered there came tumbling back on top of me. I stopped. I wobbled. I reached out to the gatepost to re-balance myself. And then I walked straight up the path to the front door.

I knocked. There were footsteps coming to the other side of the door. There was a pause, and then the footsteps went away. I waited, glanced down at the toe of my boot, which was tapping. I think I even smiled a little. Then the footsteps came back and the door opened. Marion.

She said: 'Alizia. How are you?'

I managed to be simply cold and nothing more than that. I said: 'Is Jem here?'

'I really can't tell you where he is.'

I stared at her. I tried not to tremble and I kept up what felt to me like a cold, cold stare. All I said was: 'Marion. Jem is my husband. I need to speak to him about arrangements for our child.' I said it in a quiet, slow voice.

She stood there with her arms spread out, her hands wedged one against each jamb. She was in a bulky orange jersey, her own creation: it made her look a bit like one of Jem's Figurines. They couldn't . . . oh my God that's what the Figs were! I glared at her: she glared back. I ducked and dashed, my shoulder caught the edge of her stomach, then I was past her. I paused for a moment at the stairs: up or down? Down: the answer came at once. I clattered down (a voice was echoing after me, 'Je-em') just slowing at the bottom as I turned. The Playroom . . . but there he was. He was sitting at the kitchen table. He was wearing a dressing gown I had not seen before. He was wearing slippers.

That was a peculiar moment! He was about four yards away from me. You would have thought I would want to attack him or strangle him or cry – and I am sure those impulses were in me somewhere, they must have been. But the odd thing was that what I mostly felt was here was someone I knew very well. I didn't feel like I was going to collapse – and I didn't feel I specially needed my new inner toughness either. It just seemed so very everyday. It was like hundreds, no thousands of times at supper, or breakfast, or sitting somewhere or other, or just walking along. There was Jem who was my husband. He was looking at me with a look I knew.

But also – and what I felt this mainly was, was not so much upsetting as just puzzling – he seemed to totally belong there in this other person's Interior – in this Interior that was not . . . I was about to write 'ours' but I suppose now the accurate word is 'mine'. He simply looked at home. At that nondescript table. Among those quite interesting but tatty '50s chairs with their bright pink cushioned seats and formica backs. With that everyday kitchen clutter around him. With those crumbs on his lip, and with that piece of toast and red jam in one hand. Above that cork-tiled floor.

I still hadn't found anything to say. But it turned out there was actually something more than puzzlement inside me, because what I said in the end was: 'You shit.'

'Alizia . . .'

'No, not Alizia, you. What have you got to say for yourself? Speak. Give me some words. Why do you think I'm here?'

'. . .'

'I'm here because of Poppy. Remember her? She is your daughter.'

'I know she is my . . .'

'Oh do you. That's funny because she turned up on my doorstep the other day. Not with you.'

'She was with . . .'

'I don't care who she was with it wasn't you. Do you know how long she was gone for? Five days. Five days and eighteen hours. You didn't contact me. You didn't contact me.'

I was beginning to cry, not because of him but because of the memory of that horrendous time. I was tensing my jaw, I was pushing my nails into the flesh of my thumb but it wasn't working

– but then a sound came from behind me: 'Alizia,' Marion was saying. I turned, and the tears stopped. I was tough again.

'Shut up,' I said.

'Alizia, try to stay calm, I know it's . . .'

'Shut up! Shut up!' She did. She took a step backwards. I turned back round to Jem. He was sitting on the edge of his seat now, his hands pressing down on his knees. He was rocking slightly.

'I have come here because you need to see your daughter. You should have got in touch but you have not and that is why I am here. I suggest that on Saturday afternoon you pick her up, and take her out somewhere to play, and bring her back before or after tea, as you wish. Do you agree?'

'Yup.'

'Good.'

'I left you a note.'

'Your note consisted of five words. If you were a human being I would have thought you might have more than that to say. But you don't have anything to say to me, do you?'

'Not really.'

'Not about the cruelty of kidnapping my child. Not about ten years of togetherness chucked away. But that's all right. I really don't care any more. I really don't. I've tried and tried, for ten whole years I've tried and the result is: nothing. You're just the same fucking selfish lump. Obviously I didn't know that when you asked me to marry you. But now I do. It's the one thing I thank you for. The only one.'

After that I simply said: 'Goodbye,' turned, and walked out. I didn't give Marion a glance. I didn't want her to think she deserved one.

So that was my scene. That was all I said to him. And to begin with I felt totally triumphant, when I was outside in the cold, striding along, my breath making dragon puffs. That was good, I

220

said to myself, you told him, you stayed quite dignified, not bad. You showed that fucking bitch of a fucking ex-friend too. Those two skunks they can squirt their own stink at each other and groom all they like those two fucking animals, oh, Marion can brush against his stinking balding greying hairs all she fucking likes . . .

I won't go on. It is peculiar, in a crisis like this, how words swirl and zoom around you, through you, uncontrollably, yelling themselves out just in your head most of the time – luckily – but sometimes out through your mouth as well. There are the words you speak on purpose, some of which you later wish you hadn't said. There are the words that, afterwards, you wish you *had* said. And then there is this pattering, nagging, swearing, shouting stream of words-in-the-head that surfaces, apparently, whenever it feels like it. It brings pictures with it too. For instance, I am not, let me assure you, someone with particularly voodoo tendences. But I have found myself, at the end of a pleasant evening spent maybe chatting with Carla and Simon, suddenly in a dark cave with two wax dolls of you-know-who laid out on the earth in front of me, illuminated by the flickering light of a fire. I sit cross-legged and chant and spit and then with a knitting needle I prod and I poke and I jab and I thrust and this glorious cackling gabbles through me, and then . . .

Oh, I don't want to write it. It just seems silly, written down.

Another strange thing was: the mood swings. For instance, right after making my speech to Jem I was, as I said, very 'up'. But then as I walked along and the minutes passed my legs seemed to weaken and my body sagged. The gush of words in my head slowed down – which was good – but what came instead was this terrible flat grey emptiness, a plain made of cardboard which stretched on and on. I struggled forward. Eventually I reached the steps of my house. I clambered up. The door slammed shut behind

221

me. I went through into the sitting room and sat down on the Kuramata, but at once I felt not worthy of the Kuramata and slithered to the floor. My Interior was all around me. But what was the point of it now? There was the Spiritual Landscape. It looked drab and cheap. The Kuramata was too aggressive and Jem's chaise longue was useless with no Jem to sit on it – and the colour-scheme of carefully selected complementary soft tones made me think of a heap of rags, a pile of rotting leaves. What good was the Peace Place now? And how could the Whiteness work any more when the energy of the home life around it was going to be so radically reduced? It was all no good. I just could not bring people together and make them love me. I could not hold on to anybody. Why not? What was wrong with me? What was wrong? This so-called 'Design for Life' had done absolutely zip to stop my life being ripped up and trampled in the mud. Pathetic. Just a fucking waste. Those dangling dumb life tools like four of Cristophe's ancient hams, like carcasses. My energy was up again: I jumped up and grabbed at one of the steel ropes and pulled and pulled. I wanted to tear it down. I wanted to pull the whole place down. I yanked it this way and that way and this way until it hurt my fingers: it was too strong for me. Now I was tired again. My arms ached. I sat some more. I calmed down. And then I became aware of the clock ticking. I saw the time, and I went to collect my Poppy.

Carla and Simon have been so supportive. I am very grateful to them. But really it is Poppy who has mainly got me through this difficult time. There have been all the hugs and cuddles, which have been very healing for us both. But also it has been helpful to me just to watch her. People think of children as being fragile, and in a sense of course they are. But also – they are indomitable. At least, Poppy is. She kept on playing, even though she was so sad about her daddy having deserted us. Something would catch her eye, she would be drawn to it and – kerching! – in a moment she would be totally absorbed. What is so charming, and also rather humbling, actually, is how she can conjure up anything, anything at all, just by using her imagination. Here is a piece of string but for Poppy it is a snake, no, it is a cup of tea, no, it is a dragon flying high up to its mountain lair. I am sure to some extent this is what all children do all the time. But Poppy did it so intensely, almost as if she was trying to work something out. Perhaps our hardest moment of all in this dark, dark period was when she came home from nursery and found her daddy's pottery materials were gone. Her little face wobbled when we were standing hand in hand and she saw the empty Studio. But something kept her brave. And what she did next was so sweet! She went and got some cuddlies and sat them around the place, on the worktops and on the shelves that she could reach. 'Their house now.' And when the plastic moulding of the Funnel Office ended up in our back courtyard because Marion and Jem had sold and moved to some hovel in Wales (they wanted their new baby to be born into the 'heart of nature') – as soon as Poppy saw it she ran inside and set about clambering up. I shouted to her to stop; but then I thought: Why not? Now I have filled the little circular floor space with cushions, and the Funnel Office has been re-imagined as an inside-out climbing-frame. Poppy pulls herself up on what were once the inset bookshelves, and slides down the sloping walls.

As I lived through this difficult but also beautiful time with Poppy, I realised my feelings about, well, I will just say 'Interiors', since you understand by now how much that word means to me – that my feelings about Interiors were shifting again. The Designs I had created were still all around us, but we were living in them in such a different way. Not only Jem's Studio and the Funnel Office/Climbing-Frame, but also Poppy's Bedroom, which I now slept in too, on a camp bed in the corner, and the old Master Bedroom and Ensuite, which I never went into except to find clothes, and the

Sitting Room, which had become very much a Poppy-and-me place where we did quiet things like reading stories and just chatting. I liked reclining on the Spiritual Landscape; Poppy liked Jem's old chaise longue – which I thought was fair enough, I didn't mind – and nobody ever much sat on the Kuramata: we had pushed it back against a wall. This was fine – except I started to feel how much better it would have been if I had created a more flexible Design in the first place. Because the fact is that any Interior is – at some stage – going to be used differently than the designer intended. Even my post-Bleunet ideas of rotating floors etc. now seemed too grandiose, too monumental. I began to dream of a new, low-key, pared-down and, above all, changeable style of Design with fewer fixtures and more moveable items. Fabrics would be centre-stage since they are easily adjustable. Everything would be low-cost, so it could if necessary be totally re-done. And the Interiors would where possible use recycled materials. Designing for Life (even including Death) is all very well. But what I hadn't realised when I came up with that ambitious Magic Motto all those years ago was quite what a shifting thing Life is. Interior Design may be the Makeover of Minds – but only up to a point. Minds still have the power to go their own way: and what a mess they sometimes make of it! Here, at last, is a new Magic Motto, no.13:

✓ Design For Life: Design For The Unexpected.

Bit by bit I shared these new feelings with Simon, and also with Carla. Ideas began to flower around us. Increasingly I came to feel that this new direction would be very difficult to reconcile with a continued attachment to IntArchitec.

So, when Fisher told me that in his opinion, and in the opinion of the Board, it was time for us to go our different ways, I really didn't mind that much at all. We sat for a while in his Sitting

Room/Inner Sanctum. I didn't argue: we barely even talked. By then I knew so well what he thought, and he must have known so well what I thought, that there wasn't any point. Actually he said as much. But what he also said, which I was grateful for, was this: 'I respect you, Alizia. I do think it will be rubbish, this new Adaptable Design you have been talking about. There is obviously no place for it at IntArchitec. But maybe you are the one who will be seen as right, in the judgement of history. That is what neither of us will ever know.'

He stood up solemnly and reached out his arm to shake my hand. I shook it, and turned, and walked carefully out; but then when I was out in the corridor what happened was that I grinned and grinned and skipped and twirled, and ran out happily on to the pavement where people were loitering and rushing and stopping and chatting and going wherever it might be to do . . . who knows?

IntArchitec has kept the copyright on what are really my trademarks: Home-is-Harmony and the Hints of Home-is-Harmony range. But perhaps that is for the best: a new name for a new beginning! Now we are the Alizia Tamé Design Collective. Myself and Carla – who has recently graduated – and, yes, Simon. I was so touched when he decided to take the leap after me. Sweetie that he is, he had been deeply offended by the approach Fisher made to him when I was off having my crisis: he was shocked that Fisher thought he might do anything so – as he saw it – treacherous as help to edge me out. Actually, I think he must always have felt a little at odds with IntArchitec, just as I had done: the truth is, I started my journey out of there (albeit slowly) pretty much as soon as I arrived. But now, the three of us, in Allsop Road: what ideas we have been having! There are our 'Cardboard Compacts', created (or rather, *re*-created) from compressed, recycled cardboard: individually, they can be used as stools or little tables; but groups of them can also clip together horizontally into a bench or vertically to form a storage unit and/or table. We have worked with scents (the air is an often-neglected part of any Interior), and with easily changeable chair covers (you get dressed in different clothes every morning – so why not dress your chairs?).

As time passed, we found we were getting increasingly irritated by:

• The Walls

So hard! so solid! so predictable! Of course, we have done what anyone would think of and designed a range of low-cost, exceptionally flexible screens. There is no shame, sometimes, in taking the obvious route. Then, more excitingly, we started to 'blend' the idea of Wall with the idea of Lighting. Lights, of course, are often used to change the feel of a space – and often they are mounted on Walls: spots, and up- or down-lighters. But why shouldn't the Wall simply *be* a light – in other words, be totally covered by a luminous screen which could change colour according to your mood? A lovely idea – only Simon pointed out that the environmental consequences could be devastating. 'What about blinds' – he said: 'Why do blinds only ever go on windows?' A couple of strokes of the pen, and he had sketched the blueprint for our 'Wall-Blind' system. Simply fit one of our units along the top of a wall that particularly oppresses you. Load it up with a selection of beautiful papers, even artworks; and you can draw down whichever combination of colours and textures appeals to you at any particular moment. This concept had the cheeky simplicity which is often the hallmark of design brilliance.

Of course, news of the formation of the Collective soon got out. Commissions started to crowd in, but what really pleased me was an invitation from my old college to show the students some of our new ideas. We decided on a performance that all of us would be involved in: a kind of mime to demonstrate the versatility of the 'Wall-Blind' system and the 'Chair Clothes', with 'Air-Shape' fragrances continually altering the atmosphere. The audience would sit on Cardboard Compacts and the event would be punctuated by 'Move Moments' when people would change places and the Compacts would be reconfigured. This was all very much Carla's baby – so let me hand the keyboard to her.

*First I think of Simon who is a little rotund in form. It is his duty to operate the 'Wall Blinds' and I decide he must bow with a flourish. For demonstrating the 'Clothes of the Furniture' we will be an ensemble: like the Wild West for the denim fabric, and very English, with our noses in the air, for the grey and pink tweed. I did not want to, but Alizia commands me, for the 'Air-Shapes', to perform a solo. For 'Peace-Place: Evening' I am slow, like a reverent religious. For 'Home Office Clarity' I am a woman of business, and for 'Morning Mist' I am wandering, with swimming arms. After six days, we are ready. We arrive at the door of the building and I am so excited. Students await us to help us prepare. Here is our stage: we set up the 'Wall Blinds', we position the still-naked chairs. We prepare our selves. The audience expects something truly special. And it is!*

It was lovely that we had such a success. I was filled with happiness by the sparkling faces of the students, and the long, long applause, and then the really interesting questions they asked, and the buzz of conversation as they drifted out along the corridors. Still, the real test of any concept must be how it works in practice. So we were lucky that Stan's unfortunate situation gave us the opportunity to dry-run our key concepts, even though I have to admit this came about in rather an awkward way.

227

You remember how comparatively together Stan had seemed when Jem and Poppy and Marion and Doris had gone missing? Well, when they all returned, and Marion told him, in no uncertain terms, to 'skedaddle', he got very upset. In fact, he literally went to pieces. For a while we put him up on the chaise longue, but even when he had moved into a bedsit he kept on coming back to Allsop Road – partly just for the company but also, at least this is what he said, because he found that revisiting the 'scene of the crime' was helpful to him. Actually, that wasn't quite the whole story – as I discovered when, one day, I came in to find him slumped on the Spiritual Landscape. His head was on the fabric, his hands were over his face, and his purple-framed glasses were resting on a nearby undulation. He was sobbing.

'Oh,' I said. 'Stan.' I didn't know what to do. I went over and knelt down: 'Stan, it's all right.' He just writhed and sobbed some more. After a while I felt uneasy so I said: 'I'll get a tissue,' and went out: when I got back he was at least sitting upright again. But the pain was still coming out of him in low groans. He was hugging himself and rocking to and fro.

'Here,' I said. I perched on a rise beside him.

He took the tissue and blew his nose noisily. In a friendly way I rested my hand on his shoulder.

'Stan you were brave that night. You really were. You helped me. I'm sure you can be brave again.'

There was a howl and then he had lunged and was nuzzling into my breasts, damply. I didn't know what to do, so I stroked his thinning hair. It was awkward . . . but I didn't want to seem cold!

'Oh Alizia, you are so wonderful.' He was nosing up under my chin. This made his voice sound gulpy. I could feel his mouth moving. 'Marion envied you. In a sense, you are the final cause of this whole predicament. I really admire you. And she knows that. Jealousy can really drive a woman. Jealousy of her husband's dreams.' He had lifted his head now. He was looking at me – no, looking into me. He was too close.

I got my hands on his shoulders and pushed him away.

'Stan,' I said. 'No. Come on. It's not right.' I stood up and moved to the Kuramata.

He apologised at once, but still, it did seem that it would be a good thing for all concerned if he got a little bit of help to build a new life for himself and move on. All things considered, it seemed best if we gave the lead role on this project to Simon.

*It was a really very sensitive situation. Stan was in a fragile condition and it was very wise of Alizia to let me 'front' the project. Obviously my own feelings were rather affected by what had happened. But I was also confident I would be able to keep myself under control.*

*At first it was rather tricky to get Stan to be at all helpful. He kept saying he just wanted a white box. I said couldn't he see that that was reminiscent of Alizia's Whiteness and didn't he realise that part of the whole point of what we were doing was to squash that inappropriate infatuation of his stone dead. Well, I didn't say that in exactly so many words, but nearly. But he said really it wasn't anything to do with that at all, he just wanted somewhere that was sort of nowhere; empty, and calm.*

*Very well then: we had to see what we could do. On balance, Carla and I agreed that it was OK to paint the bedsit white so long as it wasn't a pure white like in the Whiteness but rather a soft, organic 'off-white' with a brighter 'new white' on the ceiling to give a little bit of an 'uplifting' feel. For the floor: tatami mats. For sleeping, and sitting on: two single futons, one in a corner and the other against the wall opposite the window. The one in the corner was going to be for Doris so we marked it out by sticking a soft woollen fabric to the walls. This would be a lovely welcoming cue for her whenever she arrived for a visit. And when she was not* there, it would help Stan feel that that corner of his space still belonged to her. After a lot of discussion we also decided to give Doris's futon a 'flexible' touch. This was, that if ever Stan needed, it could be moved next to his futon and joined on to it with velcro strips – to make it possible for him to receive more 'adult' company in comfort. We had come to the conclusion that it was very important for him to keep this possibility alive.

For a practical low-level table-cum-desk we employed Cardboard Compacts that could be moved or disassembled as Stan wished, also providing practical storage. It was true he would have to get the hang of sitting and working cross-legged in the Japanese style, but we decided this would be no bad thing in terms of his flexibility and general fitness. To increase the vital element of 'reconfigurability' we installed one of our (actually, my) Wall-Blind Systems. This was very generously loaded up with all sorts of colours and designs including bright red for an emotional 'rush' and a blue arrow for when he needed to strengthen his sense of direction. Developing the same theme, we also installed 'moveable walls' which were actually big white cotton veils attached to the ceiling. If Stan wanted he could raise these for an open-plan look, and he could also lower them to form partitions. It is true the partioned spaces would be rather small, but then we were having to very literally cut Stan's coat (or actually floor-space) to suit his cloth. We also agreed that the more important factor was probably the visual point of view, with the veils giving a nomadic 'tent-like' aspect to the space. This would again emphasise the idea of moving on.

All of us in the Collective were very pleased with the finished Interior. It had a lovely distinctive look, as well as managing to make do (well, more than make do) with Stan's very limited space and budget. And, do you know what, he wasn't at all as ecstatic as I think he should have been. But then we reminded ourselves that

230

*he was probably upset that Alizia was not there (very sensibly, in my view) for the grand 'reveal'. Still, when you do something good, it gives you a good feeling. And I do believe that we, well, mainly Alizia really, have been much kinder to Stan than he had the right to expect.*

Actually, Stan *was* grateful. He emailed me a little video clip of himself reclining in his new draped space. What he said was: 'Thank you, Alizia. I feel I'm setting out over the empty desert. Who knows, maybe there is somebody new out there for me. Thank you, friend. That thing when I was in your house. It wasn't right. I was all poetic justice. I do think it's excusable: I was in a bad place. But all the same I didn't behave ethically. I forgot to respect you as a person. And that's bad. But now, I'm in a different narrative – don't worry. I'll think of you – as a wonderful friend!'

I forgave him, of course. But I still wasn't sure I quite trusted his view of things. Not even of himself! He did seem to be able to switch 'narratives' rather quickly. And actually we haven't really been in touch over the last few months. Partly, there is a feeling of embarrassment – whatever he says. But also, what would either of us talk about, except Jem and Marion? Or else, not talk about them . . . which would be even worse. But in a sense, this silence just shows that the Interior we created for him has been a success. We wanted to give him a space where he could feel like a valued, independent person again. And the fact that we haven't heard from him at all probably just shows that that is what we have done.

Anyway, one of the real joys of my life at the moment is watching the Interior of Allsop Road adapt itself more and more to our new working practices. As a Collective, we find we like to work, not just in my Home Office, but in all the different rooms of the house. Partly this is for practical reasons. When there are three of us tossing ideas to and fro, with different fabrics and mood

231

boards scattered around us, we need a lot of space. But also, we find that each room has something different to contribute to the creative process – and, by creating in dialogue with a Space, we come to see it differently. What this means – strangely – is that the concept of the Whole Life Space, which I developed with Jem (see ch. 4) has only really started to exist now he has left. I think the reason is that he and I created 'force-fields' which, while in many ways compatible, did have to be kept apart. He had his power base in Studio II, and I had mine in the Whiteness. However much we tried, all the other rooms ended up as a sort of no-man's-land between us. But, now he has gone, and has taken his force-field with him, I am able to feel much less defensive. There is a deep irony here. Together, we created a concept. But it is only now we are no longer '*we*', that that concept can become a reality. Magic Motto no. 14:

✓ *Sometimes, Things Happen In Mysterious Ways.*

## c. Reflective: In the Interior

Even more than the Master Bedroom and Ensuite, the space that has most resisted our new 'breakout' approach to living and working is

- The Dining Room

This is not a coincidence – because, in my view, the Dining Room is the least flexible of Interior locations. It is all about formality, slowness and ritual: people sit down in specific places at standard times and eat food which is divided into pre-arranged courses. Have you ever eaten your pudding before your main course? Can you even imagine doing that? See what I mean? See how *anti-change* the dining experience tends to be? Cristophe Bleunet was able to make something new out of this age-old formula – but he was quite clearly an exceptional talent, and in any case very sadly he has recently passed away.

The result of this permanent quality of the Dining Room is that nowadays rather few meals actually get eaten there – and many contemporary Interiors manage without a Dining Room at all. In my view this is rather a shame. I think the Dining Room is a challenge to today's high-speed lifestyles. But I also think it is a challenge we should try to embrace with both arms. Interior Design shouldn't just be comfortable. Magic Motto no. 2 – even when updated to create no. 13 – absolutely does not mean we should slavishly follow each and every lifestyle trend. Life in the full sense is sometimes stubborn, sometimes awkward, always not completely under our control. And the Dining Room embodies this 'bloody-minded' quality that Life tends to have. The Dining Room should be the Rock at the centre of any Interior – and also its Hard Place.

But I must tell you what my Dining Room is like.

The table is constructed from two nineteenth-century bathstone capitals recovered from a church, with a top made from matching stone. Nothing could be solider: the floor has had to be reinforced to take the weight. There can be no more rock-like table than this. The rest of the room complements the table. The chairs are Hepplewhites with vertical cattle-grid backs. They project age, geometry, and strength. Then there is the massy Ballard cabinet, and brass-look vertical tube radiators situated on either side of the window and of the double doors which connect the space to the Sitting Room: these reinforce the monumental feel. The walls are painted classic dark red, and above the fireplace there is a graphic Artwork by the sculptor Henry Moore. All this, as I said when I created it – and as I still think now – embodies the timeless principles of good Dining-Room design:

- Table: strong, with *no* wobbly gate legs or pull-out flaps.
- Chairs: old and, ideally, square and vertical in look (there are perfectly decent Edwardian examples if Hepplewhite or Georgian is out of your range).
- Other design cues: upright, classic.

Of course you can add lighter-hearted elements. But these should harmonise with the general feel: they should be more in the way of a grace-note than an Impish Touch. For instance – my own 'Zettel-Z' chandelier. This is light and papery – but it also keeps a lasting record of Life by way of the words that have been scribbled on to it.

Now I feel the full strength of the permanence that the Dining Room projects. It doesn't make me happy – but I do not want to do without it, any more than I want to forget everything that has happened. In a sense, every room in the house is a bit like this, or it has the potential to be: every room in the house connects me to my past. But the difference with the Dining Room is that it simply does not want to be used in a different way. Poppy and I have had a very occasional go at playing there – she quite likes to jump out at me from under the table. But, somehow, these games never manage to last very long. And, when Carla and I spent a morning trying to create in dialogue with the Dining Room, the result was – nothing at all! Part of me hates this. But part of me finds it rather comforting as well.

Sometimes, in the evenings, when Simon has gone and Poppy is asleep and Carla is up in her room, sometimes then I find myself compelled to drift, despite myself, into the Dining Room. I sit in an old chair at the heavy table, and my mind goes back over what has been. But what *is* that? *That* is what I try to grasp, and never can; *that* is why I keep on going back there; *that* is why I love the Dining Room and hate it too. Here is the room, here are these objects, solid, and very much themselves. And here am I, and there was Jem. I place my hands on the cool smooth stone and wonder what I can remember of him. So much pushes into my mind. And at the same time, it is so *little*. The bend of an elbow. And of an eyebrow. The yellow fleck in the iris of his left, green eye. The little nick of a scar on his right cheek, the shine on the slope of his nose. The sight of his back heading uphill from the car on our first trip to the clay bed in Cornwall. Hands, poised at his wheel. The sour smell of the clay, and the peppery smell of the sweat on his neck. The tones of his voice, and the sets of his face that go with them, angry, attentive, loving. And the sound of his steps when we walked down a street in the dark. And the grasp and the swing of his arms when he lifted me. And him with Poppy, and, and, and others, and others, piling in, jumping up to be noticed, and then flitting past like the flutter of an old-fashioned film projector, like the wings of a flock of birds.

I look up and there are the wings of the chandelier, the little bits of paper with their confidential scribbles. And I want to look at them again. I clamber up, reach up, and pluck and pluck and pluck, and then get down and spread out the papers like a deck of cards. Here is something someone wrote, and here is something else. And *here* are the words left from Poppy's First Birthday Dinner, that memorable evening, that evening which was really, now I look back on it, the midsummer of my time with Jem, the moment when the weather turned.

What did everyone write? Antonia said: 'Lovely dinner!' – Carla said: 'Thank you!' – Fisher said: 'Be faithful – to your vision' – Marion said: 'You do put on an excellent show' – and Jem: 'Now: can we get on with our lives?' I look at the words and what do they

235

tell me? There is a feeling that comes with each card, a tone, an expression, a smile or a frown. In your mind you look at it, you think it is a clue, you try to grasp it, you try to get to what was really going on. What was really there in Fisher's mind, in mine, in anyone's? You reach out – but as you reach the feeling fades away. The bits of paper turn back into being just bits of paper again, and I return to being just me, here, sitting at my table made of stone. There is a pile of life's litter in front of me. I sweep it to the floor.

The other day, the doorbell jangled and when I went and answered I found it was a small package, registered, from Paris. From Paris. Bleunet. Who was dead . . . then, inside me, it was like I was freezing up and melting both at once. I thought: Oh. And then: He wouldn't. And then: I really thought he was joking. And then: What shall I? Shall I? And then: What would he have liked? He would have liked me to cope. He would have liked me to rise to the occasion. So I went into the Dining Room, and very carefully, tenderly, with tears in my eyes, I placed the package on the table.

That evening, when Poppy and Carla were in their rooms, I got dressed up in a black Alaia dress which I hardly ever wear to go out in because I'm not completely sure I can carry it off – but I do love the feel of it: it's my sort of private favourite dress. I went down to the Dining Room. I got a knife and fork out of the cabinet, and a wine glass. Then I went to the kitchen for a bottle of the kind of mineral water which was Cristophe's drink of choice for when he wanted to really appreciate a dish for what it was. Then I sat down. I placed the knife and fork on either side of the package, I opened the bottle and poured. I waited, I don't know what for, but then a vision of blue sky popped into my head. I got my thumbs inside the sellotape of the squashy white packaging and ripped. Inside the wound was a little grey cardboard box. And inside that was a little polished wooden box with a hinged lid which I opened – and there, held upright in two little clips was a sliver of something purplish. It was like a thick crisp or a cut-out bruise. There was no note, only a label in the lid which read, I remember: *Flexor carpi radialis, tranche 3*. I brought my hand towards it and pressed it between index finger and thumb. It was waxy and it gave a little. A shiver went up my arm and into me and my mouth went dry: I reached for the water and drank. I said to myself: 'It's only a teeny bit. Don't need the knife and fork.'

I tried to compose myself. I remembered Cristophe's liveliness and his drive, I saw his bulging eyes and his gesturing hands. I remembered what Jem had been up to while I was so absorbed in the Paris commission but then I put that out of my mind and concentrated on Cristophe again. I remembered the high-up open kitchen, the wind up there, and the echoing noise of the streets, and the fleeting birds like scratches in the sky. I took the crisp and stuck it on my tongue and sucked: it tasted just sort of salty; then I bit into it and it was soft but also chewy like smoked fish. Then I chewed it some more; and then my whole stomach rose up against it like some sort of geyser and it came spurting out and splatted on the table. This wasn't good enough: this really wasn't right at all. I took the knife and scraped it up. I rinsed my mouth and I was going to have another go; but then I was retching again and I had to rush downstairs and round and along to the Downstairs Convenience where my supper came heaving out of me in slithery lumps. I bucked and retched and vomited and puked and retched and spasmed and spasmed; and then I stopped. I was sweaty and shivering and I was on my knees and there was something sticky on my fingers. I looked at the slimy half-chewed bit of Cristophe: and then I chucked it in and flushed.

So that was a complete balls-up. That wasn't what Cristophe would have wanted – and it's not the sort of thing that's meant to happen in a Dining Room. And yet . . .

Well, what it makes me think is this:

At least he had a vision. At least he had an idea. At least he tried. He did something quite extraordinary. I couldn't handle it. But I am glad I had to face it. I am glad I had to have a go.

And that is so different from Marion and Jem. Did you read that horrid, horrid letter she sent me? It came through the door the day after she graciously delivered Poppy back to me, on behalf of the man who had previously been with me. You would have thought it was enough to simply take him, wouldn't you? – without having to explain, as well, why that was totally the right thing to do for all concerned? It is so wrong. She is so, so, so wrong. She is not my 'friend'. I don't need to be told how to love my Poppy. She didn't bring my Poppy back out of friendship for me. It's bollocks what she says about looking out of the window and seeing me and my Poppy and how her heart swooned. What she was doing that day was fucking telling Jem that she was pregnant so she could get her fangs back into him just as he was coming back to me.

It was not 'meant to happen'. God how I hate this talk of Nature and its power. The Darkness! The Ooze! The complacency of it! So is it 'Natural' to be selfish? To live a lie? To trample other people? To do what the fuck you want to do and say you had no choice?

Even the most primitive hominids decorated their Interiors. They wanted to be in a better place. A place that would help them. That would give them something to live up to. That would make them try. That is what Interiors are for. To make Life better. To make it Beautiful.

In an Interior, you can wear soft clothes. You can walk around in socks. You can sit comfortably. You can feel at home. You can be in the same place together with the people you love. Isn't that wonderful?

Interior Design helps you know yourself. It helps you see what works for you.

But vitally, Interior Design is also about other people. A well-designed Interior is a gift. People come into it, and they can open up. They can pay attention to one another. When you speak, your voice is guarded by the walls, bounced here and there so all its different tones can sound. And that is what you get when you listen to other people speak too. Think of how a well-designed Interior situates people in relation to one another. How it guides the light to fall on their faces. How Impish Touches or other details stimulate the senses and the mind. Interior Design is all about thinking the best of people – and trying to make that best come true.

Of course it doesn't always work. Perhaps it even never works completely. But, that's not a reason not to follow Magic Motto no. 15:

✓ *Do Keep Trying!*

In fact, I wonder if there isn't something rather magic about the moment when it all goes wrong. The Cristophe moment. Or the long, so painful moment Poppy and I have lived through in Allsop Road. The moment when a Vision does not come true. And the magic thing is: it makes space for a new Vision. For you to set about imagining, again!

What is wrong with Marion and the other people like her? The ones who scorn Interior Design? Do they not have love? Are they simply not interested in other people? Have they never sat in the warm and the dry while the rain came down outside or the wind swept by – and thought, what I think, every time I step in from the street and push the door bang shut behind me, and sense the aroma of my house, welcome the feel of the air, the colours, the sound of my step on my floor – and know that all the other rooms are above and below and around me, with their harmonious forms and

239

tones, and that people I like have been in this space, and that people I love belong here:

How wonderful it is to be inside!

## Magic Mottoes

13. Design For Life: Design For The Unexpected.

14. Sometimes, Things Happen In Mysterious Ways.

15. Do Keep Trying!

## A NOTE ON THE TYPE

The text of this book is set in Linotype Sabon, named after the type founder, Jacques Sabon. It was designed by Jan Tschichold and jointly developed by Linotype, Monotype and Stempel, in response to a need for a typeface to be available in identical form for mechanical hot metal composition and hand composition using foundry type.

Tschichold based his design for Sabon roman on a font engraved by Garamond, and Sabon italic on a font by Granjon. It was first used in 1966 and has proved an enduring modern classic.